Beyond the Secret

By

L J Walls

MAPLE
PUBLISHERS

Beyond the Secret

Author: L J Walls

Copyright © L J Walls (2022)

The right of L J Walls to be identified as author of this work has been asserted by the author in accordance with section 77 and 78 of the Copyright, Designs and Patents Act 1988.

First Published in 2022

ISBN 978-1-915492-99-9 (Paperback)

978-1-915796-00-4 (E-Book)

Book cover design and Book layout by:
    White Magic Studios
    www.whitemagicstudios.co.uk

Published by:
    Maple Publishers
    1 Brunel Way,
    Slough,
    SL1 1FQ, UK
    www.maplepublishers.com

Part 1

Chapter 1

Edith hummed to the radio as she pulled plates and cereal boxes from various cupboards. The ancient VHF radio crackled and faded as her lively movements around the small kitchen interrupted the signal. The whistle of the steam kettle threatened to drown out the weather report completely and so she snatched the pot off the burner to hear the forecast. Snow showers were expected on the west coast of Ireland and Edith bent forward to peer out of the kitchen window. She disagreed with the forecast.

'Not a chance,' she murmured to herself. She could see only dark grey rain clouds gathering in the distance and her eyes caught sight of her neighbour's washing on the line. A slither of apprehension snaked its way down her spine. The limp white linen had been hung out the previous day. Edith hurried to finish Jerry's breakfast so she could go and check on her elderly neighbour.

Jerry was oblivious to the weather warning, whistling kettle and the abrupt cessation of his grandma's perpetual humming. He lined up the condiments on the table and prepared his troops for yet another battle. Edith had admonished him once already, because, in an earlier skirmish, the salt stopper had come loose, and snowy granules now littered the tablecloth and floor.

Edith relayed cereal and milk to the table and was about to pluck the bottles from Jerry's fingers when the doorbell rang. As she swished wide hips down the hall, she yelled at Jerry to clear up his mess. Her daughter stood on the doorstep with her head buried in an oversized handbag. The young woman had deposited her son at breakneck speed a few minutes earlier and driven off.

'I forgot Jerry's coat, ma, sorry. Wasn't sure if you'd be taking him out today.' Angela thrust a small anorak into Edith's arms and without waiting for a reply, turned, and hurried back down the steps to her car. 'It's gonna be chuckin' it down soon enough.'

'Ay, it will that, don't you be speeding now with the lateness.' Edith waved off her daughter and pulled her cardigan tightly round her body and was about to step back into the warm cottage but froze mid-stride. Her eyes fell on the solitary milk bottle still standing on her neighbour's doorstep. She remembered her earlier concern over the washing and stepped over the low wall separating the two cottages and rapped loudly on the letterbox.

Edith knew her neighbour's routine as well as she knew her own, they had lived side by side for over twenty years. Washing out all night and milk still on the doorstep at this hour was odd. There was no reply and Edith crossed her chest in silent prayer and peered through the windows hoping to see something to dispel her growing sense of dread. The curtains were pulled so Edith rapped her knuckles frantically at the windows. She called out to her neighbour and bent to peer through the letterbox into the shadowy hall.

'Mary? Mary? It's Edith.' Her shaky voice echoed in the empty space. She held her ear to the oblong gap, hoping to hear the TV or some movement from Mary's kitchen. In between calling out, she held her breath, listening for any sound from inside the tiny cottage. Intrigued by the commotion, Jerry emerged from Edith's house and tugged at

4

her cardigan as he stood on tiptoe and copied his nana trying to peer through the letterbox.

'Jerry! Mind your own … you cheeky devil.' She took his hand and pulled him inside. 'Watch the Lion King, Jerry; while I'm knocking at Mrs White's.' She took a disk from a shelf and handed it to her grandson. As she left him to his movie she pulled the lounge door firmly into its frame, not wanting him to follow her out again and hurried through her house to the rear alleyway that connected the row of cottages.

Edith prayed her neighbour's door would be unlocked. When she tried the handle and the door creaked open, fear stalled her advance. She called out her friend's name in a voice that rose in pitch with each repetition. Her pulse thumped at her temple, and she shuffled reluctantly further inside. As she approached the living room the stifling heat from the gas fire that had burned for too long beckoned her inside.

Mary White was slumped forward in her armchair; her glasses lay abandoned on the floor. Edith put a hand to her mouth to stifle her wail and picked up the glasses. She wanted to straighten Mary up in her chair but was unable to lift her. The dead weight was too much. She turned off the blazing fire and picked up the telephone.

Chapter 2

The daylight was fading so Lucy swung her chair away from the table and turned on a lamp. She stretched and rubbed at dry eyes. She didn't need to glance at her desk calendar to know there were only two days left for her deadline. This paper was Biochemistry; she had only two more months remaining in her pre-clinical years at medical school. The workload was relentless, but the end of term and summer holidays were in sight.

She reached into a small fridge for a coke and decided she needed to make a call home. She shuffled through books and papers on her desk looking for her phone. Home for Lucy was a sleepy coastal village on the West Coast of Ireland which she had never ventured far from until she'd left for University in Cork.

Her watch showed seven forty-five and she imagined her grandma settling down for an evening watching her favourite soaps. A tap at the door distracted her search and her best friend's face, complete with a phony grimace peeked around the door.

'Don't suppose you have any painkillers? I feel a headache looming.' With a mouth full of coke Lucy beckoned her in and pointed to her rucksack hanging on the door as the location for some pills.

'Apart from the headache, how you going?' said Lucy. Her friend hailed from the opposite side of the Atlantic and the two girls had become firm friends after they had roomed together in their first year. Janey's light blonde hair, bright blue eyes, and spirited personality were in complete contrast to Lucy's long, almost black hair, pale complexion, and serious manner.

'Two more months Luce! I'm knackered, I 'm never gonna to make it to Clinical, I'm sick of the stinking, worthless, thankless, profession. Who'd want to be a doctor anyway?' Janey threw herself onto Lucy's bed and covered her eyes melodramatically.

'Bad day then, huh? Well, how about we forget these pills and console ourselves with a pint or two in the pub?' Lucy said it with a hidden smile knowing that was probably the real reason Janey dropped by her room at almost eight o'clock.

'Are you sure, are you done for today? I mean I know how upset you get when we have a deadline to meet, and you haven't had enough kip.'

'I'm doin' okay, should have this one wrapped up by tomorrow afternoon.' Revealing an ulterior motive, Lucy swung open the fridge and pointed inside. 'Anyway, the cupboard is bare, and I haven't eaten anything since twelve thirty!' With that, Janey swung her legs off the bed and with a high-five at Lucy, the girls headed out.

They walked to O'Connell's, an off-campus watering hole that offered students discounts on food and drinks. As a result, the pub was filled most evenings with medical students, lecturers, and university staff. The girls did a quick scan of the pub and seeing no familiar faces, settled into a booth opposite the bar. Lucy wondered if they would bump into Tim Hatcher. He was one of the regular patrons in the pub, and he and Lucy had been an on-off item for the last few months, but a busy exam schedule had strained the relationship. Meeting occasionally in the usual student hangouts with the rest of the gang was a typical date. Tim was in his final year of medical school, so his time was spent on wards with his patients, and it was not uncommon for a fifty-hour week to be followed by just a couple of pints and then a very long sleep.

The barman, recognising the girls, walked over with two half pints of lager.

'Quiet tonight, Rory, is there something we should know?' Janey smiled and pulled on her drink, raising a cheeky eyebrow. The girls knew that the Blue Bear, a few streets away had started a drinks happy hour every Monday night. The marketing ploy lured patrons on what would otherwise be a generally very quiet night and it was where the girls suspected their counterparts were.

'We do not need cheap gimmicks in here, not when you have something sooo gorgeous to look at for no extra charge.' Rory pointed at his face and pursed his lips. As he turned and walked away, he added a swagger to his gait for dramatic effect. The girls laughed loudly and tongue in cheek agreed with him.

'If your assignment is almost finished then it looks like you've got a free weekend ahead. What plans, Tim on the menu?

'Well actually ...' Lucy was fingering her beer mat and glanced up at her friend's face to gauge her level of attention. Janey was looking at her expectantly, there was no going back now.

'I'm going to tell Tim we should cool it, for now at least. It's just not going anywhere; we don't have any time together and when we are ... it's just ... dull.' She blurted the words out trying to convince herself, as well as her best friend.

'That's a real shame I thought you guys were so ... suited.' Janey's voice was flat and belied any element of surprise and

8

Lucy realised that her friend had already guessed something was adrift with her romance.

'He is going to make a fantastic doctor, Janey, much better doctor than a boyfriend and it's his final year, time is a scarce commodity for those guys.' Her eyes didn't meet her friend's. Lucy had an ulterior motive for untangling herself from her fading romance, but it wasn't one she wanted to share with her best friend just yet.

Chapter 3

It took several seconds before Janey registered the annoying beeping was not her alarm clock but her phone. She fumbled through various pockets, cursing as she tried frantically to locate the phone before the caller was diverted to her message service.

'Hello.' Janey sank back down onto the bed she had just stumbled out of but stood to attention when she heard her name curtly and succinctly questioned.

'Janey Stucker?'

'Yes?'

'I'm the assistant to the principal's office. I was wondering if you could help us with something?'

'Yes.' Janey's voice was hesitant, but an adrenalin surge kicked her heart rate up a notch. The principal's office, what had she done? Questions stumbled into her head but before she had time to formulate the words, the caller spoke again.

'We've had a call from Lucy White's family doctor this morning and there is some very bad news that we need to deliver.' Janey froze. 'We understand that you are Lucy's friend. Her grandmother passed away this morning I'm afraid. We have asked the chaplain to go and see Lucy, and we were wondering if it were possible for you to join them?' Janey went cold. She cleared her throat.

'How? Why?

'The chaplain has more information than I do I'm afraid.'

'Er, okay, yes ... of course, I'll go and see her right away.' She hung up and covered her face with shaking hands. She was trying to process the terrible news herself and wondering how she would deliver it to her best friend. She realised she needed to get to her friend as soon as possible and scrambled to pull on some jeans and a t-shirt and hurried blindly through the campus corridors towards Lucy's room. On the way she dialled Tim's number hoping the administrator had thought to call him too and she wondered if he was also heading to Lucy's room meaning she might not be the one that had to break the awful news.

'Shit.' The call connected straight to his voicemail and Janey left a garbled message and stressed for him to call her as soon as possible. Whatever Lucy had said last night about dumping him was irrelevant now. She would need all her friends around her at a time like this. Janey hovered in the corridor outside Lucy's room. Where was the chaplain? He would know what to say, how to deliver the words, he had probably done it many times before, this was his wheelhouse.

'Coward,' she whispered to herself, 'You are a coward.' Lucy could open her door at any moment and walk right out, and then she would feel foolish. Her hand clutched at the phone in her pocket, and she tried to control her thoughts and her breathing. She wondered about the circumstances of the death and the possible cause. Lucy hadn't mentioned anything about her grandma being sick.

Her phone began to ring, the noise startled her and terrified that her friend might hear it, Janey walked quickly into the garden.

'Janey, I'm on my way over, are you there now?' Tim's authoritative voice calmed her a little.

'Yes, I'm outside now, waiting for the priest, chaplain ... whatever he is.'

'You haven't told her yet?'

'No'

'Jesus Janey!' Tim cursed. She knew his opinion of her was not very high to start with but now she felt she deserved every ounce of his contempt.

'Tim,' Janey's voice broke, 'I can't tell her Tim, I just can't.' She felt her eyes welling up and tried to pull herself together. Tim's voice returned more tender and very calm.

'Okay don't worry; I'll be there in ten minutes. What was it anyway, coronary?'

'I don't fucking know; they didn't tell me anything.' The pitch of Janey's voice rang high with near hysteria 'The priest is supposed to be here, they didn't give me any information.' Her yelling attracted glances from passing students and she lowered her voice. Her own grief was threatening to overcome her, she wanted to cry but she was determined to hold it together until she had consoled her friend. 'I think he's here, there's a car pulling into the courtyard.' Hanging up abruptly, she rushed towards the red ford fiesta and before the chaplain could gather his things from the passenger seat, Janey had opened the car door and introduced herself.

***

Lucy was seated at her desk and bent over her laptop, she looked up and smiled as her friend's face appeared round the door, but the smile froze in place as she took in her friend's grim expression. The chaplain followed Janey through the doorway and Lucy subconsciously recoiled. The room was small but with three bodies and the weight of unconfirmed grief, the walls closed in even more. Lucy was aware of her hands being taken and felt cold bony fingers holding hers. Sentences seemed garbled as if she was hearing them under water. She shook her head to clear the thoughts; questions

12

forming on her lips. For a few seconds, she didn't believe what they told her. Denial. The first stage of grief, she knew that, and she was also aware that the mug of sugary tea that Janey placed in front of her was no coincidence either. The sugar would combat the surge of insulin caused by shock. Tim arrived and held Lucy; she held him tightly back afraid that her legs would not support her by themselves.

'Massive coronary.' Tim's voice cut through her mind fog. 'She wouldn't have been in any pain. We can go as soon as you like.'

'When did she die?' Lucy somehow found herself sitting on the edge of her bed unsure of how she got there.

'Sometime in the night. Your neighbour found her this morning.'

'Yes, but when did she pass?' Her voice was brittle and bare of any emotion. She wanted to know if her grandmother had died in her armchair, or in her bed, the small details were somehow important to her. She remembered her abandoned call the previous evening and guilt rippled through her. She'd left her grandmother to die alone, many miles away.

Lucy could hear Janey talking in the corridor; from the muffled conversation, she could make out that Janey was arranging term leave and making plans to submit her almost completed assignment. Tim had already told her he'd arranged time off and she knew they had discussed a rota so she wouldn't be alone.

Janey eventually returned to Lucy's room.

'My god Tim, what have you given her? She looks awf...'

'I'm fine! Please don't talk about me as if I'm not here.' Lucy sat up on the bed and faced her friends.

'You look tired, are you in pain honey? Did you take some pills?' Janey wondered if Tim had given her a sedative.

'I want to go home, please come with me.' Lucy's eyes sought out her best friend's and Tim saw that as his cue to intervene and announce their plans.

'You girls get a bag packed, I'll go over to my place, grab my stuff, fuel up the car and I'll be back here to pick you up in half an hour.' The girls listened to Tim's footsteps fade down the hallway.

'I can pack your things, why don't you have a nap? Forty winks? I'll wake you when Tim gets back.' There was no argument from Lucy, she lay back and allowed Janey to pull the duvet over her.

***

St Augustus stretched and yawned, disgruntled by the sudden disturbance as his master stood up to answer the telephone. Father O'Reilly shuffled around in his tartan slippers looking for somewhere to put down his dinner. He decided against it; the fat, ginger tomcat had one eye on his plate and would have had no hesitation gobbling down the fish supper while his back was turned. He made his way down the narrow hall, with its uneven flagged stone floor and was about to place his tray on a sideboard when the ringing stopped.

'God bless my old bones!' The priest cursed and mumbled unholy expletives all the way back to the living room wondering if he might be able to finish his dinner without interruption. It was the third time today that a caller had rung off before he could get to the phone.

'Has to be the Yank, impatient, those Yanks.' He muttered to St Augustus, who gave him a bored look. The cat had now stretched his full length across the warm and recently vacated sofa, so Father O'Reilly settled himself into an armchair instead and fixed his gaze back to the TV set loudly blasting a

14

quiz show from a corner of the room. The cat, indignant that the fish pie was not coming his way, stood up, turned around a couple of times assessing the various cushions and curled himself into the warmest spot.

The old priest had called the States earlier that day. It had taken him all morning to find the number he hadn't used for over twenty years, and he was relieved when it still connected. An American accent delivered a pre-recorded message which satisfied him that it was the agency he'd hoped to reach. Father O'Reilly reported the death of the elderly Mrs Mary White, he gave the date and time of death and with an afterthought added that the cause of death was of natural causes. Finally, he asked if somebody could call him back, he was unsure of the protocol and what he might be required to take care of.

The rest of the day the priest had busied himself with his usual obligations. Knowing that a death in the community would draw more parishioners than usual to the small church for quiet prayers and contemplation, he'd made sure the candle dispenser was full and that prayer books were handy on the end of the pews. He would visit the granddaughter tomorrow, perhaps in the late morning. He knew Mary White and the girl well, he had become the child's de facto godfather when the small family had arrived in the tiny village and had a particular interest in their welfare. He knew Lucy would be kept busy with a stream of visitors for a few days; Mary White was a popular member of the community. The priest was engrossed in his quiz show as the telephone began to ring again. Father O'Reilly frowned, swore at St Augustus, and slammed his fork down to hurry down the hall again.

**

Driving rain welcomed Tim and Lucy as they left the hilly moorland that edged County Candula and navigated the narrow winding lanes that led to the lower coastal road. The coastal route hugged the Atlantic and connected many of the ancient fishing villages dotted along the shore, most of them similar in size and character to the one where Lucy grew up.

Lucy was sleeping, her head rested on a scrunched-up jumper propped against the window. When the car pulled up outside her grandmother's house Tim nudged her awake and as she gazed up at the dreary little cottage, pain shadowed her face. She didn't try to hide the shiver that overcame her despite the relative warmth of the car.

'I'll go in and get the fire on.' She watched Tim race up the steep steps two at a time; his head cowered from the driving rain. Steps her grandmother had found troublesome lately. Lucy knew this although the old woman had never complained. As she sat cocooned in the car, watching the rain lash and trickle-down the windscreen, she wondered what other things had become difficult for her grandma, things she hadn't noticed. Tim was struggling with the lock, and she was distracted from her melancholy to go and help him. She impatiently took the bunch of keys from his hands and smiled with satisfaction as she inserted the correct key and the door opened curtly. Her short triumph evaporated as the familiar scent of her grandma overwhelmed her and tore into her heart.

Tim walked ahead through the small cottage, and she heard him filling the kettle. Lucy stood at the bottom of the stairs; she hated this place now, she hated being here, everything had changed, and she felt like a stranger in the place where she had grown up and lived her entire short life. She summoned the courage to climb the stairs and stood tentatively outside her grandmother's bedroom. Placing her fingertips on the door she gently pushed it open but remained rooted to the spot. Grief overwhelmed her as she scanned the room, the dresser with a hairbrush, comb, and perfume all neatly arranged. A pair of slippers neatly lined up by the bed and a nightgown folded on the corner of a pillow. A sob escaped from her, and she fell to her knees. She gave up fighting the tears and sobbed violently until she was too exhausted to move.

Chapter 4

Lucy refused to open her eyes. She couldn't remember going to bed, she only remembered the hot drink being handed to her while she sat huddled on her grandma's bed. Tim must have given her sleeping pills. She didn't know the time and she kept her eyes shut tight against the daylight, against the knowledge that her grandmother had died. She covered her face with the faded bedspread as if it were a shield. Several minutes passed and she listened to the sounds of cupboards being opened and closed. She knew Tim had found the central heating control because the plumbing creaked and popped as hot water flooded through the pipes.

She fought the numbness in her limbs and eventually pulled back the bed covers to drag out bare legs. She had to concentrate on putting one foot in front of the other and wondered just how many pills Tim had given her. She pulled a gown tightly around her shoulders and headed downstairs.

A steaming mug of coffee was presented to her and then Tim, without speaking, leaned back against the door, and observed her through furrowed brows. His frame filled the doorway almost completely; grey sweats and a damp fringe told her he had been out for a run. She took a cautious sip of her coffee, wary of burning her lips.

'Thank you. I will drink every last drop.' She gave a weak smile and he nodded.

'And I'm making you toast.' She stayed quiet about her lack of appetite; she didn't have the energy for an argument. If she forced down a few mouthfuls, it might keep him quiet.

'Where did you run to?'

'I went to the top of the cliffs and then back down through the lanes. I picked up some fresh stuff from the bakery and … a few of the old dears from around the village are popping by today.' Lucy could feel his scrutiny. 'I can be the bouncer if you're not up to it. I had the rosary beads brandished at twenty paces and a holy water shower all before breakfast so I understand if you're not ready for that I can make some excuses for you today.' She giggled at the image.

'No, it's fine, they will only come back tomorrow if they can't pay their respects today, I suppose. If you can cope with them all, so can I.' He put a hand over hers and squeezed gently.

'Better get that toast down you then, you're going to need the energy, and … there's things we need to organise.'

The day passed with a stream of visitors to the cottage and each one came with a plate. A mountain of homemade pies and stews developed on the kitchen counter. One of the first to arrive was the doctor; he told Lucy he suspected heart failure; her grandmother was on no medication and the coroner would confirm the cause of death in short time. Father O'Reilly followed his flock in the early afternoon. The old priest was her grandmother's closest friend and he was the one who would lay the old widow to rest. While Lucy was distracted with a neighbour, she overheard him give Tim the details of the funeral home. When Lucy finally saw the last visitor to the front door and closed it behind her, she felt weary.

'I think I might take a walk over the tops. Get some fresh air in my lungs and run off all those custard creams before I start on the cabbage and bacon.' Tim gestured with a nod of his head towards the kitchen and the mountain of gifted food. Lucy wrinkled her nose.

'We need a dog.'

'We need an elephant to get rid of that lot!'

'I'll freeze some of it.'

'I won't be out long.' Pulling a sweatshirt over his t-shirt, kissed Lucy on the top of her head and headed out.

***

The undertaker said the middle of the following week would be the earliest for the funeral. Lucy didn't want Tim around all that time. She planned to dispatch him back to Cork as soon as possible. She brewed coffee and toasted bread, and it was not long before the smell lured him down.

'That air from the moors last night must have done you some good, you're looking refreshed.' Lucy noticed the dark shadows from beneath his eyes had lightened. Days and nights spent inside hospital corridors, with little natural light, and minimal sleep gave all the staff a grey waxy complexion. 'I called Janey this morning and she said she was coming up on Monday.'

'Great.' He bit a slice of toast in half.

'And I called the undertaker, in Kearis. He said Wednesday or Thursday was possible for the funeral.' Tim looked up with raised eyebrows, but she continued, 'I want it as soon as possible, and they said it should be straight forward enough with the coroner's office. I'm going to go to the undertakers this afternoon to arrange things.' She continued at speed so he couldn't interrupt. 'I'd like it if you could come with me today, but you needn't stay here all week. If Janey's coming on Monday, I'm not going to be alone for long ...'

'I'm not leaving you for four days.'

'If you go home tomorrow that's only two days, and I've got so much to sort out I'm going to be too busy to notice

20

I'm alone.' Contemplating her plans with his head bowed and hands gripping his mug, his sigh signalled his capitulation.

***

Tim drove his battered white Renault into Kearis with Lucy sitting by his side. Her half-hearted endeavour eating breakfast earlier had stirred him to attempt to feed her again before their appointment at the undertakers. He pulled into a parking space and nodded at the row of cafés overlooking the town's busy boulevard. They headed for the first one with free tables. Warm, humid air greeted them as they stepped inside. The babble of conversation and a background tune from a radio afforded Tim some privacy for the conversation he planned to have with Lucy.

'Luce, have you given any thought about paying for the ... ' He was interrupted mid-sentence by an old couple who caught sight of Lucy across the room.

'Oh, my love, my pet, how are ya?' The old round woman was closely followed by an even older man, and they hobbled over to offer their condolences. Tim had overlooked the fact that Lucy would be acquainted with many of the customers in the cafe. The town was small, not as tiny as the village where she grew up, but still a place where people knew you and your business, whether you wanted them to or not.

Tim tried again to have a conversation with Lucy but after the third such interruption he gave up. He let Lucy chat with the other patrons offering their prayers and commiserations.

'Yes, my lovely, you take good care of yourselves now, she was a good, good woman, and she has a fine resting place up there with tha ma. So, she does.' Tim noticed Lucy's dignity had started to fray and he took control again.

'We really must be off now actually, Lucy, or we'll be late.' He pretended to notice the time and rose to pull out her chair. He steered Lucy away and extracted her from the café with an overdone gallantry that left the gaggle of elderly women charmed.

Lucy's tears rolled silently at first, controlled until they were on the other side of the door. Then in the sharp breeze, Tim turned her into his chest and held her trembling body tightly to him as she cried. Having to deal with the grief of losing her grandmother was heart-breaking enough, but the reminder of her mother was too much.

Lucy was an only child, her father had left when she was a toddler and her mother died when she was five years old. Mary White had raised her granddaughter on a small pension and what she could earn from taking in laundry and mending. It had been a struggle for the old woman. The house was warm in winter and there was always plenty of food on the table, but the terraced cottage only ever received essential renovations. Its peeling paintwork and patched up roof embarrassed Lucy when she first invited her university friends home, and she'd always yearned for brothers and sisters. The whole lane was full of children, and she had many friends but felt a constant pang of loneliness not having the company and comradery of siblings.

***

The undertaker's office was a large Georgian building that stretched out into two wings either side of a portico supported by two Corinthian columns. A white gravelled drive sliced the finely manicured lawn in two identical rectangles and led the eye to a highly polished brass plate by the door that told them Leyne and Sons had been Funeral Directors since 1860.

'Not quite as old as the building, but not far off, eh?' Tim whistled under his breath. 'These guys have it all sussed out, just look at this place ...'

'Shush.' Lucy whispered as they entered the building. It was dark inside and her eyes took a few seconds to adjust. As they walked into the lobby a middle-aged woman approached them. She wore a tailored pale blue suit and over-powdered complexion and a large multi-jewelled pin glinted on her lapel. The exquisitely groomed woman made Lucy aware of her own shabby appearance and she glanced down at her worn jeans and hand knitted jumper. If the receptionist was aware of Lucy's self-consciousness, she pretended not to notice and instead took Lucy's arm and gently guided her toward a sofa.

'Lucy White?'

'Ye ...'

'Please take a seat.'

'I'm very sorry we're late ...'

'... No, no dear. No need to worry yourself about that.' A manicured hand came up to silence Lucy. 'And you are Mr?'

'Timothy Hatcher. I'm a close friend of Ms White.'

'I shall let Mr Leyne know that you're here, can I get you tea or coffee?' The lady floated back to a reception desk and Lucy expected her to make a telephone call, but she tapped at a keyboard and was back in no time to present them both with a glossy folder.

'There you go, my dear. This is a comprehensive list of all our services, many people don't really take things in right away and you will find all the answers to your questions in here. Mr Leyne, that's Tirlough Leyne will be with you very shortly.' She offered them both a genuinely warm smile and Lucy decided she had one of the worse jobs anybody could possibly have. Much worse than being a doctor; doctors only occasionally dealt with the relatives of the deceased. She wondered what it might be like to be surrounded by misery and grief every working day of your life and she offered the woman a reticent smile. Tim flicked through the glossy pages in the brochure and his eyebrows arched as he appraised pictures of gleaming Mercedes and Limousine's alongside traditional horse-drawn carriages. Lucy surveyed the computers and telephone equipment on the reception desk. Each piece of hardware was the latest technology but encased in a walnut veneer, so it didn't look at odds with the old building.

'Would you care to follow me please?' The receptionist was back, 'Mr Leyne will be with you any moment.'

They were shown into another room. Gold and cream drapes framed double aspect windows which showcased another immaculate courtyard at the back of the building. The receptionist closed the door and left them alone. Tim whistled as he surveyed their surroundings and then his attention was drawn to the coffee table which already had a silver tea tray laid out on it.

'That was quick.' He nodded at the tray complete with dainty biscuits arranged on a plate.

'Maybe it's been here for half an hour waiting for us.' Tim put his hand gingerly against the pot.

'Nope.' His raised eyes brows and pursed lips told Lucy it was hot. 'Do you think it's too late for a career change?' he said, gesturing to their surroundings. 'I wonder how many of these rooms they have. And have you seen all these Merc's?' Tim held the brochure up as he flicked through the pages. He took two of the biscuits from the plate and put both into his mouth. Lucy ignored him, she was feeling empty and his obsession with the cars and décor was starting to annoy her.

Tirlough Leyne rattled briefly on the door and entered. He fixed his best smile as he quickly appraised the room and its occupants. Lucy White stood at the window and only partly turned to acknowledge him. The girl's body language and her disengaged expression told him she hadn't fully accepted the death of her grandmother; she didn't want to be here. At thirty-nine Tirlough had been in the family business for twenty-three years. He was a seasoned professional and an expert at judging people and situations. He summarily determined the man in the room was not close to Lucy. He was seated on the large sofa a few meters away but may as well have been on the other side of the courtyard. The doctor's notes he had, indicated that Mary White had, to his knowledge, only one living relative. He laid down the laptop and stack of papers and held out his hand.

'Miss White, we've been taking good care of your grandma for you. She is in very good hands here.' Lucy shook his hand and then took a seat on the sofa as far away as possible from him. He flicked open his own copy of the glossy brochure and pointed out his various family members posing beneath the pristine white campanile at the front of their office.

'You have already met my mother, Sheila, and we are all here to help you through this upsetting time. Is this your first experience of planning a funeral?'

'Yes.' He saw that the direct question made Lucy nervous.

'First things first then, there's a list of everything we need in your pack. We can take care of notifying any banks and insurance companies for you if you prefer. We take care of that once we have the death certificate.' From his pile of coloured cardboard folders, he pulled a sheet of embossed paper and laid it on the coffee table between them.

'Do you know if there are any provisions for a burial plot?' Lucy shook her head, ignored the paper he offered and walked over to the window. He had lost the girl's attention so shifted his questions to the girl's friend. Tim Hatcher asked the questions until Lucy interrupted.

'Is she over there, Mr … Tirlough?' Lucy nodded in the direction of the building across the courtyard. Tirlough was relieved to have her back in the room. He stood up and joined her at the window.

'No, my dear, those buildings are the garages and the stables for our Jock and Seabald. The Chapel of rest is downstairs if you would like to visit your grandma.'

'She's here?' Lucy considered the fact for a few seconds and then confirmed she would like to see her grandmother. Tirlough noticed she didn't seek any accord from her friend.

'I can come with you if you want.' Tim seemed uncertain and Tirlough stepped in to ease his clear discomfort.

'I can take you downstairs while Mr Hatcher waits for us up here. …' He put his body between the couple and nodded in Tim's direction. Tirlough took Lucy's elbow and guided her through a maze of corridors before leaving her to wait in a small conservatory. A bubbling fountain drew her attention and she moved closer to the raised Koi Pond to get a better look at the fish. The friendly little things bobbed towards her, and she guessed it might be feeding time; big mouths hinged open and closed like little opera singers in full flow.

Voices invaded her scrutiny of the Koi and she turned expecting to see Tirlough, but the voices belonged to a family being ushered into a nearby room. A middle-aged woman dressed in a black wool overcoat, accompanied by a teenage daughter, and perhaps, though she could be mistaken, a son, who appeared to be in his early twenties. They were close, holding onto each other. Collective grief, Lucy suddenly felt very lonely. The desire for a family to share her loss sliced through her and a stab of sadness jolted at her soul. They had each other and she was alone. She was the only person missing her beloved grandmother. She was suddenly overcome by a strong desire to be close to her grandmother and say a last goodbye.

When Tirlough returned she offered him a warm smile and he silently guided her to a room and held open the door. Her eyes fell on the casket in the centre of the room.

'Thank you,' she whispered but the door had already closed softly behind her. She stepped cautiously up to the body unsure of everything. For a second, she stared at a stranger but knowing the dead rarely resembled the living person they had been, she moved closer. The facial lines and wrinkles that once held a lifetime of stories were now relaxed. Her grandma's skin had been skilfully painted and powdered to hide any pallor. Hairstyles were often guessed at, she knew that, but she smiled affectionately, her grandma would be pleased with the style they had worked on her, 'glamorous', she might have called it. If there was one thing, she was always unhappy about it was the hairdressers in Anchora. Having been in her prime in the fifties, she was a fan of the American movies and the bouffant hairstyles of the starlets on the big screen. Lucy put a hand out to stroke the wispy threads. Her fingers touched her grandma's face accidentally and the cold skin frightened her enough to make her pull back her hand. She was overcome by an overwhelming yearning to have her grandma alive again, just for a short time, for a hug, or a few last words, and Lucy had to concentrate hard to get breath into her lungs. She took hold of her grandma's hand and held it tight and kissed it. She pressed her lips firmly against it as she cried an apology for not being with her for her last moments and not knowing about her health problems. She cried for having been a burden to her grandma and she cried because she'd lost her mother so young and needed her now. She cried for the great-grandchildren her grandma would never see, and she cried because she wanted her back for just one more moment. And she cried because she did not have anyone to tell.

Chapter 5

Lucy scribbled her list of errands onto a journal as Tim peered over her shoulder and both jumped when the clatter of the door knocker interrupted their concentration. Tim groaned and cursed as he headed down the hall to greet the latest caller. The stream of visitors had eased off but not ceased completely.

The latest guest announced herself as Mrs O'Malley. She told Tim she'd been a neighbour of the Whites until her son had moved her into a newly built assisted living apartment in Kearis. He stood back and held the door open for her and the woman squeezed her ample body past him. She bear-hugged Lucy and then proceeded to settle her weight into an armchair. When she pulled out her knitting Tim gave a silent sigh heavenward and retreated into the kitchen to re-boil the still warm kettle. He thought he'd stay out of the way in the kitchen and read the papers, but after a few minutes he thought he overheard a strained and testy tone develop in Lucy's voice. He decided to go back and be more supportive. The constant stream of visitors was taking its toll on Lucy.

'So, it will just be you and tha cousin in the funeral cart then ma love?'

'Tim is my boyfriend Mrs O'Malley. I already told you there is no cousin!'

'Yes, I know who Tim is.' The old woman gave a nod in Tim's general direction. 'I mean the young 'n' that comes by at Christmas time. Don't know about last year ... wasn't ...' She mumbled something inaudible to herself but then raised her

28

head as if remembering. 'A couple of years ago? Can't speak about last year, was in my new apartment building by then.'

'I don't have any cousins, Mrs O'Malley, you're getting confused.' Lucy's impatience was barely controlled, and her insult clearly stung the old woman.

'Well, my dear, I do not understand why the good Mrs White would go to a length to tell me her handsome young visitor from America was a cousin of yerself if that never was the case.' The old woman stood and thrust her knitting bag back under her arm and waddled back to the front door.

'Now then I'll see myself out, god bless yers all I'll be in the church for the funeral so I will.' Tim made sure to escort her down the steep steps and when he returned to the lounge, he found Lucy pacing the living room with her hands on her hips. She was clearly annoyed, and he tried to lighten the mood.

'Whatever you said worked!'

'I haven't got a clue who she was talking about, I know she's getting on but ... what do you think about this cousin? She keeps going on about him, like he is a real person, like my grandma would tell her that. Dementia?'

'Me or her? ... oh, Jesus! I don't believe it.' They both grimaced in unison as the door knocker walloped.

'Can we pretend we're out?' she whispered, her eyes pleading. Tim headed for the door again.

'Stay out of the way. I'll invent a headache or something and say you can't be disturbed.' He wished he'd thought of this earlier. The clattering letter box turned out to be just another sympathy card. Tim opened the door in time to see the rear end of a small boy scrambling back through the hedges. The path was clearly the long way round for him. Lucy opened the card, and without looking at the front or reading the verses, she put it on the mantel with the others.

'Couple of doors down,' she acknowledged to Tim.

'I figured the kid took a short cut through the bushes.'

'Oh, that'll be Billy then, I used to babysit for him, and his little sister. That's nice.' She glanced at the card again, to see if the children had signed it, but no, it was just their mother.

'I expect his ma' will be at the funeral.' Lucy sat down next to him and leaned her weight into Tim, he saw his chance.

'About the funeral, Luce.'

'Yeah.'

'Well, I've been meaning to tell you, but haven't had a chance. You know if you need some funds I can borrow from my dad. I don't know how you are fixed, and those sharks over in Kearis don't come cheap. And I know you want to do things properly.'

'Thanks, Tim,' she smiled absentmindedly. 'Somewhere there's some old jewellery. I'm going to sell it.'

'What jewellery?'

'It was my ma's. I haven't seen it in years but I'm sure granma didn't sell it already. I thought I'd have a look for it tonight after I've dropped you at the station.'

'What kinda jewellery?

'Well, there's a watch and my ma's wedding ring. It's a large rock, it's gotta be worth a bit. I remember gran saying she was keeping them because they would bury us both.'

Tim stayed silent. A wedding ring and watch wouldn't bring the kind of money she needed for the funeral. Lucy had never really spoken much about her father, but he doubted the man had the means to lavish expensive jewellery on his wife. He hoped her expectation of lost heirlooms wouldn't leave her too disappointed.

***

30

Lucy waved at the train until it disappeared and then headed back to her borrowed car. She took advantage of having a car and took the long scenic route back to Anchora. As she drove across the open moors, she ignored the driving rain and opened the windows to feel the wind. The elements lashing at her face were somehow cathartic and it was dusk when she finally arrived at the cottage. The dark and empty home caused a ripple of acute sadness. The other cottages in the lane breathed the warm yellow glow of habitation and reminded her that she was all alone. Loneliness was a new experience and she gazed up at the cottage with a new perspective. Her grandmother had been her best friend, mother, mentor and her inspiration. Now that she was gone where did she belong? There was nobody to impress with high grades, nobody to notice if she did not come home at the end of term.

Lucy shrugged off her coat and slung it over the banister. With this new perspective, she walked from room to room, gazing at the tired decor. The stampede of people passing through the cottage over the last couple of days had left its toll and she ran a finger over the dust covered furniture. She sat in her grandma's chair and fingered the worn fabric where many cups of cocoa had rested and wondered if this tiny cottage in this sleepy village would continue to be her home.

Chapter 6

The banging dragged Lucy's sleep-drugged mind back to consciousness. She'd fallen asleep in her grandma's armchair and had to stretch her aching and stiffened limbs before she could move properly. The caller hammered again on the front door, and Lucy cursed as she hurried to put a stop to it. As she passed through the hall, she pulled an old cardigan from the coat stand, hoping it would cover her crumpled appearance. She opened the door to find a large hairy hand level with her face, its owner was about to grab the doorknocker again. Lucy squinted in the bright morning light, until the face of a very large man came into focus.

'Mrs White?'

'Yes?'

'It must have been a hell of a party.'

'Eh?'

'Got the boys ere, we're ready to get started on the loft, not too early for you, are we?' His voice was deliberately slow, which irritated her, she was sleepy not brain dead.

'What party? What loft?' Lucy pulled the cardigan further around her shoulders under his scrutiny and the chill of the early morning air.

'We. Are. Here. To. Clear. The. Loft.' The way his eyes peered at her with reproach and slight amusement annoyed her. She failed to answer so he tried again. 'You called our office last week and asked for loft clearers.' The tall man rolled his eyes.

'Ah ...' Lucy realised her grandmother must have booked the contractor.

'I'm John, from Hogg's removals. I got a couple of lads in the van and we're ready to get started, we are.' She peered past him and spied a white van with large blue lettering. Two big hands clasped in front of her face, the dry swishing noise as they rubbed together made her take a step back.

'No.'

'Eh?'

'I'm too busy for this today.'

'What! But you booked us for today!'

'No, not today, thank you.' This was the last thing Lucy needed now, and she made to close the front door.

'Wha ...?' The big blue man put a hand up to the door.

'It must have been my grandma that booked you and she's erm, she's not here right now so ... another time. Hoggs, you say, hmm okay, I'll give your boss a call to re-book.' Lucy retreated a few steps back into the cottage.

'Hang on a minute missus, I am the boss. And my lads here have been guaranteed a morning's wages, not easy to get young muscle on a Saturday morning you know. You can't just go cancelling without notice just because you had a big night out yourself.'

'What! I'm not cancelling anything; I didn't book you in the first place! And I haven't had a BIG NIGHT OUT. You, cheeky git!' Lucy's voice rose with each word.

'Well, I'll send you the bill anyways. In the post!' She watched the man stomp back down the path and she stepped out of the doorway to shout after him.

'Send what you want, I'm not payin' a feckin thing!' She caught sight of two scruffy looking heads sticking out of the van windows. Impish grins slit their faces. It annoyed her even more and she slammed the front door hard and immediately regretted it. The bang would have vibrated two or three houses up the lane, and she sensed it was still very early. She pulled out the dry contact lenses she had fallen asleep in which were now scraping her eyes with every blink, and rummaged for some glasses. When she glimpsed at her reflection in the mirror by the door she gasped. Swollen, red eyes peered back at her and she remembered crying herself to sleep. Her skin was dimpled from the seam of a cushion where she'd rested her head and her hair resembled a bird's nest after a storm. She recalled her drive across the moors with the windows wide open, and grimaced. She resembled a creature from a sci-fi movie. No wonder the caller thought she had been at the booze.

***

Lucy dumped her shopping in the boot of the car and hopped into the driver's seat. The contractor and his elves had called at seven-thirty, so she took advantage of the early start and made inroads into her ever-growing to-do list. Not wanting to disturb her neighbours any more than she already had that morning she swerved the vacuum cleaner and headed into town. She hoped the early hour would circumvent acquaintances and do-gooders, but it had slipped her mind that old people were early risers. She bumped into several people who wanted to chat, pass on their condolences, or ask about the funeral arrangements. Confirming the funeral date and time became a priority, and this was now moved to the top of her list. Next stop was the vicarage to sort out the mass.

Father O'Reilly was more than just the local priest; he was her grandmother's closest friend and had played a big part in Lucy's life. When they had first moved to Anchora, Lucy's mother was grieving for her dead husband and the priest helped the family adjust and settle into the village. Then when a couple of years later Lucy's mother died too, Father O'Reilly became an even more influential figure in her life.

As Lucy grew up and became inquisitive about her parents she learned to go to the priest. It was no use asking her grandma, she avoided the questions with a nonchalant remark or claimed that her memory was failing her. *'No point in brooding in the past, and those ghosts there, it's the future that's important.'* Father O'Reilly was the one who filled in the blanks on her family's past and answered the questions she had about her parents' early deaths. The priest had visited Lucy the day before and they had made a date to plan the funeral, so he was expecting her.

Car wheels crunched on the gravel as Lucy pulled up to the old rectory. The house was like most of the buildings in Anchora, sturdy and pretty, but weather-ravaged and in desperate need of renovation. The large garden was overgrown, and weeds poked through the stones on the drive. Lucy knew every nook and corner of the vast gardens because she had played in them throughout her childhood, usually while her grandma helped with a church fete or jumble sale.

Lucy rang the doorbell and considered the unkempt garden with despair. A shuffling noise from inside made her turn and she pinned a smile on her face in readiness. More shuffling and still the door remained closed. Her smiled faded to a frown and she was about to peer through the letterbox when the latch released.

'Hiya Father, I was getting worried for a second there, what took you?'

'Ah, you young 'n's, always rushing about. My old bones don't like this cold weather ya know.' He turned and headed down the hall; Lucy followed him into the living room where she was hit by the heat from the fierce coal fire burning in the hearth.

'St Augustus!' Lucy grabbed the fat cat and swung him up in the air before cuddling him close under her chin. The cat purred with the attention. Lucy was the only person St Augustus did not bully. If anybody else had tried to swing him about like a chandelier, they would have lost their eyes, even Father O'Reilly himself. Mrs Reardon, the housekeeper who came a few days a week wouldn't dare shift him from his spot on the sofa. That was where Lucy plonked herself down now and the cat lolled about on her lap showing off his belly for a tickle.

'It's very warm in here you know.' Lucy observed the blazing fire and then to Father O'Reilly, 'Might do you some good to let in a fresh breeze.'

'And next ya gonna tell me that the place is too big for me, and I need some help with the garden?' He was acting like a grumpy old man, and it amused Lucy.

'Somebody been rattling you then?'

'Ah, only the parish busybodies, they think they know better.'

'I see, well, in that case, I'll keep schtum.' It occurred to her that she had not yet been offered a cup of tea, so she scooped up St Augustus and carried him like a baby into the kitchen.

'Are you still on that posh stuff Father?' she shouted through to the lounge as she busied herself with the tea making while cradling the cat in one arm.

'Yes, my tea caddy is the one with the black lid.' Lucy sniffed it and guffawed, pulling a face and sticking her tongue out to the cat.

'You want a whiff?' She offered the opened tea caddy towards his face, and the cat leapt free and slunk moodily out of the kitchen. Lucy hunted at the back of the cupboard to where she knew the best biscuits were stashed and pulled out three Viennese swirls, then on impulse reached for two more.

'I bumped into Mr Connolly in town this morning.' She spoke with a mouthful of biscuits. 'Naomi's pregnant again.'

'Sweet Jesus, bless the poor woman and all those little kiddies she's got already, that'll make eight now, or seven, I … I'm losing count I am.'

'Hmm.'

'Anyhow, what do you mean in town this morning? It's early enough as it is now.' Father O'Reilly nodded in the direction of the carriage clock on the mantel.

'Yeah, tell me about it. I was woken up at seven-thirty this morning by a bunch of house clearers! Come to clear out the loft, they said.'

'What? … getaway. Scavengers! The poor woman is not even buried yet, she's not.'

'Apparently, grandma booked them last week.' A frown appeared on the old man's face as his mind considered this information.

'Yeah … can't remember … Hoggs! from Kearis. He had a couple of lads in the van from what I could make out, not sure how much stuff they were expecting to get out of it. Nobody's been up there in years. I think I was about thirteen the last time we got a ladder up there. We started keeping the Christmas tree under the stairs when gran's knees got dodgy. Do you really think they could be scallywags, on the make?' Lucy dunked and gobbled biscuits between sentences. 'Heard through the grapevine about gran's passing and think I've got family antiques up there?'

'Well now, I'm not so sure, Hoggs is a respectable firm enough. Sure, there aren't any pests up there? And your ma called in the wrong people?'

'Pests?'

'Birds nesting, mice, or the like?'

'Oh, holy Jesus, Mary and Joseph, I didn't think of that, do you think it could be rats?'

'Maybe not, if you've got 'em the whole lane would have 'em, and somebody else would have mentioned it by now, I'm sure.' The priest was gazing into the fire and the flames reflected in his eyes.

'True, well, I'm not asking the same guys to come back, made a bit of a spectacle of myself I did, being so early and all.'

'No need to rush into anything, for now, concentrate on the funeral, you can get the house sorted later.' Father O'Reilly gazed at her over his mug. There was a strange look on his face. It was a look she had never seen before, and she couldn't fathom the thoughts and feelings behind it. It made her uneasy and hesitant to pursue any further inquisition on the matter.

'Hmm.' Lucy was non-committal; she was already thinking who she might call to borrow some ladders.

Chapter 7

The broth had warmed Lucy and the daytime TV show and saggy old armchair were working their usual magic and making her sleepy. She fought the fatigue, finding the jewellery had become a priority because she needed to know her budget for the funeral so she could get on with the arrangements. Until the items were valued, she was unsure about which casket, flowers or headstone she could order. The loft contractors had aroused Lucy's suspicions and she wanted to find the valuables before she allowed anyone to go poking around in the cottage.

She stood in the doorway of her mother's old bedroom and let her eyes scan the room for a possible location of a jewellery box. The room had not been decorated in decades. The delicate flower print wallpaper was faded in patches where the sunlight fell on it. Peeling corners had been glued too many times for Lucy to remember. The events of the last few days had brought back memories of her mother and Lucy imagined her now, sitting at the dressing table applying her make-up and perfume. She remembered the bottle of scent, a sleek black atomiser, a prized possession that she had held onto for years after her mother had gone. This bedroom now served as the designated guest room, but it was still always referred to as her mother's room. The furniture was the same as the décor, tired and old-fashioned.

Lucy pulled over a chair so she could reach the boxes piled on top of the wardrobe. She came across some old scarves and hats she had used for dressing up as a child.

In other boxes, she found old toys, vinyl records and tatty envelopes full of well-used dress patterns. Her eyes stopped roaming when she found a battered tartan suitcase behind some boxes. She pulled the case forward and tested its weight before lifting it down. The thing was covered in dust, and she turned her face away as the movement unsettled the decades' old powder. The case was no bigger than a large vanity case and she tried the clasp. She was relieved the lid popped open easily and delighted as childhood memories flooded back as she handled once cherished dolls, she hadn't laid her eyes on in over twenty years.

Further inspection revealed nothing of any value, an old iron and numerous board games. Lucy tried to replace the dislocated boxes and cases as she'd found them but her impatience at not finding the jewellery was beginning to bite and she unceremoniously stuffed some items back haphazardly. After she had explored every drawer and cupboard in her mother's old room she reluctantly decamped into her grandmother's and opened the walnut wardrobe. Her grandmother's scent escaped and once again grief knotted the muscles in her stomach. She fingered the small selection of dresses hanging from the rails and stroked the stack of neatly folded jumpers but her emotions, threatening to distract her from the task at hand, were pushed away and she focussed hard to avoid another descent into despair and sorrow. Through her tears, Lucy spied an old tin chocolate box on a top shelf and her eyes widened when she pulled off the lid and found exactly what she had been searching for.

The glittering pieces of treasure thrilled her just as much as when she had first laid eyes on them as a youngster. She turned the watch and the tiny diamonds on the silver cocktail watch sparkled as they caught the light. Small italic lettering on the face declared it to be a Cartier. Lucy felt a pang, having to sell this beautiful thing would be a big disappointment.

As Lucy twirled and examined the timepiece, she noticed an inscription on the back.

Katherine Sinoli, my beautiful bride.

Sinoli? She was stumped. She said the name out loud a few times, it didn't jog any memories. Her father's name was Cooper, had he given her mother a pet name? And bride? A wedding gift, she surmised, and hoped the inscription wouldn't devalue the watch, maybe it could be polished out or the back replaced. The tin box also contained some black rosary beads and a smaller cardboard gift box which she recognised as containing the wedding ring. She tipped it onto the carpet.

The rock was a large oblong clear stone. She whistled at the size of the gem. Lucy knew very little about jewellery and even less about diamonds, but she knew enough to recognise that this ring was valuable, and her grandmother had alluded to that fact many years ago. The stone was far too big and too extravagant for her taste, but she slid it onto her own finger to scrutinise it by the window. Her mother's hands were smaller, she could only get the ring as far as her knuckle on her wedding finger. There were no inscriptions on this, and she made the decision to sell only the ring and keep the watch if she had that luxury.

Lucy stuffed the jewellery into her pockets, raced downstairs and leafed through the telephone directory until she found the pages listing jewellers. She found two shops in Kearis, but the town was small and small towns held no secrets. Word might get around that she was selling the family heirlooms and she didn't want her financial affairs gossiped about. Lucy decided to widen her search. There was a bigger town twenty miles away. If she timed it right, she could get there and then collect Janey from the train station in Kearis as arranged, on her way back.

Chapter 8

Lucy had to concentrate to navigate the one-way traffic system through the ancient market town. The town had become a mecca for shoppers since its recent addition of a modern mall and drew shoppers from all over West Ireland. The narrow streets and ancient boulevards didn't accommodate 21st-century traffic very well and when Lucy eventually found a carpark, she tried to soothe her frazzled nerves and checked the tatty piece of paper with a scribbled address.

She found the store easily; its name was emblazoned in silver italic letters across a deep blue façade. Gold, silver and expensive looking gems winked at her from the brightly lit window. The price tag on the items intimidated her and Lucy's instincts were to keep on walking. As she was about to turn and walk away, she noticed a small sign that said, "Valuations for Insurance and Probate" and before she knew it, she was inside the shop.

'Good morning, dear. Can I help you?' A skinny man in a pinstripe suit appeared from a back room.

'My grandma died, and I need her jewellery valued ... I'd like it valued please.' The words tumbled out, they sounded robotic, but she was nervous in these surroundings. She dug into her pocket and pulled the ring from the cardboard box and placed both items on the glass counter. The assistant gasped almost inaudibly and snatched up the jewellery and placed it gently, seemingly to her, overly dramatic, into a velvet-lined tray. Lucy sensed she had committed a faux pas which added to her discomfort.

'I'm not sure if I want to sell both items but I need to raise some money for funeral expenses. It kinda depends on the value, ... how much will a valuation be?' The man said nothing but continued his scrutiny of the ring through his jeweller's loop. Lucy felt embarrassment clawing at her complexion. She had no idea why she had not just asked for a valuation and left it at that. He didn't need to know the reason she was here or even how she had acquired the jewellery. She pretended to be surveying the display cases while he swirled the ring this way and that. Lucy took a sneaky glance at his face to glean a clue as to what he might be thinking. He eventually lay both items back in the velvet tray and offered her a wide smile.

'Is there a box with this watch?' Lucy shook her head. 'Not to worry; I need to make some calls and it will be a few days before I can give you an accurate quote on that.' Lucy frowned and opened her mouth to speak.

'Both items are quality pieces, Miss ...?'

'Lucy.'

'Lucy. I will need to consult with a colleague about this watch. These timepieces are very collectable, it may have been a commissioned piece, made to order. The ring I can value today, a written valuation is thirty euros.' Lucy nodded as if to give him the go-ahead to proceed with the valuation, but he hadn't noticed. 'Emerald cut, 3 carats, superb clarity, platinum shank.' He continued to put the ring through some scrutiny and swapped his lens equipment and subjected it to a device of some kind. He repeated the words 'superb quality' as a whisper to himself.

'I'd put a retail value of about twelve or thirteen thousand euros. For insurance purposes, you would be looking to cover the maximum valuation of course.' I can write that up for you. The jeweller seemed to be waiting for her to say something, but Lucy had lost control of her jaw. When she became aware she was gawping at the tall skinny man, she snapped her mouth shut. She was sure if she swallowed, she would choke on her own saliva, so she just nodded and pulled out her purse to find thirty euros.

The jeweller took the euros and disappeared behind a heavy blue curtain, Lucy scrutinised a display of earrings, not seeing any of them. She was too stunned at the ring's valuation. When the man returned, she cleared her throat and tried to appear nonchalant as he handed her a sheet of paper.

'Of course, the valuation reflects current market prices which can go up and down, and we don't pay retail prices but if you are looking to sell the ring then I can consult with my partner to see what we would be willing to offer.' Lucy needed some fresh air, and she almost snatched the embossed letterhead from his fingers and scooped up her now incredibly valuable jewellery from the counter. The jeweller gasped as Lucy stuffed the items back into her pocket.

'Madam would you care to purchase a box for the ...'

'Nope. No. Thank you. Not today.'

'Miss, Lucy, ..., those items are very valuable, the watch looks like it may possibly have been a commissioned item and you might want to be careful not to get it scratched or lose the stones.' He opened a drawer and extracted a small velvet bag, the same royal blue as the store livery and handed it to Lucy, 'You had a box for the ring I believe?'

'Oh, yes, I see, well ... thank you.' She replaced her very expensive ring back into the cheap cardboard gift box and the watch into the velvet pouch he gave her. 'Thank you very much.'

'Take good care of them. At a very prudent first estimate, I would estimate the watch to be at least twice the value of the ring, dear. Should you wish to sell either item please do not hesitate in coming back to see us.'

'I'll have a think about things, and I'll let you know.'

Lucy chided herself for not researching the stuff online before bringing them here. She understood why he had baulked when she tipped the jewellery onto the counter. She delicately pushed the pouch deep into her pocket and kept her hand clasped around them like a cushioned vice. She had planned to browse the shopping arcades before heading off to collect Janey but knowing what valuable cargo she held she instead walked quickly back to her car. Some vexing questions were running through her mind. Had her grandmother known how valuable these pieces were? And how could her father have afforded such expensive jewellery?

Lucy listened. The buzzing went on for a while and then switched to voice mail. Janey's messaging system asked her to leave her name and number and Lucy excitedly relayed the day's activities into a machine. As she repeated the value of the ring over the line, she caught herself and anxiously scanned the car park to make sure nobody could overhear. As an added security measure, she flicked the door lock and continued to squeal into her mobile phone.

'Call me when the train gets in, I'll be in the carpark.' She chirped excitedly and then hung up. She was relieved she wouldn't have to sell the watch; the ring would be more than enough to cover the funeral expenses. Her grandmother was right when she'd told her the jewellery would bury them both.

Lucy scanned her phone for the undertaker's number and proudly ordered the flowers and casket that she liked but initially thought would be too expensive. She reversed the car out of her parking space and headed back into the busy one-way traffic system.

Chapter 9

The borrowed black wool wrap-around dress and high heels didn't suit Lucy. She was used to wearing jeans and boots and had the gait to go with them. Normally she would have blankly refused to wear such things, but today it suited her to act out a part. The previous day Edith and her daughter had brought piles of clothes for both her and Janey to try on and select for the funeral. As the day arrived Lucy had risen before dawn and was now dressed and sat in quiet contemplation at the window waiting for Janey to stir and the day to start. Eventually she heard her best friend's heavy tread coming down the stairs.

'Is my watch lying to me?' Janey drawled through a yawn as she surveyed Lucy's hair and wardrobe. Lucy didn't shift her gaze from the hilly vista.

'No, I'm just up early. Couldn't really sleep so I decided to get everything sorted. Somebody is bound to turn up early. You know what old folk are like.' She spoke in a monotone, indicating her disinterest and anxiety about the day ahead.

The funeral was scheduled for ten thirty and it was a short walk to the church, but Lucy had ordered two funeral cars. Lucy, Janey, Tim, and Edith would go in one car, a handful of her grandma's elderly friends that couldn't manage the walk would go in the second.

'Oh, I better get myself showered then. Have you eaten?'

'Yeah, I had some of the sandwiches as I made them.' Janey glanced into the dining room. The table was covered with a white tablecloth and stacked with plates of sandwiches, pies and cakes, all covered with cling film. Janey moved to get a closer look and stood wide-eyed with her hands on her hips.

'Wow. The fairies have been.' She muttered this to herself, but then yelled over her shoulder. 'Have you left anything for me to do?' There was no reply and Janey lifted the film from one plate and took a fondant fancy for her breakfast. She was evening out the pile so the theft would go unnoticed when from right behind her Lucy spoke.

'Janey Stucker you should be ashamed of yourself! That's hardly a nutritional breakfast and those are for later!' Janey jumped out of her skin and nearly dropped the cake. She stuffed the whole thing into her mouth before Lucy could whip it off her. Lucy laughed and tried to squash the cheeks stuffed with cake.

'I hope you choke on it!' Lucy giggled as Janey tried in vain to keep the cake in her mouth despite the onslaught from her friend and her own spluttering laughter. Lucy retreated into the kitchen as Janey, still laughing, bent down to pick up pieces of yellow icing off the carpet.

'Coffee with your cake, madam?' She went to fill the kettle and tried to keep the smile off her face. 'Leave that mess, I was going to run the vacuum around anyway once you were up.'

'Ah, well there is something useful *I* can do then. What time did you start all this?' Janey still on her knees nodded in the direction of the buffet.

'Hmm, not sure. There is one thing that you can do.' Janey liking the idea of being useful raised her chin in expectation. 'Could you take Tim's car over to Kearis and collect him from the station about nine thirty? If I go, it's pushing it a bit, in case anybody shows up here early.'

'Erm ... hmm. Okay.' Janey mulled it over, her reluctance was nothing to do with Tim. She wasn't used to driving manual cars and driving through unfamiliar narrow country lanes on the opposite side of the road than the one she was used to driving, filled her with dread. She pushed the rising anxiety to the back of her mind and reluctantly nodded. She mentally drove the route and got mixed up somewhere. 'You'll have to draw me a map.'

'Yeah, I did already, but don't worry, you will only have to drive it one way. Tim can drive it back from the station.' Janey was grateful for her friend's telepathic skills.

'He'll have to. He won't want to see or hear the damage I'll be inflicting on his gearbox!' Lucy laughed again and Janey smiled knowing she had pulled her friend from the melancholy she had found her in five minutes ago.

***

All the villagers had come for the Mass, but Lucy didn't turn around so was unaware that the frigid old church was full with standing room only at the back. Sitting with her hand enclosed in Tim's wide fingers and her best friend next to her she felt lonelier than she had ever been in her life. Something had gone forever, and she was unsure how her life was supposed to endure. Father O'Reilly's voice washed in and out of her conscious hearing. She stood up when everybody else did and knelt and sang at the appropriate times.

When Janey walked up to the pulpit to deliver her reading, Lucy didn't hear the words. It didn't matter. She had picked out the reading and she had heard her friend rehearsing it copious times the day before. Now she knew it by heart. Janey returned to her seat next to Lucy and they continued a never-ending routine of standing, sitting and then kneeling for prayers until the pallbearers eventually moved in to pick up the coffin. Lucy panicked momentarily and reached out for her grandmother before Janey's arms pulled her back.

'We'll follow in a minute, Luce.' Janey told her in a church whisper. People stood up to leave and the choir muffled Lucy's sobs. The bright daylight momentarily blinded Lucy as she followed the coffin out of the dark church.

Some mourners peeled off and made their way out of the churchyard. Lucy followed the priest and her grandmother's friends to the burial plot. In her unfamiliar high heels, she was extra cautious in navigating the worn and uneven flagstones slippy with damp moss. Granite headstones glittered with the frost and neatly cut grass around the stones looked as if it had received a light dusting with icing sugar. Lucy began to tremble when her eyes found the deep black hole where her grandmother would rest. She tried to control her emotions until Father O'Reilly had finished his prayers. His prose sent warm plumes of breath into the cold air. When the coffin was lowered into the grave Lucy turned and fled back through the cemetery. She heard Janey calling after her, but she didn't want to see the coffin disappear into the cold ground. At the edge of the churchyard, she leant against a gatepost and waited for Tim and Janey to catch her up.

Through her blurred tears, Lucy noticed a sleek dark car parked further up the narrow lane that ran around the graveyard. A young man stood watching the burial. With Lucy's scrutiny he turned to walk away but glanced back and when they made eye contact, his pace quickened as he strode back towards his car. The words of her neighbour came flooding back to Lucy and her interest was piqued.

'Helllooo.' Lucy bellowed as loud as she could. The stranger was some distance away and she waved an arm in a wide arc to catch his attention. He gave a final glance over his shoulder as he ducked into the vehicle. She was slightly perplexed that someone might come to the funeral and not introduce themselves. She tried to catch the car.

'Hey, helllooo ...' Her shoes and the icy path restricted her speed and the car drove away before she could get anywhere near it.

'Who's that?' Janey said breathlessly as she jogged up to her friend.

'Do you think he could hear me? He must have been able to hear me. Why didn't he wait?' Lucy watched the car disappear and turned to her friend with puzzled eyes.

'Do you know him?' Janey asked

'No. That's so weird.'

'What's weird?'

'Something Mrs O'Malley said about 'a cousin' coming to the funeral.' Lucy glanced at Janey, but Janey's eyes were looking in the direction the car had taken.

'I thought you didn't have any other family?' 'I don't!'

'So, who the hell was he?'

'I have no idea. He completely ignored me! He saw me and then just drove off!' Lucy folded her arms across her chest trying to keep her irritation under wraps. She was indignant and Janey knew enough not to get her riled. Instead she tried to change the subject.

'Who's Mrs O'Malley?'

'She used to live a few doors down from us.'

'Maybe he came to the wrong funeral. I'd be embarrassed if I'd come to the wrong one and I'd defo run away without talking to anybody.' She hooked her arm under Lucy's and glanced back towards the grave.

'Do you want to go back down there and say goodbye?' She nodded in the direction of the grave, where Tim was still talking with the priest. A couple of neighbours remained at the grave holding their rosary beads with bowed heads.

'No, I'll come back tomorrow to sort out the flowers. We should get back to the house really, there might be some people waiting to get inside to the warm.'

***

The cottage felt warm and homely after the dank church. Muted chatter and bodies filled all the available space in the small rooms. Borrowed chairs occupied every corner and Lucy had to squeeze her way through bodies to distribute her sandwiches to anyone unable to get to the table. She also had an ulterior motive; she was looking for Mrs O'Malley. There was no sign of her ample frame in the kitchen or dining room, so Lucy made her way to the sitting room. As she squeezed through the throng of bodies, she caught Janey's eye. Her friend grimaced at her and Lucy pretended not to notice her dilemma; she needed rescuing from old man Roddy. Janey's ability to decipher the Irish dialect was sometimes a struggle and Roddy's patois meant he was probably the worst person she could get stuck in a corner with. However, she would have to suffer a little while longer. Lucy's priority was to find and talk to Mrs O'Malley. The mysterious stranger at the grave had raised some questions and Lucy wanted answers. Could this be the mysterious cousin she had mentioned a few days ago?

The front room was stuffed with as many people as the other rooms, all the chairs were occupied, and several children were taking up floor space. Tim was sitting on the arm of the sofa charming the ladies, old and young; they hung onto his every word. Edith's daughter Angela seemed to be particularly captivated by Tim and could only take her eyes off him when she was distracted by Jerry brandishing porcelain ornaments he'd lifted from the fireplace. Lucy spotted her target in her grandma's armchair, and there was little hope of having a private chat with so many people around.

Lucy offered around the sandwiches, there were few takers, so she put the plate on the coffee table. Jerry made a beeline for the pile and his mother relaxed as his attention had been diverted from anything breakable. Lucy lurked and waited for an opportunity to engage Mrs O'Malley in a private chat.

The afternoon dragged on; the mourners thinned out and Lucy had started to put more than a tipple of brandy in the teapot in the hope it would make the rest of the old folk sleepy and nod off. It had the opposite effect. Folk were instead getting merry, and it was the final straw for Lucy when somebody suggested a singsong. She wrestled a bottle of whiskey from old man Roddy and announced that she would be clearing away the buffet. If anybody wanted to continue their commiserations, she would be putting a few Euro behind the bar in the local pub. The mention of the pub did the trick and old bones were stirred. A mass exodus to the pub followed.

Lucy spotted Mrs O'Malley being helped with her coat and grabbed it off the kindly helper so she could monopolise the old woman.

'I'm sorry for being blunt the other day when you called round, Mrs O'Malley. I think it was just ... all this getting to me.' The old woman stopped trying to stuff her bulky arms into her coat sleeves and turned rosy cheeks to look at Lucy.

'Tis the shock, you know, can short-circuit the brain. No, don't you worry about that ... we've lost enough around here to know what grief does ...'

'Yes. Erm ... thing is, that cousin?' Lucy interrupted Mrs O'Malley otherwise she would not have got a word in edgeways. 'Well, I'm sure he turned up here today, at the funeral.'

'God bless tha ...'

' ... but you know what, it's so embarrassing, well, I can't remember his name. Haven't seen him since I was a young 'un and, well I felt so rude.' Lucy expected Mrs O'Malley to volunteer some information, but she might have left it too late. The woman was inebriated and beyond any coherent questions. Lucy could smell the liquor on her breath and so she tried a more direct route.

'When did you last see him visit gran?'

'Hmm, let me see, well he always came around Christmas times, and I've only been in my flat these last few months, must 'ave been, erm ...' Lucy was holding tight to the swaying Mrs O'Malley and Father O'Reilly appeared in the hall.

'I think we had better get you into a taxi.' He interjected into the conversation.

'Mrs O'Malley was just telling me about my "cousin", from America.' Lucy's eyes also directed the question to the priest.

'Ah you've all been reading too many of those Mills and Boon books, tall dark strangers 'n' all.' Father O'Reilly did not look at Lucy and instead hurried Mrs O'Malley into her coat.

'Father there was a stranger at the burial this morning, I tried to speak to him, but he ran off.' The door knocker rattled and interrupted her flow. Lucy opened the door to find one of her old school friends on the doorstep.

'Kieran, how are you doing?'

'Hiya Lucy, I've been summoned to collect tha ma. I'm so sorry to hear about your granma.'

'Thanks, Kieran, I heard you were in church this morning. I'm sorry I didn't get a chance to see you earlier.'

'Ay no worries, your ma was the best jam butty maker in all Anchora. How would I dare miss her send off? Ma, come on, I left the car running.'

'We might make it down to the pub later if you fancy a pint.'

'All right, yeah, I'll see you there. Mrs O'Malley, would you care for a lift? I can go by your flats no problem.' Lucy had no chance to protest, she had not finished with Mrs O'Malley, but the last of the mourners were ushered into Kieran's car and there was nothing she could do about it. She shut the front door on them all and leaned against it with a sigh. She could hear Janey giggling in the dining room and went to see what was going on. Tim had collapsed on the table with his head on his arms feigning exhaustion.

'Any of them left?' Lucy said as she cast her eyes over the destruction in the cottage.

'Just the one under there. He passed out a couple of hours ago, we thought it best to let him sleep it off.' Janey pointed under the table and Lucy, horrified, bent to lift the tablecloth. Her friends both roared with laughter at her gullibility.

They chatted about the day. Tim told the girls, how at one point during the afternoon, fed up with making tea, he had decided to announce that they had run out of milk and somehow, like by magic little old ladies appeared in the kitchen laden with pints of milk under both arms. He had given them another hour or two and then decided that the kettle sprung a leak and hence be unusable in the hope they might all toddle off home.

'So, it was your fault the Whiskey came out!' Janey shrieked.

'That's what kept them all here longer! The sing-along was the final straw for me. They'd be here all night if they had started the singing, you know that,' Lucy told Tim.

'Maybe that might not have been such a bad idea. We could have crept out and gone to the pub without them. They would never have noticed us going,' he said.

'Oh no! I forgot about the pub.' Lucy groaned and rubbed at her eyes. 'Do we really have to go down there?' The day had taken its toll and a sombre note had returned to Lucy's voice.

'No, 'course not, honey. Everyone will understand if you're not up to it.' Janey saw the fatigue on her friend's face.

'I can pop down there, show my face, buy a few pints, maybe put a few Euros behind the bar for later arrivals,' Tim announced, nodding to himself at the idea.

'That's a good idea, us girls can get on with clearing up this place.' Janey cast her eyes over the carnage of abandoned plates and glasses.

'Don't even think about it, Janey, it's down to me to clear up all this shite. You go with Tim, keep him company in the boozer.' She spoke with a wry smile, 'I know you actually wanted that sing-song anyways.' Janey was about to argue but caught a silent plea in Lucy's eyes and figured she wanted a bit of space. The house had been full of people all day and knowing Lucy as she did, she figured she would be craving some quiet time, so she agreed.

***

Father O'Reilly rode in the back seat with Mrs O'Malley. Kieran re-tuned the car radio from a rock station to an easy listening one for the sake of his passengers.

'How is she coping, Father?' Kieran's eyes sought out the priest's in his rear-view mirror, concern for his old school friend causing creasing to his brows.

'Well now, she's getting through it with all our help Kieran. Not having any family left is hard. We all need to keep an eye out for the lass, especially in these next few weeks. It's going to be a lonely time and will take some adjusting. Being in that house all alone ... well ...'

'Ah yes, very strange that'll be, I'll say.' Kieran's mother agreed from the front seat. Knowing the other passengers could hear him Father O'Reilly lowered his voice and leant into the large woman sharing the back seat with him.

'Mrs O'Malley, I think Lucy is in a very fragile state of mind at the moment.' Hesitating so that he was sure he had her full attention.

'Oh, she is, to be sure.'

'And all this chatter, about this cousin. I've heard it mentioned, and well I can tell you for certain Mrs O'Malley; there are no distant family members of the Whites, here, or anywhere else in the world.'

'But ...' the old woman tried to intervene, but the priest silenced her with a firm hand on her knee and continued his sharp whisper.

'Any gossip to that effect is only going to give the poor girl some false hope to cling to. And that's a very cruel thing to do, Mrs O'Malley. And I know for a fact such a fine Catholic as yerself would never want to cause distress to somebody grieving now.' Mrs O'Malley had her mouth open waiting for the priest to finish, but the priest cast her a look that silenced her words and her thoughts. In no uncertain terms he had warned her to keep quiet and she closed her mouth with a nod.

The car pulled up to the vicarage door and the priest got out. He said his goodbyes and waved as the vehicle pulled away and wondered if he had done enough to quieten the old woman. The story sounded plausible. Mrs O'Malley had noticed an infrequent visitor to the Whites' and so Mary would have had to invent a cover story. Father O'Reilly sighed and turned to make his way inside. It had been a long day and St Augustus would be surely dancing for his dinner by now.

***

Tim and Janey walked down the steep hill towards the local pub. A light rain had made the flagstones shiny, and the moon silhouetted the distant hills against a twilight sky. Other than being slightly larger than its neighbouring properties the pub was not much different from any of the other whitewashed cottages that lined the main road through Anchora. The orange glow coming from all the windows and the faint din of many chattering voices signalled it to be a public house instead of a private residential dwelling. Tim spoke first.

'It's nice to be out of that house.'

'Yeah.' It was quite oppressive; Janey had been so concerned about Lucy's thoughts and feelings she had not given Tim a second thought throughout the day. 'It was a hard day to get through. Do you think she's gonna be okay?'

'Sure, I don't think we should be gone for more than an hour or so because I imagine this pub is going to be very smoky.'

'No, I don't mean now. I mean tomorrow, next week, next month?' Janey asked and Tim slowed his stride.

'She's gonna be fine, Janey, at least for the next few days. You're still around, right? After that, I don't know. It depends just on how good a friend you're gonna be because you and I both know she doesn't want me in her life in the longer term.' Tim stopped walking completely now and looked squarely at Janey. They both seemed as shocked as the other that it had been spoken out loud. Janey struggled to find something to say, but she could not deny it and Tim took this as a confirmation, and he started walking again.

'Lucy doesn't know what she wants right now, Tim, but I do know she is concerned about taking up your time in your final year.'

'It doesn't matter, I can give her time, space, whatever she wants. I just get the feeling you're going to be featuring in her future more than I am. I don't want a big discussion about it. You asked, and I told you the facts.' Janey bit her lip, this was the Tim she knew, the one she didn't like very much. He had been in hiding for a few days and she wished he'd stayed in his box.

'This is a great pub, have you been in here before? They are all really friendly.' She tried to move the conversation on from its awkward arrest.

'As opposed to not being so friendly out here?' Tim raised an eyebrow and gave a crooked smile at Janey.

'Ur huh.' She nodded.

'No, I haven't been in here before, and they are going to be friendly anywhere you are. You're American, you're a novelty in this small place.' Tim's grin widened and he pulled open the door for her. 'Come on, you're doing all the talking.'

Janey relaxed a little as they walked into the busy pub. News of Mary White's funeral had spread far and wide and several of the patrons raised their pints in a salutation and commiseration. Somebody stepped up to offer the new arrivals a drink.

'What will it be, my friends? A pint of our black stuff or a drop of the harder stuff to warm yers up?'

'Thank you, but Lucy has asked me to buy you all a drink on her behalf, she's not feeling ... ' Tim spoke loudly hoping the crowd might hear what he was saying. The landlord saw Tim struggling to be heard above the chatter and rang the bar bell to silence the rabble. The room went quiet, and Tim thanked the landlord and turned his attention to his audience.

'As many of you know, Mary White was buried this morning, and Lucy has asked us to come and buy you all a drink in her memory. She is not up to it herself; it has been a long day and so we are here on her behalf. Landlord ...' Tim passed over a wad of notes and asked for two pints. It started the ball rolling and the landlord struggled to keep up with the orders being shouted over the bar.

***

Lucy put a hand in to test the temperature and found it was perfect, then climbed into the bath. She slid down low into the tub so only her face protruded above the water line and let the hot liquid envelope her taut muscles. The day had been a test of endurance and she was glad it was behind her. She lay listening to her own heartbeat under the water. If she closed her eyes and concentrated, she could pretend the last few days had never happened. Her lids were heavy from the lack of sleep and her head filled with a lifetime of conversations with her grandmother. She lay there and let memories replay in her mind.

The murmur of next door's TV could be just about heard if she held her breath. If she could hear theirs then surely, they would have been able to hear her grandmother's and did they now notice the silence? Did they miss her grandmother as much as she did? She closed her eyes and listened to the ghost voices of the last twenty years reverberating around the tiny cottage. Never having known the house so quiet and empty like this caused a stab of grief. Lucy called out, as she had done a million times before.

'Ma ...' It was barely a whisper, and she cleared her throat. 'Granma.' She felt a cold stone of anguish knot in her stomach when no reply came back. The silence tormented her and forced a wail from her lungs. 'GRANDMA.' A holler like this would have brought reproach in the past. *"If you want me, come down here and speak to me here. Stop yer yelling around the house, its bad manners."*

Edith had turned down her TV.

'Oh my god!' Lucy jumped out of the bath, donned a large rough towel, shoved wet feet into slippers and hurried downstairs. She waited expectantly for a knock at the front door. Edith would be worrying about her now. It was the nature of these small cottages. If you sneezed somebody would know. Sure enough, the shrill of the telephone jolted her and Lucy held the knowing smile out of her voice as she answered.

'Hello.'

'That you Lucy, my love?'

'Yes, Edith.'

'You could have woken the devil, with that there hollering my dear. I'm just getting the child into a blanket, and I'll be right round ...'

'Oh no! I'm sorry, I'm so sorry It didn't occur to me Jerry would be sleeping there tonight, Edith. I'm ... sorry, I was just having a mad moment and all ... it's the silence ... it's just getting to me a bit.'

'Yes, my dear, I know ... I'll come and keep you company, no trouble at all.'

'No. Really, it's okay, I've just run the bath and I'm going to plop myself right into it just now. Don't you be getting yourself a chill by coming outside. I promise I'm fine, and Janey and Tim will be back from the pub soon enough. I'm sooo sorry for waking the child.'

'Oh no. Takes more than that to disturb this little kitten, but if, you're sure.'

'I am.'

'Okay then, take care yourself, I'll be round in the morning.' Lucy put the phone back on its hook slowly. From two doors up Mrs O'Malley had noticed an annual visitor but from next door, through walls thin enough to yell through, Edith hadn't? Lucy grabbed a dirty glass from the table and a half-empty bottle of brandy and headed back upstairs to her bath.

Chapter 10

Lucy despatched Janey into Anchora with a list of errands while she waited at the cottage for her old school friend to deliver a set of ladders. Since the contractors had turned up to clear the loft her mind had been preoccupied with getting up there and inspecting its contents. Finding the jewellery had raised more questions than answers and she wanted to see why her grandmother, after all these years, had decided to get the space cleared.

The day after the funeral Lucy had stalked the narrow alley behind the cottages, peeking over her neighbour's stone walls looking for ladders that she might borrow. She found nothing so turned to the faux leather telephone directory on the hall table and leafed through dog-eared pages until she came across a school friend who was now a decorator.

Janey had assumed the role of a health and safety officer and made Lucy promise to wait for her return from town before climbing ladders and lugging boxes about. Lucy was already hopping with anticipation and knew it was unlikely she would honour her friend's request, but while she waited, she busied herself with some housekeeping. It at least stopped her from waiting expectantly at the window.

Just as she finished washing breakfast pots and wiped the soap suds from her arms the door knocker clattered. She threw the tea towel onto the counter and skipped through the house. Leo was given a warm welcome, ushered in and proffered tea as the two friends exchanged gossip. Lucy was away so much she always had to catch up. Who was seeing who, who had moved in or out of town, who was engaged, married, divorced, or buried? Leo's news was on the list.

'So it won't be long before the pitter patter of tiny feet is sounding for you two!' Lucy grinned. Leo lugged an aluminium ladder upstairs and positioned it against the loft hatch.

'Are yer sure you don't want me to go in first? That hatch might be a bit sticky if it hasn't been opened for a while you know. Might need a good firm shove.' His scrutiny of her puny muscles made her agree to him popping the hatch door.

'Hmm maybe you should, and check if there is anything moving about up there, will ya?'

'What! What do you mean moving? Have you heard anything?' Leo jogged up the ladders unperturbed no.

'Nope, but I'm just being cautious. Don't rats go for your neck?' Lucy shuddered.

'Sure, you're ready? They might come jumping out, better close all the doors. You don't want 'em running amok around the bedrooms.' The look on Lucy's face made Leo chuckle and he struck a firm blow at the hatch which thrust the door upwards. Before she could speak his head disappeared into the dark square and his voice came back muffled.

'Got any electricity up here?'

'Mm', she tried to remember. 'Yeah, there is definitely a light, somewhere.' Lucy was straining her neck back to try and see inside the loft. Leo pulled his body up into the dark space and then a yellow square replaced the black void.

'The light switch is on a beam to the left, for future reference. But you might want to bring a torch up here though, the corners are dark, it's all boarded.'

'Okay. Any rats?' Lucy was expecting a quirky reply or a sarcastic remark to her obvious nervous question, but Leo stepped out of view and there was a silence for a couple of minutes until he reappeared at the square hole again.

'Not even any old bird's nests up here. A load of old boxes, books and toys by the looks of it. You sure you don't want me to start bringing a few down?'

'No, it's okay. Me and Janey can manage the ladders between us.' Leo switched the light off and jogged back down the ladder leaving the hatch open.

'Do you want me to close that up again? It should be easy enough to open now it's been cracked. I could just wedge it a bit. Might lose a bit of heat if it's left open.'

'No need, I'm going up there soon as Janey is back. Thanks, Leo. I really appreciate this you know.' The friends hugged, and she promised to get the ladders back to him soon. Leo's happy and easy-going chatter had brightened her day, but she was eager to close the door behind him and scramble up the ladder and get into the boxes that her grandma had wanted shot off.

Halfway up Lucy gripped the sides of the wobbly aluminium ladders and contemplated the steps she had just climbed. She fretted momentarily about getting back down. Leo had made it look so easy. It was too late now, she was almost at the top; she could see the naked light bulb hanging from a beam and she located the light switch, took the last few steps, and stretched up to click it on. Leo was right. The light didn't reach much beyond the centremost of the loft and she cursed. In her eagerness to get up here, she forgot his advice about a torch. The loft was also freezing cold, and she rubbed her hands together as she surveyed the fragments of her grandmother's lifetime. The dim light illuminated a few boxes closest to the loft door and she pulled one over to thumb through it. She rummaged through old magazines and children's books. She marvelled at the illustrations; they invoked a swell of nostalgia for her childhood. If she re-read each one of them her progress would be slow going, so she started to pile them into stacks of keepers and ones to throw out.

After several boxes of books, she turned her attention to a pile of black plastic bags. They were lightweight and she imagined they contained clothes or bedding and she could just tip them through the hatch to examine downstairs. She watched each one fall to the landing below with a gentle thud then turned her attention to a suitcase which contained an almost identical but smaller version inside. The luggage was very good quality and in super condition. She reflected that her grandmother must have forgotten about them because she'd bought new ones for Lucy when she left for university. Her grandmother was a frugal woman and would not have wasted good money on non-essential purchases.

The smaller case was filled with papers and envelopes; she pulled out a couple of old photographs that caught her eye. One was a semi-circle of nuns outside a vast brick building. Her mother and grandmother were standing among the nuns and smiling for the camera. Lucy's head peeped shyly from between her mother's skirt folds and from the brightness of the photo and the summer clothes her family wore it appeared to be a hot summer day. She estimated she was about two years old, but she could not summon any memories of the time and place. Another photo showed her grandmother and her grandfather sitting side by side on a bench outside a shop. The couple held hands and appeared to be very much in love. She was puzzled that this beautiful photograph was stuffed away with old papers and not, like the one her grandma had of her grandpa, in a frame beside her bed.

Lucy worked her way through stacks of papers and tried to arrange them into neat piles folding and scanning through them as she worked. Sometimes she laughed as memories resurfaced. She found old school reports, postcards, and birthday cards. Her light and wistful mood darkened as she found some of her mother's medical reports and hospital records. She understood the medical prognosis and the shorthand scribbles of various doctors, and it dragged her back to the memories of when her mother was ill. The reality of seeing the details of her mother's illness spelt out in black and white shocked her to the core.

The medical records started from when the family had moved to Anchora, and Lucy followed the documented decline in her mother's health and wondered why her grandmother or Father O'Reilly had not intervened to stop her drinking and the inevitable spiral that resulted in her early death. Lucy put the paperwork to one side, blinking hard and swallowing back tears. Father O'Reilly was right; it was too early for her to be clearing the house. She was revisiting ghosts of the past when one had only just been put to rest. She remembered his introspection when she talked about clearing out the loft and thought now that she understood his caution.

Lucy's hands were covered in grey dust, so she wiped her tears away with the cuff of her sweatshirt and resolved to finish this small suitcase and leave the remainder of the boxes for another day. Another dig into the small case exposed a tightly tied wad of letters. The blue and cream envelopes were sealed and bore no address but had her grandfather's name. Lucy fingered the envelopes in awe. She reluctantly removed the ribbon that held them together and felt a flicker of guilt cross her conscience and she shivered in the frigid temperature of the loft but continued to pick at the corner of a pale blue envelope.

The first one was dated June 1985. Lucy would have been two and a half years old, and she scanned the words.

My Darling Michael,

We have a home now, a tired little place near the Ocean, just like the place we started out from. I sometimes go to the Ocean knowing you're just across it and I pretend to myself that it is only a couple of miles, instead of thousands. I think of you, Joseph, and the babies every single minute of every single day and my heart is heavy. Katherine is not coping very well and there is nothing I can do to ease her pain but try to hide my own and be strong for her and for Sive. December seems such a long time ago and I thought then that in a year or so we would be muddling along, living with our memories and be thankful that we had some happy times all together. But I know now that this will never happen. I will always wonder what you are all doing. I will always have a deep void in my heart and my mind because you are all far away and I can't be with you. I wish desperately that the little ones are all okay and pray each day that you are still a part of little Sine's life. I hope so much that you can forgive us, and I promise I will do my best for our Katherine and Sive.

xxxxx

Lucy's head spun as she re-read the letter and tried to comprehend what she had read. She read the small letter several times and tried to get a fix on her horizon. She felt as though it had shifted. The writing was her grandmother's, but she was writing about strangers. She tore open another envelope.

14th January 1985

My Darling Michael

This is far harder than I ever imagined, it would ever be. I miss you all so much, and so does Katherine. We have new names now and the agent says that he will pass my letter on to you, but I must not mention our location, or any facts about our new life and it pains me to think that you will never ever know what becomes of us. I know that you are all safe and well, I have word at least of that much.

We are supposed to just forget everything and move on, but it is so hard, and I pray for strength from God that he can forgive us all. We are being taken care of by good people and I'm told we will be moved again in a few months when the trial is over. We will get our own house and I'm hoping then our lives will be more settled for Sive's sake. Kiss Joseph and Laura and the children for me, I hope that at least some good comes of Katherine's testimony. I will love you forever.

xxxxx

New names? Lucy tried to make sense of the words she was reading but could not understand any of it. From the first letter she had jumped to the conclusion that her grandmother might have been having an affair and that somehow, her lover had another family. But this one mentioned an agent and new names. It was sounding weirder. Lucy's hands shook as she pulled at the final envelope. Her mouth was dry with the anticipation of what might be in the last of the little envelopes.

12th December 1985

Michael

Katherine is so tortured by her guilt and grief and has become very sick. Her drinking is now constant, and the doctor has told me it may be too late for her now. I cannot bear to see her wither away before my eyes. If I take away the drink, she stays in bed all day and just wails. I'm so terrified of what this may be doing to Sive. The only time Katherine holds the baby is when she is drunk, the rest of the time she can't bear to look at her and I can understand that she just sees Sine as well. I don't know what to do, Michael, and I am praying as hard as I have ever prayed before. If Angela dies, then what am I to do? They tell me Sive will not be safe if we come home, they will want her back and will stop at nothing to get her back if they can find us, but how can I do this all by myself? I miss you so much and I can only go on with this if you tell me that it is the best thing to do for Sive.

Please help me, your darling Rene

xxxxx

Lucy was trembling hard. She had never heard her grandmother complain about anything or ask for help in her life and this letter was just begging for comfort and guidance. She felt light-headed so rested her head in her hands until she had brought her breathing under control and her vision steadied. She put the letters in date order and re read them. If she was Sive, why had her mother hated her and who was Sine? What could she have possibly done to cause so much revulsion? And why did her grandmother sign herself Rene? There were no answers forthcoming, only more and more questions.

New feelings for her grandmother and mother started to manifest and the adrenaline that arrived with the growing anger spurred her flight. Lucy groped for the ladder. She had to get out of here, get out of this loft and out of this house that she suddenly hated. The aluminium ladders rattled loudly as Lucy's unsteady body carefully tried each step in autopilot. She snatched up her keys from the table in the hall and grabbed at the front door. Running outside she took the steep steps two at a time, and she almost mowed Janey down as she fled the tiny cottage.

'Whoa! You're in a hurry.' Janey's face held a puzzled smile as she manoeuvred backwards on the narrow path to let Lucy career to a stop. The bulging bags she was holding dropped to the floor as she took in Lucy's shocked face and trembling body. Janey's smile disappeared and her eyes widened as she took hold of Lucy's arms.

'What's the matter? Where are you running to?'

'I... I don't really know, I just wanted to get away.'

'Get away from what?' Janey eyed the cottage and was aghast to see Lucy had fled leaving the front door swinging on its hinges.

'Who's here?'

'Nobody, I ... I found something in the loft.'

'What?'

'Some letters.'

'Letters! Well what's in the letters to make you want to run away like a wild banshee and leave the front door swingin' on its hinges?' Janey did not wait for an answer. She had one of Lucy's arms firmly in her grasp and was steering her in the direction of the house. 'You better show me these letters.'

'They're in the loft I think, I can't remember where I left them.' Lucy sank into a chair and ignored Janey's grumbling about her going up the ladder while she was out. Lucy stared at her feet, pain and confusion numbing her senses and let Janey's word's wash over her.

Janey returned to the table with the letters and sat across from Lucy. She read the first one gingerly. Lucy scanned her friends face trying to remember which particular words she would be digesting. At first, Janey's face registered confusion and it took her an age to read the letters. Eventually a clenched fist came up to cover her mouth and suppress any words. When eventually Lucy felt her eyes on her face, she thought her friend appeared as if she was seeing her for the first time, there was intrigue in her expression. When she eventually spoke, she was almost inaudible, but Lucy hung on to every word.

'Fuck me! You're in a programme.'

'A programme?'

'Your mom ...' Janey grabbed the second letter and scanned it again. 'Your mom testified against someone. Someone dangerous by the looks of it. The government can put people in a witness protection programme if they are at risk of ...' the sentence trailed off. Lucy felt every hair on her body stand up. She knew what Janey was saying made sense. It was the only logical explanation, but she refused to believe it.

Three small letters had just changed her entire universe and she was frightened to her core. She sat mute, unable to articulate the questions racing through her mind or the feeling of utter betrayal by her grandmother. As Janey started to piece together the information in the letters, she read and re-read sentences out loud, trying to fit the pieces together like a puzzle.

'Katherine and Sive? Are you sure this is your grandma's writing?' Lucy offered a sad nod in Janey's direction, but her friend didn't notice. 'Strange that your mom didn't get a new name. But you must be Sive.' She did look at Lucy now.

'Hon? Are you okay?' Lucy didn't answer and she continued at speed, 'Your grandpa was Michael, but who is Joseph? And Laura ... and the children?' Janey stopped as she noticed Lucy's hands trembling. She moved around the table to hold onto Lucy and hug her.

'It's my family, isn't it? These people are my family, and I didn't even know they existed. Why has everybody lied to me all my life? What did I do? And why did my mother hate to look at me?' Lucy spat the words through gritted teeth. She wanted to scream but she did not have any strength inside her to do it. 'Janey, why didn't grandma tell me?'

'I don't know. It must be big.'

'Big?'

'Whatever or whoever your mom testified against.'

'How am I gonna find out?' Lucy frowned as Janey let out a long breath from puffed cheeks.

'We need the internet. Who's the nearest neighbour with the internet? What about Father O'Reilly? He must know something.' Janey shrugged.

'Yeah, he helped us settle here, so he must know something.' Lucy jumped up and grabbed her coat before Janey could stop her.

'Wait! Do you want me to come with you?'

Chapter 11

Lucy walked the short distance to the vicarage in autopilot. The wind blowing into her face made her cheeks burn but she didn't notice. She hunched into the wind, stuffed her hands deep inside her coat and speculated over the words in the letters. One thing had become clear she was never supposed to find these letters or her grandmother's secrets inside them. Mary White must have known her time was short, and tried, in vain, to get rid of them.

Half-way through her trek to the vicarage, she was tempted to turn back and search the loft again. She had left a few boxes unopened and wondered if there were any more clues to her past waiting to be uncovered. As Lucy's feet crunched over the driveway, she noticed the grim-faced priest waiting for her on his porch. Lucy didn't speak, she was unsure where to start, but any words were negated as the priest spoke first.

'Janey called me.' His voice was despairing, and he wrung his hands together. Lucy studied his eyes, and they confirmed his complicity. This was another blow and she numbly walked past him into the living room and sat down; not in her usual spot on the sofa with St Augustus, but she took the seat opposite the priest's armchair by the fire. Even the cat sensed that something was amiss; he didn't leap over the furniture to greet Lucy but sat up and surveyed the scene from his sofa. Lucy gazed intently at Father O'Reilly, and he shifted in his seat and avoided her eyes, a pained expression clutched at his face. 'Lucy I...'

'Shouldn't that be Sive?' The venom in her voice surprised them both and the priest recoiled as if he had been physically struck. She watched him swallow hard before he acknowledged her question.

'Sive, yes. That was your name.'

'And Irene, Joseph who are they? Just made-up names or made-up people?' Lucy tried hard to control her rising temper. This man, whom she had known for as long as she could remember, had lied to her all of her life. He had given her the first communion; he had confirmed her in God's house, with a false name, a lie. The priest sighed and gazed into the fire as if he was trying to remember. She noticed he suddenly appeared old to her. She was looking at a very old man and she loved him desperately despite his betrayal.

'Your grandmother was Irene. I can't remember her married name, not sure they ever even told me that, but your mother was always Katherine. Katherine Sinoli.' A jolt of recollection sliced through Lucy; it was the engraving on the watch. 'You were born in America, in New York.' The priest paused and waited for this to register with Lucy. She merely blinked. She was numb and torpid with shock.

'Your father, he was a crook. The whole family ...'

'My whole family?'

'Yes, your whole family, on your father's side anyway. They were murderers, gangsters. Your mother had to leave them; she might have been murdered too if she hadn't got away. Your grandmother left with her to help her with the bab ... you. She knew your mother wouldn't be able to cope on her own. She was a broken spirit; even before you all left America.'

'Why didn't you tell me before?'

'Your grandma never wanted you to know. She thought it would be safer...'

74

'Safer! Safer not knowing my father, what kind of twisted monster harms their own children?' The priest raised his gaze from the fire to look at Lucy and she felt a chill run down her spine at his ominous expression. She was unsure of how to continue, and some time passed in silence. Lucy was trying to process the revelations.

'The letters I found mentioned 'Joseph and the children, and Sine' who are they?'

'Your grandma also had a son; he was married with a couple of kiddies, I think. Two children, or one on the way. I don't remember their names.' Lucy felt a renewed stab of pain at each of the revelations. She had longed for a large family, and now finding out that she had cousins and aunts and uncles all along was a hard truth to absorb. 'Your Ma made great sacrifices for you, child. She gave up her whole life for you and your mother. It wasn't easy for her to leave behind a husband she dearly loved and a son and grandchildren. Knowing she would never ever see them again.'

'Why?' Lucy felt tears stinging her eyes now.

'Because if that family had ever found you, that evil family your mother married into, if they had found you then they would have killed your mother in retribution and anyone in their way. God only knows what would have become of you, raised inside a family like that. Your mother gave evidence in a trial you see; she put your father and his cronies behind bars for a long time.'

'Why did she do that?'

'They are monsters, Lucy. You were born into a family that has no respect for human life and the normal laws of society. Your mother ... when she realized, eventually realized what she was married to, the mistake she'd made, wanted something better for you. She witnessed ... well, she saw unholy things and ... had no choice. She had to get away and get ... you away from your father.'

Lucy tried to control her emotions, she was vying between hating her mother, her grandmother and this priest for keeping this secret.

'Why did grandma never send those letters?'

'I don't know. I didn't even know there were any letters until today.' The priest slumped in his chair, his voice was broken and exhausted.

'I can't believe they just left, you can't walk out on a whole life and never have any contact ever again. You should read those letters, Father. Grandma is tortured, she's begging for help!' Lucy's tears were flowing profusely now. She put her head into her hands and expressed a low groan. St Augustine fled from the room with alarm. The priest tried to console Lucy with a tender voice, and he took Lucy's hands into his own, but she snatched them back. He shuffled over to a cabinet and poured an amber coloured liquid into two beakers handing one to Lucy. Lucy swigged hers down in one go.

'Lucy, there's something else.' Father O'Reilly perched himself on the arm of the chair facing his charge. She felt the apprehension in the priest's voice, and she wanted to tell him to stop. She had heard enough secrets and the dread seeping through her veins forewarned her of a monumental revelation that she couldn't forestall.

'You have a brother, a twin brother.' The priest bowed his head as he finished his sentence. His guilt for holding the secret was tangible to Lucy. She gagged and coughed up the liquid that had been offered to her a few minutes earlier. She felt hands hugging her shoulders but was unsure if they were her own or the priest's. 'Your ma tried to leave with both of you but somehow, your father managed to snatch your brother back.' It took many minutes before she could speak. Eventually she wiped at her eyes and nose with the tissues the priest had put in her palm and sniffed.

'Was that him, at the funeral?' Lucy tried to recall what the stranger looked like. He seemed to be around the same age, he appeared to have an athletic build, but she had not taken much notice of his face. Could she have been just yards away from her own brother?

'I doubt it very much Lucy. You'd be in very grave danger if any of your family knew your whereabouts.'

'So, you're telling me ... I have a twin brother, an uncle, a couple of cousins, at least, a father, grandfather, all living in America. And you never thought to tell me.' Her voice had started vehemently but dissolved away as she finished the sentence.

'Your grandfather died in nineteen ninety-two. We got word of that at least, but that is all we ever heard. Lucy, I'm sorry ...' The priest tried to embrace Lucy, but she pushed him away and fled the stuffy living room. She flung open the front door and without a look back at the concerned old priest, she strode into the grey drizzle as sobs took hold and shook her body. She heard Father O'Reilly's cries behind her as he tried to follow her, but his pace was no match for her driven fury and his desperate calls were lost in the wind.

In nineteen ninety-two Lucy was eight years old. There had been a terrible accident in Anchora. A bus had careered onto a pavement mowing down several pedestrians. She recalled her grandmother weeping; the mourning was protracted. Lucy remembered many nights when her grandmother thought she was sleeping, she had crept to the stairs to listen to the quiet weeping. She understood now that her grandmother's grief was not just for those people but for her own husband. She had hidden her secret personal grief behind the mass sorrow of the community. She had learned more about her grandma's life in one afternoon than in her entire life. The woman she thought she knew, had secrets and chapters of a life, and loves that Lucy had no knowledge of, until now.

She started running. There was no destination, but she found herself eventually on the beach. She ran until she thought her lungs would combust and then at the ocean edge she stood in the surf and screamed in rage and fear until she had no breath left in her body.

Exhausted, on the sand, she gazed across the Atlantic and imagined her grandmother doing the same, as she had written in the letters. She perched her numb body against a breakwater, oblivious of the lashing wind and rain and stayed there until the inky black tide teased at her toes and threatened to swallow her whole.

Chapter 12

When Janey replaced the receiver, she tried to imagine how Father O'Reilly would break the news to Lucy and how her friend would ever come to terms with the new knowledge of her identity and heritage. She tried to call Tim but reached his voicemail and left a message for him to call her urgently.

The cottage was in disarray, black bin liners were strewn all over the landing and papers and books covered the table. The open void in the ceiling beckoned her and she climbed the ladders to see for herself the hiding place where Lucy had found her stash of secrets. Janey tried to tidy up as best she could, stacking boxes and bags to clear a path on the landing and bring down books and piles of paperwork but her endeavours were interrupted with the shrill of the phone. She climbed out of the loft as quickly and raced to get the phone before the caller rang off. She was hoping that Tim might have picked up her message but the hollow voice on the other end of the line belonged to Father O'Reilly.

'Janey, Lucy ran out on me, has she come home? I'm worried about her.'

'No, she's not here. What happened?'

'I told her about her family, she is really shaken, and she just ran out into the wind. She has no coat and she's had a terrible shock. My old bones couldn't keep up with her.'

'Which way did you see her heading?' Janey was at the door and looked up and down the lane for any sight of her friend.

'She went towards the beach.'

'Okay, I'll find her. Don't worry Father. Stay home.'

'She won't be in a good mood. She is very angry, what I told her frightened her.'

'Is she in a programme, witness protection?'

'Yes. The American authorities had to hide them from her father. Lucy didn't know any of it.'

'This would be a shock enough for anybody, Father, anytime, but now, especially just after her grandma's ...'

'I know, I know.' The priest sounded heartbroken, and Janey wondered if a man of his age should be going through this much stress too.

'Father, are you okay? Do you want me to come over there first?'

'No, no I'm fine. You go after Lucy. I'll be grand. She has a brother, Janey. I had to tell her she is a twin, she is very upset.' Janey took a sharp intake of breath but quickly tried to disguise her own shock.

'Well okay, stop worrying. I will find her. She will be fine ...' Janey doubted her own words but tried to sound positive and kept her tone light. 'Stay indoors. I don't want you roaming the streets looking for her in this weather. And one other thing ... I might want to get my hands on some sleeping pills, do you know where I can get some without a prescription?' Janey's mind was working with a speed and calmness that impressed even her.

'Doctor Kelly. He will bring some over. I'll give him a call.'

Janey flicked through Mary White's telephone directory on the hall table, while the priest talked.

'Yeah, I've found the number - Doctor Kelly. I'll call him and I'll find Lucy. Try not to worry, I'll let you know as soon as we're back.' She pulled on an anorak, grabbed a spare one for Lucy and headed out.

***

Father O'Reilly paced the narrow hallway whispering prayers to himself. It was a terrible way for Lucy to discover the shocking secrets of her family. Mary White had given up so much, sacrificed her whole life so that her granddaughter could have a normal upbringing and never know the true horrors of her origin. In the end, it was her own miscue, with letters she had written and not destroyed, that exposed the secrets. Father O'Reilly was a firm believer in destiny and would have normally accepted the crisis as God's wish, but somehow, he could not shake the impending feeling of doom. He felt a dual burden of guilt having kept the truth from Lucy and fear about what the future would bring for her now and he wanted to sit at his altar and pray hard for Lucy, but first, he had one more telephone call to make.

This time the telephone number came easily to hand. He had called the same number only a few days earlier and had no idea he would be calling it again so soon. The U.S. Marshal's Service had returned his call within twenty-four hours of his last message. An administrator had confirmed his identity and thanked him for the communication. The shortness of the call surprised the priest. He'd expected more questions about the family and the circumstances of the death or at least a request for the death certificate. Only when Lucy started to question the identity of a mysterious stranger at the funeral did he consider that the Americans might have come to Ireland to verify the death of a witness in their protection programme for themselves.

As he dialled the number again, it crossed his mind that the American might still be on Irish soil and wondered if he may get a visit. As the automated call system clicked and beeped the priest waited to leave his message and in the clearest voice he could muster, delivered his news and asked if somebody would call him back as a matter of urgency. He was unsure of any protocol going forward. The priest replaced the handset and stood by the telephone, the wind outside had picked up, he could hear it howling and heavy rain had begun to lash at the window. He prayed Janey had found Lucy and steered her home.

***

Janey hunched into the wind and pulled the waterproof jacket tight around her waist. She hurried in the direction of the coast road. When she eventually reached the beach, she sought a high vantage point and scanned the shoreline for her friend. Having a fifty-fifty chance of choosing the right direction Janey chose to head south towards some cliffs that jutted out from the headland. She reasoned that this was a shorter distance and if she didn't find Lucy by the cliffs then she could quickly turn back and go the opposite way.

Her calls were lost in the wind. The beach was vast and any one of the rocky coves could be hiding her friend. She'd considered rounding up a few neighbours to rally a search party but then dismissed this idea because it would lead to questions that Lucy might not want to answer. The last thing her friend needed now was interfering neighbours, she needed time to come to terms with all this new information herself first.

As daylight started to fade Janey's anxiety levels cranked up. Surely Lucy would not be so stupid to stay down here after dark, in this weather. A search in the dark would be futile. Janey trudged the length of the beach to the cliffs and then back again to the point she'd started from and headed North. Her voice was raw from shouting Lucy's name. Eventually she reluctantly turned to head back inland and return to the coast road. Her clothes were soaked from the rain and the spray blowing in from the Atlantic. As she passed the vicarage, she noticed a dagger of yellow light peeking from between roughly drawn curtains and it crossed her mind to call on the priest. She had no good news to tell him and decided it would only worry him more so kept walking towards the cottage.

The babble and laughter coming from the crowd inside the pub added to her depression. The joviality caused a stab of envy of the patrons inside enjoying a habitual and uneventful evening whilst the life of her best friend had just been torn apart. As she made her way up the hill back to the cottage, she hoped to see a light inside, signalling her friend's return, but the house was in darkness. Janey got out of her soaked clothes and sat on the bottom stair. With fingers still numb from the cold she tried Tim's number again. Janey knew he was going to find this as unbelievable as she had, and she was glad at least that Lucy was not here while she made the call.

'Hello.' His reply echoed which told Janey that he was still at the hospital and was probably taking a risk having his mobile switched on, let alone taking a private call.

'Tim, can you talk?'

'God! I've been trying to call you all afternoon. What's going on, Janey? I got your urgent message and I've been worried sick.' She could tell he had moved to another room to take the call; the echo was not so pronounced.

'Tim, I don't know where to start ...'

'Try the beginning.' His interruption was short and rude, but Janey ignored it.

'Okay. Just listen.' Janey paused and took a deep breath. 'We found some letters in the loft when we were clearing it out, and, well, it turns out Lucy is not, in fact, Lucy White. It appears she is an American citizen in a witness protection programme.' Tim's laugh was genuine and very loud.

'What have you two been on all afternoon? I am actually quite busy you know.' Janey could hear the grin in his voice and the rumble of laughter told her he was genuinely amused.

'No, Tim! listen it's true. Lucy found some letters her grandma wrote twenty something years ago which didn't make any sense to her and so she went to confront Father O'Reilly about what she found. It turns out he knew. He's known all along; she even has a twin brother! Anyway, now Lucy has gone missing. She's major upset, and I can't find her. I've been looking for her for ages. I've been up and down the beach, all over the village ...' Her voice trembled and she let the pent-up emotions out as she talked at speed. 'Are you there? Tim?'

'Slow down. What did the letters say? Whose letters, are they?' Janey tried to remember the words and then remembered that they would still be in the dining room. She read each one in turn out loud to Tim.

'Fuck me!' Tim whispered when Janey finished. Both were silent and she could understand why he was speechless. 'FUCK! ME!' Tim was pacing the room, Janey could hear his footsteps, 'I can't believe it!'

'Imagine how Lucy feels! this is HER life.'

'Where is she?' Tim's voice now held a hint of stress.

'This is what I have been tryin' to tell you, I DON'T KNOW! what shall I do?'

'She's gotta be ...

'Oh god! Oh jeeze ... she's back ... I'll call you later!' Janey snapped her phone shut, and rushed forward to embrace her friend, her emotions of relief rendering her speechless. As her arms wrapped around her friend's shoulders, she felt the freezing flesh. She pulled her into the front room and fumbled desperately to get the gas fire started.

'I've been looking for you out there for hours. Where have you been? Are you okay? God, you're freezing, Luce. Get your wet clothes off. NOW!' The monologue ended with such force and volume that Lucy was stirred to action. Janey suspected there was no retort or reply from her friend because her face was too frozen to formulate any words.

An afternoon outside in the rain and wind could easily lead to hypothermia. Her friend's movements appeared laboured, and she was not shivering. Janey checked Lucy's pupils and questioned her friend, she watched her speech, her cognitive performance. Her fingers were already wrapped around her friend's wrist

'Where were you, Luce?'

'The beach,' she answered with barely a murmur.

'Why did you go to the beach?'

'Erm, I just needed to think.'

'How long did you spend at the beach?' Janey measured the response to her questions while tugging at Lucy's clothes. She cursed her friend and left her briefly to race upstairs to find dry clothes. She returned with pyjamas and a duvet that she had dragged from her bed. Janey ignored the incessant ringing of the phone while she stripped and then swaddled her friend in the dry things and wrapped a warm towel around her damp hair. She called Tim and the priest and then she made tea and sat on the floor in front of her friend and watched her drink.

Everything had changed for Lucy. She had grown up thinking her father was dead and that she was an only child; she had been told lies by the people she loved most. Janey checked for anger in Lucy's face but could see only a lost stare shadowing her eyes. She had not yet asked what had transpired at the vicarage, but the details could wait for another day. There had been a fundamental shift in her friend's life, and it would take some acclimatization.

Once Lucy had drunk enough tea to bring the colour back to her face, Janey searched out a hairdryer and unravelled Lucy's long dark mane and dried it gently. She scrutinized her friend's shiny black hair with the new insight of her ancestry, and she silently wondered if Lucy's twin brother would look like her and she tried to imagine a male version of her best friend.

'I have a brother.' The words came clearly, she was proud to make the announcement and Janey was unsure how to respond. 'All these years, I had a twin, and nobody told me. Can you believe it?' It wasn't a question. Janey stayed quiet. 'All my life ... I always wanted a brother or sister. Did you know that?' Her voice was not so clear now and Janey suspected her friend might be about to cry.

'Brothers aren't all they're cracked up to be, Luce. Trust me on that score.' She tried to lighten the mood and get a smile from her friend. 'I'll kindly donate any one or all of mine.'

'You wouldn't. You wouldn't really. You love each of them more than the world.'

'You're right. Oh Luce, I'm so sorry ...'

'You had the opportunity to know them and love them. I didn't. But now I know about him, I guess I might have a chance to make up for lost time.'

Janey stopped brushing her friend's hair and took the chair opposite.

'Is that a good idea?' she asked softly.

'It's my twin brother, Janey! I'm going to find him.'

'It could be too soon, Luce. You have a lot of things to come to terms with, you're still grieving for your ma. Give it some time. Let things ...'

'Twenty years is more than enough time. They had no right to separate us and feed me bullshit!'

'There's a lot to take on board, don't make any rash decisions.' Janey leant forward and took her friend's hands. 'Let's get all the facts, the whole story, all the details about why your grandma kept this hidden. She wouldn't have done it for no good reason Luce. She was hiding something, hiding you from something. Keeping this from you caused her great pain. She wouldn't have done it for no good reason. Did Father O'Reilly have any insights about why your ma was hiding?'

'Oh, sure! Loads. My family is awash with murdering criminal scumbags. I can't remember his exact words, but he laid it on thick that they were gangsters of the worst kind.' Lucy was in pain. Janey didn't want to add to the pain. It would have to be a soft persuasion. Warning her off the very thing she had yearned for all her life would be futile. The best she could hope to do was delay Lucy from making any big decisions until she had time to assimilate the revelations.

Chapter 13

Lucy rapped on the vicarage door. She had crept out of the house without waking Janey. Her conversation with Father O'Reilly the previous afternoon had only left her with more questions than answers and she had returned to the vicarage for resolution. There was no reply to her knocking and so she lifted the letter flap and yelled in.

'Father, it's me, are you in there?' Only St Augustine answered with a meow, and she let the letterbox clatter and turned on her heel. She was frustrated and mentally re-strategized her day.

Lucy was going to America. Her friend's caution had done nothing to dampen the desire to find her newly discovered family, but she needed money for the flight and accommodation while she searched for them. Her bank account was overdrawn, she had her student loan and now there was the funeral bill that had to be paid. She needed to sell the jewellery quickly, but she would cost her trip first and then decide what she would sell. She left the vicarage with a purposeful stride and headed for the bus stop all the while keeping one eye on the road leading from her cottage in case her best friend should awake and try to stall her plans.

Lucy chose the seat at the back of the bus, huddled up with her gaze fixed firmly out of the window, to ward off any unwelcome conversation from fellow passengers. She didn't see any of the hills of county Candula or notice the vehicle stopping to collect more passengers from endless tiny hamlets; her mind was on another continent. Her impatience was bubbling over when the bus finally pulled into the modern terminus in the centre of Kearis and as she disembarked, she noticed a couple of acquaintances from neighbouring villages. She was in no mood for polite chit-chat so managed a brief nod and quickly headed to the nearest travel agent.

She thumbed through the racks of brochures until a young woman seated behind a desk raised her eyes from the screen and asked if she needed any help. When she declared an interest in New York she was directed to a stand that displayed brochures for mini-breaks and the glossy pages showcased dazzling photographs from many of the world's major capitals. She pulled a couple from the rack and took a seat to examine them in more detail. The assistant walked over and peered at the pages that held Lucy's attention.

'Have you been to New York before? Can I recommend some hotels? Some attractions? When are you planning on travelling?'

'Hm, I'm just browsing at the moment. Ta though.' Lucy flipped through the pages to find the tiny price grid. She baulked, the cost was too high . Selling the ring would cover the funeral expenses but these hotel rates would eat through the rest of the money in no time. Even though she had access to more money than she had ever had in her life she'd inherited her grandmother's frugal compulsion. She stood and gave a wide smile at the woman.

'I'll take these away and have a good look at them tonight if that's okay, and then call you in a day or so.' She took the card the woman offered and darted out of the door. She knew a smaller independent agent a couple of streets away. Its window advertised low-cost deals and she thought it was more likely to accommodate a low-budget trip, so she headed in that direction.

***

Father O'Reilly was disturbed after Janey's call. He heard how the girls had stayed up long into the night talking and no matter how much Janey tried to dissuade her best friend; Lucy's yearning to search for her brother and father was persistent. Now she had disappeared again, and Janey was calling the usual suspects in her search for her friend.

He found it difficult to focus on his usual parish duties and his favourite afternoon quiz show didn't hold its usual appeal. It was the priest's worst fear, and he knew it was the reason Mary White had kept the truth hidden from her granddaughter. Mary must have felt her time shortening and knowing that the last vestige of this terrible secret lay in those unsent letters she had tried to get rid of them. She had attempted, in vain, to remove any possible trace of her granddaughter discovering her provenance because she knew Lucy would have the desire and determination to find her family.

Father O'Reilly paced the lounge waiting for another of his calls to be returned. When the telephone did eventually ring, it jolted him from his worrisome thoughts and he hurried to answer it, hoping it would be the Yanks, and knowing that they rang off much too quickly he spurred his old bones down the hall. An American accent greeted him, and he was glad his housekeeper had already left for the day. He was free to talk at length and in private to this U.S. Marshal.

The Marshal was surprised that after two decades the girl had only just been told of her original identity and he cursed under his breath when the priest told him she now wanted to find her family.

'There are no half measures with the witness protection programme, Father O'Reilly. She's in or she's out. If she decides to find the Sinolis', she's on her own.'

'She'll be safe do you think? It wasn't her that put the family in jail, her mother was the one to testify. She was a baby ...' Father O'Reilly was trying to find assurance for his worse fears.

The agent rattled through the procedures, what would happen to Lucy if she left the witness protection programme in a monotone. The words came without feeling or inflection and when he finished and the priest remained quiet, he added:

'Do you understand what I'm saying, Father?

'Yes, I understand but what harm do you think there might be if she meets her family?' The priest's brow was furrowed as he spoke the words. He knew the answer but needed affirmation from the agent.

'Father O'Reilly, we spend our time helping people leave and hide from the mob! I have spent my entire career helping people escape their grip. She needs to know why she was put in the programme. If she goes looking for them, she's gonna end up in a whole heap of shit! Do you understand?' The Marshal spoke with a bored but slightly annoyed tone. To them Lucy was a number, a statistic, the Marshal was slightly irked but otherwise uninterested in Lucy's ambition. The priest lowered himself slowly onto the chair beside the telephone. He quietly resigned himself to the outcome that Lucy would leave Anchora and he was fearful of what that might mean for this beautiful young woman. He had known Lucy since she was only two years old, and he loved her like she was his own daughter. He knew her loneliness and longing for siblings, and he knew of her envy for her friends with their large families. He had attended the countless tea parties she hosted with her teddy bears and dolls all lined up around the table posing as pretend brothers and sisters. It had stung him to keep the secret of a twin brother and he knew there was nothing in the world that would stop her finding him now.

Chapter 14

Steven Dolph dropped his canvas duffle bag on the marble concourse at Newark airport and pressed his phone. He wanted his girlfriend to answer, not her mother; the jet lag from two transatlantic flights in as many days had taken its toll and he couldn't be bothered with small talk. Nobody answered and his irritation intensified. He had really wanted to see Maria today, the cramped conditions on the aircraft had put him in the mood for a workout in the bedroom. Now it would have to be the gym. He dialled his office to confirm his arrival back in New York.

The job hadn't gone great; he was supposed to be in and out to confirm a death. No contact, just verification, but one of the mourners at the funeral had eyeballed him and tried to strike up a conversation. If he'd been on home turf, he might have engaged in a brief conversation to divert undue attention, but here, in this small village on the West coast of Ireland his accent would have stood out, so he had quickly ducked into his rented car and driven off fast, probably too fast.

This was Dolph's fourth year working with the U.S. Marshal Service. This trip was a boring routine job and he'd drawn the short straw. It was just a whole load of paperwork and sitting around on long flights, he preferred to be more active out in the field. It was unusual for witnesses to be in protection abroad, foreign authorities didn't like it and getting relevant paperwork was an expensive and protracted exercise. He wasn't sure why these women had been exceptional cases, possibly because they were dual passport holders. The truth was he didn't really care. The case was ancient to him, the fun stuff had happened over twenty years ago. The files told him the main protectorate had died soon after being relocated. No suspicious circumstances, just a slow suicide, which was a regular occurrence in the programme. Only a handful could handle the complete disconnection from their lives and families.

He was in such a hurry to get away from the funeral that he almost forgot to get an up-to-date photo of the daughter for the files. He drove the car some distance from the churchyard and jogged back to get a long lens shot of the girl as the funeral party left the cemetery. He was also in a hurry to get away from Ireland. The small guest house smelled of boiled vegetables and the stench was beginning to permeate his nice suit. The TV in his room was so small he had to sit directly in front of it to watch anything and the few channels he could tune into were more boring than watching four walls, so he drove directly to the airport and hung out in the airport bar until his flight was due.

Dolph threw his bag into the back of a cab and climbed in. He tried Maria's office as the taxi pulled away from the airport, maybe she was working late.

***

The cardboard files slapped onto the desk a bit louder than Jodi had intended. She put the urgent messages on top of the pile, and she would have tapped a long red fingernail on them, but the recipient was not at his desk.

'Where's Seth?' Jodi asked another colleague over the low partition. The man didn't answer; he did not even take his eyes from the screens in front of him but instead jabbed a stubby finger in the direction of the coffee machine. Jodi huffed and headed in that direction. Laughter and loud voices confirmed Seth's presence at the coffee point before she had even turned the corner. Jodi poked her head around the doorway and gave a toothy grin that revealed chewing gum between her incisors.

'Two urgent's on your desk Seth.' Jodi nodded a hello at the other marshals in the room.

'Oh yeah, what we got Jodi?' Seth sighed and jumped the queue for the vending machine.

'The Ireland thing we put Dolph on 's gone bad, and Baltimore has an incident with a kid in an accident. Turns out she needs a blood donor, and she's rare, the hospital wants family donors.' Jodi wrinkled her nose in sympathy at Seth's predicament and turned to leave.

'Hang on.' Seth called out to Jodi as she waddled away. 'What's wrong with the Irish thing? Isn't he back yet?'

'Yeah, he's back, got in yesterday. Due in for his debrief any time now.' Jodi hollered back disinterested. If Seth had bothered to read his e-mails, he would have seen the message she sent him yesterday when Dolph checked in on landing.

'Well tell him I want to see him pronto, I …' Jodi didn't hear the rest of his sentence. She quickened her pace to evade his usual procrastination.

Seth was one of the old-timers; with almost forty years of service on his clock, his colleagues whispered that he was a dinosaur of the Marshal Service. Too old to be out in the field he was now tied to a desk and co-coordinated several hundred Marshals across the country. The US Marshal Service protected thousands of witnesses under the WITSEC programme. Individuals to whole families were relocated all over the U.S.A in return for their testimonies. A small number of protectorates were located overseas but this group was a political hot potato, so it wasn't done often. Witnesses were given new identities and helped to assimilate into their new life. Some witnesses stayed in frequent contact with their designated Marshals, but most were weaned off constant babysitting and received only an occasional visit from an agent when their files needed updating. All protectorates had access to an emergency number and if they thought their identity was compromised, they could be moved at very short notice.

Seth had been around long enough to remember the time when U.S. Attorney General, Robert Kennedy, vowed to bring down every organised crime family in America. It had become too powerful and the various syndicates across America were posing a major risk to the U.S. economy and its perception of legitimacy around the world. The result was the witness protection programme. It motivated witnesses to testify and bring down major crime figures. Large inducements were offered in addition to a lifetime of anonymity and security for witnesses and their families.

Seth was a key player in the Marshal Service in the 1980's when a wave of informants turned on their crime families and organised gangs started to implode. Within a decade he saw all the major heads of mob families serving time behind bars and he helped the informants disappear. The steady stream of informants turned to a torrent in the late eighties as mobsters broke their code of silence and testified against each other. Seth had first-hand knowledge of almost all major cases, and he knew that the small family relocated to Ireland in the eighties had been key contributors in one of the biggest trials of the decade. The wife of the head of the Sinoli family had given evidence which was instrumental in the downfall of several senior mob figures.

He had no idea how this ancient case could have become a problem now; the case was twenty years old and two out of three of the protectorates were deceased. His workload was large enough without old cases turning live again. Seth had put a young Marshal on the case to verify the details of the death in Ireland and then get his backside up here and update the file. Now he was pissed that something had gone wrong. Seth glanced at the messages on his desk.

Date: Monday March 23, 2006.

Witness: 4,497. Liaison Officer: Tailor Seth/Dolph Steven.

Location: Ireland.

Communication received from local contact advised that the granddaughter (INFANT WITSEC 4497. 1984) of recently deceased (WITSEC 4495. 1984) found personal correspondence and is now in possession of her original identity. No knowledge that she was in US Federal Witness Protection Programme until now.

That must have come as a bit of a shock. Seth mused and breathed a sigh of relief. At least it wasn't his Marshal who had screwed things up over there. Seth scanned the second message and then quickly keyed the file numbers into his computer. He picked his phone and started to dial, this one was the priority.

Date: Tues March 23, 2006.

Witness: 11,631. Liaison Officer: Tailor Seth/Panerai Simon

Location: Baltimore.

Witness has fallen (accident) through plate glass window, suffered multiple lacerations and needs urgent blood transfusions. Blood type: A rec- Hospital wants family contacted for blood donations.

'Not very likely,' Seth murmured aloud.

Chapter 15

The second travel agent Lucy visited was more in line with her budget expectations. The young assistant, not long out of college had found her cheap flights and recommended hotels that were central but away from the tourist trail so were more suited to her resources. Lucy had costed the trip and now sat in a small room in the bank waiting to see the manager.

She was nervous. The last time she had been to see her bank manager was when she applied for her student loan. That appointment was the intersection of a life-changing chapter, the beginning of a new life at university, a life outside of Anchora and the beginning of adulthood. As she sat here again, in the same faux leather chair she realised she was at another precipice. Her entire life had shifted in the space of a few short days and the reorientation caused anxiety to rear up without warning. All past events had a new perspective, there was no anchor and no constant. The deceit she had been dealt caused anger to bubble under the surface.

Janey had called, and Lucy had deflected her questions. She was in no doubt that her 'shopping trip to get some bits and pieces' would provoke an inquisition on her return and she tried to put it out of her mind until the bus ride home. She would work on a story later. This trip to New York would take considerable planning and cunning, if she wanted to swerve her best friend's and Father O'Reilly's apocalyptic cautions.

'Lucy White?' A bearded man in a nylon pinstripe suit greeted her and she stood to shake his hand before being led into a large office with mahogany furniture. She nodded to the offer of coffee. It would be her first of the day and her mouth felt dry with apprehension. She didn't want to increase her overdraft, but it seemed the quickest way to get the cash she needed for her trip without selling the jewellery for a low-price just because she needed a quick sale. Her grandmother had raised her with the principle that *'if you didn't have money, then you didn't spend money'* and what was the other one *'neither lender nor borrow be'* - she shook the citations out of her head. It wouldn't be a long-term debt; she had the means to repay it.

'I'm very sorry to hear of your grandmother's passing, may I offer my sincere condolences?'

'Oh, yes.' Lucy's mind had fast forwarded to an unchartered future, and she had to remind herself she had only buried her grandmother two short or was it three short days ago?

'We have received the death certificate and I can assure you we are working as quickly as possible to get the relevant statements to your solicitor.'

'Oh, I see. Well, thank you. I am not really looking after all that. I left it all up to Mr Leyne to sort out. I was wondering if I might, erm, well, erm have a loan. I've got assets to sell but, in the meantime, ... is it possible? Please?'

'I see. Well of course. We could arrange something on a bridging basis until the probate is finalised. But are you sure that's a route you want to take, Miss White, because that will incur interest and charges and I'm sure that your solicitor will have things wrapped up in no time at all?'

'How long?' It sounded greedy, so she added. 'How long do these things usually take? Normally? In your experience?'

'Has Mr. Leyne not gone through the formalities with you?'

'Hmm, yes I'm sure he did, but, well I've had a lot to sort out ...'

'Of course.'

'And the thing is, the house you see, I'm told it will need some renovations, updating, before it can be put on the market and I'm going to spend the summer abroad, with my friend from Uni. She's from Florida and I was thinking of getting the work underway so that things might be finished for when I come back, after the summer. Then it can be put on the market.' She realised she was rambling and promptly shut up. Selling the house had not even crossed her mind, but she thought it might highlight to him that she was good for the loan, without having to mention the jewellery. Lies had come easily to Lucy in the last few days.

'How much were you thinking of?' The bank manager frowned and leafed through his papers.

Lucy cleared her throat; she had intended to request a few thousand Euros but the story about the house renovations made this amount seem implausible and she had to make the story realistic.

'Ten thousand Euros.' Lucy waited for a rebuff but on hearing none she felt braver. 'How much is in my grandma's account?'

'Well, strictly speaking, it should really be down to the solicitor to advise you of the estate value, but seeing as you are the sole beneficiary, I don't see any harm in letting you have the bank statement, let's see.'

Lucy eyed the manger expectantly as he leafed through some papers.

'The balance stands at eighty-two thousand three hundred and twenty-one euros fifty-two cents. There will be a small amount of interest to go in at the end of the month as usual.' Lucy sat immobile for many seconds. There must be a mistake.

'My grandma has eighty-two thousand euros in her bank account?' The only outward sign of this bombshell for Lucy was the increased tempo of the pulse throbbing at her temple. To Lucy, it felt like a giant drum beating inside her head and she subconsciously rubbed at it.

'Huh, eighty-two thousand and change, that's correct, as of the close of business Friday last, my dear.'

'Where did it come from?' She took a large swig of the coffee that someone had laid before her during her monologue about the house renovations.

'Where?'

'When was it paid in?'

'Well let me see now ...' The manager reviewed his screen and tapped at some keys. Lucy suspected he knew where it had come from without having to check his files.

'We have one small annual deposit of just under four thousand Euros around November each year, and of course, that accrues interest.' He left a long pause. 'No withdrawals.' Lucy's silence seemed to annoy him a little, he wore a frown. 'The deposit looks to be international. I understand the solicitor can put a trace on it, in case anyone needs to be notified, annuity or the like ...' His voice trailed off; Lucy suspected he was getting into something that was not really his business to know about. He would know that the considerable balance only ever accumulated and was never touched. She suspected there were not many of the banks' customers who owned tens of thousands of euros in an account, never touched their money but instead lived like paupers.

'Yes. I think you might be right; I remember seeing some paperwork about something ...' She knew where the money was coming from. The most shocking thing was that her grandmother had never touched the money. All these years they had lived on a small income from sewing, laundry and babysitting. All the while there were thousands of Euros sitting in the bank. Lucy had even taken a student loan to pay her university fees while this fortune sat untouched. She needed to get out of there as fast as she could to think, to digest this news. She stood to leave.

'We can sort the paperwork for you in a jiffy. I can then arrange for a transfer to your account.'

'Ur, yes. Okay, make the paperwork. Thank you.'

Chapter 16

'Unbelievable, fucking, unbelievable!' Seth snatched the files from his desk and headed towards his boss's office. Not only had the Sinoli girl found out her identity, but his agent had been seen at the funeral and solicited the girl's scrutiny. Seth walked into his boss's office without waiting for an invitation. Laurie Bannister headed up the entire witness security division for the U.S. Marshal Service. He was another old-timer and had worked his way through the ranks of the department.

'You won't believe this.'

'Seth. What can I do for you?' Laurie didn't raise his head from the paperwork in front of him.

'I had a call from a priest in Ireland, Anchora.' Seth had to look briefly at the file in his hand to confirm the name of the village and he continued when he saw that he had his boss's full attention. 'The Sinoli girl, extracted with ...'

'Yeah, yeah, I know the Sinoli girl, what's up Seth?' Knowing his boss's penchant for getting to the point he wasted no more words.

'It's come live again.'

'What do you mean it's come live again? This case is over ... twenty years old.'

'The girl wants out. Only just been told of her extraction and now wants to meet the family.' The man seated across from Seth sat back in his chair and pulled the glasses from his nose. His eyes registered no emotion as he was mentally downloading some historical data. Seth waited, he had expected a reaction, an exclamation, a curse, something. But Laurie just stood and walked to the window and gazed out into the middle distance with a pensive expression. Seth was uncomfortable with the silence and shifted in his seat.

'Apparently, she came across some correspondence when the grandmother died. Until then hadn't a fuckin clue, so it's been a bit of a shock.' There was still no reaction from his boss and Seth tried a different tack. 'I think we should get somebody over there, try to explain things personally and why it might not be such a good idea for her to look up her scum bag family.'

'Twenty years ago ...' Laurie said more to himself, then turned and walked back to his chair. 'Who have we got?'

'Well sir, there's Dolph. He's just flown back from Ireland, covering the old lady's funeral, but I don't think it would be a good idea to send him. He was eyeballed by the girl at the funeral, and it got her all upset and started her asking questions. Fletcher did the file review for a few years but he's out with knee cartilage problem or something.'

'Dolph was seen?'

'Yes, sir. I have his debrief this morning. I'll get the file to you soon as we are done.'

'I want a list of all available Marshals over twenty fucking years old! In fact, get me a list of ANY with half a brain ... I don't care if we have to pull them off something else. I'm not having this fucked up! The debrief will be in here at ten o'clock!'

'Yes, sir.' Seth didn't waste any time getting out of the office and jumped when the door slammed behind him. It slammed with such force that half the administrators on the floor looked up to see which fool had upset the boss. Seth skulked back to his workstation with his tail between his legs. He didn't get it. What was so special about this case? this girl? that made Laurie Bannister so touchy.

Seth wished he had handed the file up through the system as was usual. He might have avoided his boss's wrath and the prospect of being raked over the coals again when he and Dolph had to go back in there at ten o'clock. He was peeved about the outburst and started to consider the reason. Twenty years of U.S. taxes had kept that family safe, and it would all be for nothing. Another failure in the WITSEC programme. Ex-government witnesses were never welcomed back with open arms into their families; even if this one had been an infant at the time, the mob would think she was a plant. Informers were dealt with swiftly by the mob. It would look like an accident, of course. The mob had become sophisticated at eliminating their traitors.

Seth opened the file and started to familiarise himself with the case. His eyes widened as he read. Twenty years ago, Seth was a low-ranking Marshal and the significance of this case had passed him by. He learned now that this case was the lynchpin to the collapse of the major crime syndicates in the 1980's. There had been a bitter feud within the Sinoli clan back in the eighties. The FBI had been infiltrating them and dividing the once powerful family. Seth's rank back then meant he had not been privy to any real intelligence, but he had heard the rumours. FBI agents had been tipping off the Sinoli brothers for years about raids and passing over intel which helped them evade arrest and increased their power base. An FBI agent had managed to turn one of the brother's wives. She testified and the whole house of Sinoli started to tumble. It transpired that as well as FBI agents, the Sinoli's had prosecutors, judges and senators on their payroll and the blowout from just one testimony rocked America. Nobody knew exactly how the wife had been persuaded to testify. The whole case was shrouded with rumours and the agents

104

and marshals involved at the time refused to talk about it then or at any time since.

Seth started to print off the case details for the meeting, he needed four copies. The file had been updated with recent photographs of the girl, so he knew the agent was already in the building and working on it. Seth would print these files himself. After the roasting he had already experienced today, he didn't want any more cockups.

Chapter 17

It was early; the girls each held a handle of the large rucksack as they walked to the bus stop. They hugged as they said goodbye and Janey hoisted her luggage onto the bus and wiped condensation from the window so she could send Lucy air kisses at the bus pulled away. Lucy tried to identify with the emotions now flowing through her mind. Her fondness for her friend had somehow lessened lately. The information she had uncovered about her origins had shifted her affections. Her overriding ambition to discover the family she'd never known consumed everything and anything standing in the way was a nuisance.

Janey was standing in her way. She wanted Lucy to proceed with more caution, research more about them before seeking them out and it created a chasm in their relationship. Lucy had managed to deflect her friend's concerns with a lie about wanting to come and spend the summer with her and her family in Florida and it was this impending adventure that stoked Janey's excited leave-taking now. What she didn't know was that Lucy was indeed planning a trip to America, but she wouldn't be going to Florida.

The lies had come easily to Lucy and this realisation slowed her pace on the damp path back to the cottage. She had become a different person and she wondered which one was authentic. The old Lucy was the charge of an elderly woman, a personality formed in a small village in a small country from a made-up persona, an identity carved from a government system which had cut through her bloodlines and denied her knowing her parentage, siblings, and her real life.

She had been heading back to the cottage but instead turned and walked in the direction of the cemetery. Lucy had not been back there since the day of her grandmother's funeral. She took a shortcut through fields and arrived at the graveside with muddy boots. The flowers had wilted and the ink on the various cards had become smudged with the incessant rain. There was nothing dry to sit on, so Lucy knelt on the wet grass and began picking dead blooms from the arrangements. She removed the cards and put the soggy paper into her pocket.

With a new insight into this woman that lay beneath she began to let her thoughts drift to the years she had spent living with her grandmother. All her memories had to be recalibrated with the knowledge she had uncovered. Lucy's part in her grandmother's life had been a mere chapter in this woman's existence and she reflected now on the prologue she had never known. The woman she thought she knew had lived on a different continent, borne children she had never spoken about, and forsaken her husband and son to keep her daughter away from a dangerous spouse. Mary White had never complained about everyday tribulations, the cold weather snap, which lasted longer than it should, perpetual rain that prevented the kids from playing outside, a leaking boiler or a gale that blew away roof tiles, and Lucy understood now why Mary White had never grumbled or griped about any of it. The angst and sorrow that she carried inside were more agonizing than anything else that time and circumstance had ever thrown at her.

Chapter 18

Steven Dolph had almost finished typing up his notes when his phone went off. He unclipped the device and checked his message, the hair on the back of his neck stood up as he read the one line of text. Debrief re-scheduled: 10 am, Laurie Bannister's office. He almost dropped the phone on the floor and his mind played over the reason why the chief might be interested in what should be a routine debrief.

He replayed his recent assignment through in his head and finding no reason why he might be in trouble, he smiled. Maybe his day had finally come, and he was up for a promotion. Or maybe a big case was about to land on his desk. It was about time; he had been bypassed by several colleagues. This was his turn he thought. He was too excited to continue typing his notes and instead picked up the phone to call his girlfriend and tell her the good news.

At 9.45, Dolph assembled the paperwork neatly on the circular table and ran his hands through his hair. He had arrived early to make a good impression and been shown into a board room adjacent to Laurie Bannister's office. Seth arrived next and Dolph thought he appeared flustered. He scanned the paperwork on the table and barely greeted the agent who had been on his team for over two years. Dolph disliked the aged Marshal. The old man was prehistoric and should have been retired years ago. Let some of the bright young things like him move up the ladder. Dolph smiled smugly to himself thinking his time was now, but as the director strode into the room his stomach turned over. The dark mood and angry expression on Laurie Bannister's face made the young agent squirm in his chair. Seth made a cursory introduction and when Laurie spoke Dolph shifted and swallowed hard.

'We have ourselves a situation here that I am none too happy with. Twenty years into a programme and then the witness decides she wants out. Your screw up in Ireland did not help.' He focused directly on Dolph and jabbed a finger in his direction. 'But that's for another time. Right now I want somebody on a plane to sort this mess out ASAP, understand?' Two heads nodded curtly but Dolph's nodding continued for several seconds longer, he appeared to have lost control of his neck muscles.

'Remind me step-by-step with a dateline.' The chief now turned his attention to Seth and Dolph shrank into his seat and unconsciously wiped the sweat that had appeared on his brow. He opened a notepad and took notes as Seth outlined the case history, he needed to keep his hands busy to stop them shaking.

Seth skimmed over the details of the testimony and trial and then moved on to the case notes that covered the family's extraction and relocation. Dolph looked up from his incessant note taking to see that Laurie didn't need reminding; the memories of this case seeming to be etched into his face and he looked haunted by it. Dolph wondered what he was burdened with.

Seth reported that the two women and one infant spent several months in a convent when they first arrived in Ireland. Their intermediary was a local priest and once the trial was over, he organised a safe house in a small coastal village. This was the final move, they'd been there ever since. There had been no need to move them again. They have no reason to believe the Sinolis' had ever tried to find them. He skimmed over the medical reports relating to the key witness and her subsequent death and then moved onto the grandmother. No known contact had ever been made with the Sinolis' or the other side of the family, although Mary White had asked if a letter might be delivered to her husband in the year following extraction. The Marshal in charge of the case had refused, in keeping with the rules of the programme. An annuity payment had been made every year for the witness's dependant and Seth sucked his lips as he noted the payment, due to some oversight, had failed to be terminated once the girl reached eighteen. He detailed the daughter's current age, education and pushed an A4 headshot into the middle of the table.

Laurie picked up the photo and gazed at it for a long time.

'So, looks like those undelivered letters were found by the daughter. This girl has a bright future ahead of her and she is about to toss it into the wind.' Laurie's voice was soft as he gazed at the A4 image. Dolph relaxed a little. 'We need a body on a plane out today, who do we have?' Dolph sat up in his chair but was ignored. Laurie instead pressed a button on a nearby telephone.

'Martha, I need a seat, JFK to Shannon, accommodation and rental car. Tonight, at the latest.' He turned back to the Marshals at the table. 'So, who we got?' Dolph raised his finger and was about to speak when Martha McLain's southern drawl sounded from the doorway.

'Only one person for this job.' Laurie's eyes narrowed as he considered the suggestion. The two younger agents waited to be enlightened and Seth was the one who spoke.

'Surely not Cavell?' Seth directed his question to Laurie, who ignored him and walked over to gaze out of the bulletproof window. 'Couldn't get him back for this one …

110

could we? I mean I know he ...' Dolph noted the dinosaur had sent a furtive glance his way and gone quiet.

'If anyone can turn her head it's him.' Laurie did not turn and address the room, he appeared to be speaking to himself.

'You think he might do it; shouldn't we keep it in the department? Plus, he's retired from the FBI now, as far as I know he has been for a good few years.' Laurie ignored Seth and spoke directly to Martha who was still standing in the doorway.

'Get a seat out from Appleton to JFK first and make it flexible, it might take us some time to find him in them damn woods.' Dolph was left to sit and wonder exactly what was going on as Laurie and Seth strode out of the office.

Chapter 19

Jim Cavell pulled off his boots and left them on the porch; he held open the screen and whistled to the dog to hurry up. Duke sniffed randomly at the weeds lining the dirt road leading to the cabin. His disinterested demeanour evidenced no unfamiliar scent, so Jim was confident there'd been no visitors while they were out fishing.

He missed the red flashing light on his messaging machine and slung his catch into the sink. He headed to his bedroom to switch on his laptop and check email. The laptop and printer competed for space with piles of books and newspapers crowding the large desk in the corner of his bedroom. Jim flicked on the device and knowing it would take a while to boot up, he returned to the fish and busied himself sorting his supper. Duke barked once at the cupboard under the sink and Jim laughed; he didn't need a watch, the scruffy mongrel would always let him know when it was four o'clock, dinner time.

The dog had run out in front of his car the previous summer and after asking around and finding no owner he had fed it for a week, which turned into two. He'd planned to find it a home with a neighbour or someone in town, but the pair had bonded, and Jim quickly realized that Duke's nose and bark were worth far more than any security installation on the market and so the animal acquired a name and a basket at the bottom of his bed. Jim poured the dog his kibble and cleared away the breakfast things that still littered the oak topped counter that divided the small cabin into a kitchen and living space.

He had bought the cabin over a decade ago but only used it rarely until his retirement from the FBI. Now he had taken up permanent residence and had plans to modernize the old place over the summer. His savings and pension were good, and he could afford something bigger and needing less work, but he valued the location of this one. It was deep in the woods, a place you would only find by accident. With his previous line of work, anonymity and security were a big concern.

Jim Cavell had put hundreds of mobsters behind bars and there was more than one price on his head, but out here, he was not unduly concerned, and he had the best nose and ears on this side of Lake Michigan in the form of the large brown mongrel who had now plonked himself on the oversized saggy sofa and was taking his after-dinner nap.

The computer finished its start-up procedures and Jim checked his emails. A message from Martha McLain sat in his inbox. Martha was the personal assistant for his long-time buddy at the U.S. Marshal Witness Protection Programme. He was also good friends with her husband whom he had worked with at the FBI. The message wasn't a personal one, it was from her office address, and he opened it and read each line with growing anxiety.

Martha referred to a telephone message and an attached file. The file was coded but he knew it was the Sinoli case file. Jim turned and glanced at the flashing red light on his phone. He was torn as to which he should open first, the file or the message, he whirled around on his chair and hit the button on the phone.

Martha's drawl greeted him warmly but then moved on quickly in a more business-like manner to the reason for her call. Jim sat back in his chair; he was dumbfounded. A twenty-year-old case had come live again, and they needed his help. A witness whom he had extracted twenty years ago now wanted to leave the programme and they asked him to go and talk her out of it. He did not need to open the file attached to his e-mail to remember every tiny detail of this case.

It had gone wrong. It was his mistake; he should have left it to the Marshals; witness extraction was their expertise, but he had insisted on being involved in this case to the very end. Because of that three families had been devastated. Jim sat for a while and allowed himself to re-live the events. The memories came easily, they always did. What was different this time is that he allowed them to surface. He felt the sudden rip, the raw agony as if the events were current. The girl would be twenty-two now. Sensing his master's anguish, Duke had slunk over and put his head on Jim's knee.

For many years he'd regretted ever getting involved in the Sinoli case, wishing that instead of landing on his desk that grey winter morning in 1976 it had been passed to somebody else, anybody else. In his mind, he had played through countless scenarios of 'what if' and imagined another life if fate hadn't dealt him a dud. He had been angry for years, but this had mellowed with the passage of time, and he took solace in the fact that at least the mother and daughter had gotten free of the mob. The girl would have a chance for a decent and crime-free future. It was the one good thing that came out of this whole tragic episode and that fact alone had eased his lament. Now, after all this time the girl wanted out! It would all have been for nothing.

There was no question as to whether he would take the case; he would do everything in his power to stop the Sinolis' getting their daughter back. Jim's brain was already racing ahead to his travel arrangements, and he looked at the dog.

'You're going on holiday, let's see if old man Jack can feed and water you for a few days.' He dialled Martha's number and threw a few items of clothing into a bag while the line connected.

***

The Delta 767 was bound for Dublin but would have a stopover at Shannon which is where Jim would disembark. Shannon airport, being the first land point in Europe after crossing the vast Atlantic Ocean was traditionally the primary refuelling point for transatlantic flights. As larger jets, capable of travelling farther without the need to refuel emerged, its purpose as a refuelling stopover meant the airport had been scaled-back since its heyday of the seventies and eighties.

It was to be a long flight and as Jim settled back into his cramped economy class seat, he hoped Duke wouldn't be tearing up old Jack's cabin too much. He leafed through the file that a courier had handed him at JFK airport, and when his eyes settled on the recent photograph of Lucy White, he stared at it for a long time.

***

It was late afternoon by the time Jim arrived in the town of Kearis and he pulled his rental car over to check the address of the guest house he was booked into. The almost eight-hour flight and two-hour drive from the airport had left him with tired muscles and he stretched weary limbs as best he could in the confines of the rental car. A highway had taken him south-west from the airport and that led him onto a coastal road, which offered a spectacular view. He didn't have time to stop to drink it in, and he felt a pang of disappointment that his visit wasn't a recreational one.

After a couple of wrong turns, he eventually found the guest house. It appeared small from the outside, but flower beds and lawns were well tended, and he was hopeful the exacting standards would continue into the interior. As Jim unfolded himself from the car a woman in a floral print apron opened the front door and greeted him before he got to the door.

'Mr. Cavalli, is it?'

'Cavell, yes, that's right, found you eventually.'

'Oh yes, we've been expecting you a while now then. C'mon in now. Been keeping your tea warm we 'ave. The middle-aged woman ushered Jim into a small dining room and indicated for him to sit in an over cushioned wicker chair. 'I expect you're starving now after such a long journey?' A crystal beaker and water jug were placed on the table. Jim neither wanted to eat or sit down but the woman hovered over so he thought it best to get the meal over with so he could start work.

The dining room was decorated with a bold and colourful flower print wallpaper, and he hoped his room wouldn't be the same, otherwise he might have trouble sleeping. The woman left the room briefly and returned with a plate covered in aluminium foil and placed it on a table under the window with a breadbasket that held two small white rolls and a knife and fork.

'Get this down ya Mr Cavell.' She took the seat opposite Jim's and proceeded to tell him the house rules and pressed a key into his hand with a large black plastic number four attached to it.

'Your room is at the front of the house. You can see the Ocean. If you have good eyes. Leave the plate when you're done, Alfie will clear that up. I'm off to the bingo, if you need anything, ring the front doorbell. Alfie can hear that alright.' Alfie, he assumed was a husband. The woman left, and Jim pulled back the foil from the plate in front of him. He grimaced as he unveiled a brown mush that had become hard around the edges from sitting for too long in a warm oven. He could make out several dried-up boiled potatoes and some waxy looking carrots, he was tempted to discard the lot and find a shower, but he scanned the room, there was nowhere to put it and he did not want to upset the woman. So he stuck a finger into the mush and found that it didn't taste as bad as it appeared.

Chapter 20

Toing and froing to Kearis on the bus was taking up too much precious research time. It dawned on Lucy that with all that cash sitting in her grandmother's account she could buy herself a car but then figured as she was leaving town soon there might be little point.

This current expedition into Kearis was to see the solicitor and expedite her grandma's probate. The irony of transferring legal title between people with fake identities was not lost on Lucy. She sat across the desk and let the solicitor do the talking.

'As there is no known Will the estate will pass to you Ms. White, as the only living relative. It's a simple process and I can take care of changing the title on the house and transferring funds to your accounts. As there is no life insurance ...'

'What if there is?'

'Life insurance?'

'No. Relatives.'

'I'm sorry?'

'What if there were, some long-lost cousins or the like, ... out there somewhere?' Lucy scrutinized his response carefully.

'Well, of course, that would be a different matter. They would have to make a claim on the estate within six months from the date of the legal notice, but the legal order of entitlement favours direct descendants. Are you expecting a claim from someone?' The solicitor checked his file. 'The Undertaker has advised me that you are the only heir and I have quoted fees on that basis. If we have other claimants the process could be protracted and ... I might have to requote.'

'Whoever really knows?' Lucy gave the solicitor a mocking wide-eyed shrug.

'Hm. Well. Should we continue with the assumption that it's just you, or would you like to wait the statutory period?' He offered Lucy a confused expression. Lucy wondered why a firm of undertakers like Leyne and Son would associate themselves with a greedy, one-man band solicitor with a tatty office over a newsagent. After the luxurious surroundings of the undertaker's establishment, she was expecting another classy setup. At least a secretary or a couple of typists. 'As the estate was your grandmother's there is some capital acquisition rules that you need to be aware of. To avoid them I would advise that you do not sell the property until ...' His sentence drifted off. Lucy was disinterested in the details of Irish inheritance tax laws and her attention was diverted completely when she felt a vibration in her jacket and began patting down various pockets on her worn combat jacket to locate her phone. She glanced at the number illuminated on the display before quickly disconnecting the caller.

'Sorry about that.'

'No problem.' The solicitor closed the files on his desk and pushed himself away from it. 'We can try to have all this wrapped up in just a few more days Ms White. I will give you some information to take away about the tax implications. You can call me anytime if you have any questions.' Lucy felt like she'd just been dismissed by the school headmaster. She mumbled some words of gratitude and let herself be guided back down the same creaky wooden stairs that she had ascended and back into the fresh air that blew along the main High Street in Kearis.

As she stepped into a sandwich shop and lined-up to select her lunch, the vibration in her pocket started again. With a handful of cash and a coke she managed to pull her phone free and answer the persistent caller.

'Lucy, is that you?'

'Hello Edith, yes, it's me.' She addressed her neighbour warmly.

'Where are you, my love? You have a visitor.'

'A visitor?'

'Yes, dear, waiting outside he is, in a big posh car, been sitting there for ages. I asked him to come on inside, into the warm but he just said he would wait in the car. I tried to ring you earlier.'

'Who is it? What does he want? Did he say what he wants?' Lucy was puzzled as to who would come to the house in a big posh car.

'I took him a brew and he asked me if you would be gone long, dear. What time might you be back?' There was a long pause and Edith added in a whisper as if she should not be disclosing the fact, 'He's from America.' Lucy felt herself stiffen. Edith did not speak for a moment either. Lucy thanked her and said she was in Kearis and would be back as soon as she could.

Lucy's gaze fixed intently on the phone in her hand as though it might give her answers to her questions. Edith knew more than she was letting on. The way she had whispered that he was an American left her no doubt the old woman knew exactly why an American in a big posh car would be sitting outside an inconsequential cottage in Anchora. It annoyed her that this was yet another person who had kept her grandma's confidence. Her mobile showed her it was almost two pm. The bus for Anchora left on the hour every hour and she darted out of the shop only to be yelled at for not paying for the coke. She launched some euros at the shop keeper and sprinted to the bus depot. As the stand came into view, she noted the absence of passengers queuing and she cursed loudly as she realized she'd missed the bus. Getting her breath back she scanned the timetables for different routes. There was a bus due in ten minutes that stopped in a neighbouring village. She could get that and cut across the fields.

***

As she raced through the meadows, she was conscious of her pace. The muddy grass would cushion a fall, but it was easy enough to twist an ankle on the uneven terrain. Children's voices sang out from a nearby playground and swings were in motion. It told her school was out, the bus journey had taken an age. She hurried over the lumpy turf and through an ancient iron kissing gate which opened into the steep lane leading to her cottage. As she sprinted up the lane, she craned her neck and searched the road for the car Edith had mentioned. There were no unfamiliar cars, she could see only neighbour's cars parked in the narrow lane. She swore loudly; her efforts had been for nothing. Her cheeks were flushed, and her lungs hurt from the exertion. She walked slowly now up the hill to the cottage, disappointed and trying to regain a steady breath. She was too focused on who the American might be to notice the girl until she heard the rumble of a scooter hurtling towards her. She lunged out of the way but there was no need. She had doubted the youngster's dexterity. The girl had steered and stopped the contraption with a proficiency she remembered she once had with her own scooter. The girl offered her a gummy grin and Lucy's frown was replaced slowly with a gentle smile. Two brown pigtails framed a freckled face. She recognized the girl as living a couple of lanes away, Lucy didn't know her name.

'Has missus White gone to heaven?' She was surprised with the straightforward question. The girl looked about six years old, she held her head to one side and a question in her eyes. She was too young to comprehend any detailed response so Lucy nodded. 'She was my friend.' The girl called out cheerily, 'See yer later.' She was gone again. The scooter hurtled down the steep hill at a disturbing speed and Lucy was disappointed she hadn't thought to ask her name, her grandmother would have known it. The condolence was so honest and direct, she wondered when it was adults learned to become cryptic and ambiguous.

The encounter with the little girl hinted at a grieving community and Lucy reflected what a huge blow for everyone it was, losing her grandma. A melancholy mood beset her again. She was so wrapped up in her own pursuit of the secrets she had not given any thought to the void her grandmother's death had left in this tight-knit village. These thoughts had distracted her from the mysterious visitor and took her all the way into her hallway, where she dropped her keys into the dish under the hall mirror. The glass offered a reflection of an older woman. Lucy's eyes had become ringed with dark circles and her skin seemed paler and thinner. She touched her fingers gently to the corner of her eyes, the corner where crow's feet would eventually become a permanent characteristic. Her dark un-styled hair hung heavily, the face that gazed back was somehow familiar and she realized slowly that she saw a flicker of similarity to her mother. She had never resembled her mother, her dark hair and eyes were a stark contrast to her mother's fair hair and blue eyes, but now she recognised something in her own face that she remembered in her mother's. Grief, she saw what it had done to both of them and realised the resemblance wasn't a genetic trait; it was a consequence of time, grief, fear and suspicion. Those emotions engraved themselves into a face the same way an artist would fashion a sculpture by cutting and digging away at the clay. A flicker of understanding struck Lucy and for the first time she could comprehend why her mother had turned to drink, to shut it all out.

Lucy suddenly wanted to see her mother's face again, with this new perspective, and she raced upstairs and pulled down the dusty old shoe box from the top of her wardrobe.

Chapter 21

For the second time that day, Jim pulled up his rental car outside the small, terraced cottage. He hoped the girl would be back by now. He'd filled his time trying to find the priest. Father O'Reilly was the WITSEC designated local point of contact. From what he could see from the file the priest had done a good job. Neither the girl nor the priest was home, and he was getting impatient. A neighbour had found him waiting outside the cottage and tried to get him to come inside until the girl returned, but he didn't want to be interrogated by a curious local so had left.

The lights were on now. He thought the cottage didn't appear as tatty as it had seemed earlier, the fading daylight hid the peeling paint and the decaying woodwork. This girl's life was completely at odds with the luxury and extravagance that her father's criminality had procured. Drug running and extortion had provided the Sinoli clan with a fortune that they had somehow managed to keep from the authorities and legitimized over the years with layers of legal business enterprises. He knew that lifestyle would be a considerable draw for a girl from this background. He looked at the tired cottage and sighed, he had hoped for a better outcome for the small family he helped twenty years ago.

He had never imagined that Katherine would die so soon, he'd hoped she would have got her life on track, eventually remarried, maybe had more kids, not this. Not a miserable slow death just two years after her extraction and leaving just her mother to raise the child alone.

The file told him, that Lucy had gone to University in Cork and was studying to become a doctor. This cheered him some, if he could stop her mission to find the Sinolis' then she would have a successful future. He eased himself from behind the wheel and hoped that the girl would have the common-sense to comprehend all that he was about to tell her. He knocked on the door and waited, rapid footsteps thumped on the staircase and the door opened. Lucy stared at him and said nothing. She did not appear to be surprised to see him and he knew the neighbour had pre-warned her. Several moments went by before Jim's quiet voice interrupted the silence.

'Lucy, I'm FBI agent Jim Cavell, may I come in?' Lucy stood motionless, the door still in her left hand and her eyes searched his face as if weighing up whether to let him in. She eventually pushed back the door and stood aside for him to pass. Jim walked into the narrow hallway and waited for Lucy to shut the door and indicate which room for him to take. There was anger in her eyes and her movements were abrupt and forced. Lucy walked past him and through into the dining room but did not take a seat, she stood in front of a window and the dimly lit room shadowed her face. He was in no doubt however of her derivation, even if he had not seen the recent photograph, he would have been able to pick Lucy out of a hundred strong crowd she was so like her father.

'I'm afraid I don't have any ID to show you, I'm actually retired from the bureau.'

'What are you doing here then?' Lucy's voice was cold.

'I was involved with your case twenty years ago. They asked me to come over here especially, once they realised there was a situation.'

'A situation! Is that what I am?' Lucy laughed.

'I'm sorry that you only found out about all this recently, Lucy, that was not up to me. I did what I had to do back then, and that was to get you all out safely. Give you and your mother a chance for a normal safe life.'

'One without a father? Is that normal to you?'

'It was your mother's decision, I just ...'

'You just coerced her into it! She testified for you! For the government! You're not telling me she just walked right into your office and said, hey, my husband's a crook can you put him in jail?' Lucy's voice faltered with emotion, and she turned and stared out of the window. Jim let the words hang in the air for a while and then addressed her softly,

'No Lucy, that's not how it happened. I can tell you anything you want to know, that's why I'm here.' He spoke slowly and quietly; he could see her fragile state of mind. 'Your mother was encouraged to give evidence against him, but we did not force her to do anything.' Jim hadn't been offered a seat and did not feel comfortable taking one yet so remained standing across the room. 'Lucy, your father is ..., you mom didn't want his lifestyle for you ... she made a choice ...'

'I should have had the choice!' Lucy spat out the words and rounded on Jim.

'I agree, once you were old enough to understand the whole situation. And I'm sure that's what she would have wanted. But an informed choice, and that's what I intend to give you now. I understand you want to go and see your family. I came all this way because I want to answer the questions that you have and tell you whatever you want to know about your family. I am the person who knew your mother the most. We could have sent any marshal or agent out here Lucy, but they wouldn't be able to tell you everything that I can.'

'Lucky me.' She sat at the table sulkily and Jim took it as an invitation to the same. 'Do you have a cigarette?'

'You don't smoke.'

'Good answer, what else do you know about me?'

'I don't know anything about you, Lucy, I just know about your circumstances.'

'What makes you think I want to hear it from you when I can just go to New York and find out for myself?'

'I also have to tell you about the implications of leaving the programme, the legal implications. You were a minor when you entered it, most witnesses know the consequences of coming out.' He watched her consider this for a moment and he thought she was struggling to comprehend the reality of her situation so he continued.

'You have no proof of your original identity; you can't just switch back and live that other life. We have to ...'

'That's not what I was intending to do.'

'What makes you think your family will believe you're who you say you are?' Jim knew there was no doubting her origins, they would recognise her immediately, but that fact would just make her more curious, so he did not enlighten her. He tried to lighten the hostile atmosphere. 'I thought the Irish were known for their hospitality.' Jim said it with a sly smile and nodded into the kitchen.

'But I'm not Irish, am I?' Harsh words, hard facts. Her body language was ready for a battle, and she was smart. Jim thought she was ready for the tough reality, no point beating around the bush.

'I don't want you to meet them, Lucy.'

'What's it got to do with you?'

'Why don't we start at the beginning?' He pointed to the kitchen and asked if there was a coffee pot, it was going to be a long story.

Part 2

Chapter 22

Katherine hoisted the giant bouquet off the reception desk and hurried along the corridor to the staff room. It was the third such offering in as many days. She was embarrassed and hurried to stash it out of sight before her boss noticed. Sam Sinoli had vowed to send her a bouquet of roses every day until she agreed to go on a date with him. The flowers entered the staff room before she did, so she did not see where the giggles were coming from until she put the flowers down.

'Not another bouquet. Oh my god, they are divine ...'

'Take them home, Joannie. We haven't got any more room in the house.'

'I can't take your flowers. It's your gift, honey.'

'Well, I'm sure there will more tomorrow.' Katherine sat down and kicked off her shoes to massage her aching feet. She was halfway through her evening shift as a receptionist at the New York City Excelsior hotel. She worked evenings in the elegant Fifth Avenue hotel to fund her daytime secretarial courses.

'Well you know how to stop them coming.' Joannie stubbed her cigarette out and stood to check her appearance in a mirror. 'Just go for a drink with him, no harm in just one drink.' She winked at Katherine. 'Don't you like him?'

'I don't want to get fired, Joannie. If I go for a drink or anything else with Sam Sinoli then I may as well go looking for another job. It's in the staff handbook. NO liaison with guests.' Katherine's colleague laughed.

'Honey, if you're Sam Sinoli's girl there ain't no rule book that applies to you. Know what I mean?'

'No, I don't.'

'You know ...'

'... That he's rich and could probably buy the hotel?' Katherine felt there was something her colleague was neglecting to tell her.

'He's a very powerful and influential man.' Joannie giggled again. 'As if old Mr Moreau is gonna fire the ass of Mr Sinoli's girl. Tsh, that'll never happen, girl ... it won't happen.' She sniggered. 'He already knows about the flowers and that Sam wants to date you.'

'He does?'

'Sure honey, that old fart doesn't miss a trick in his hotel. The walls have eyes, know what I'm saying.'

'No.' Katherine was even more confused. Was her colleague alluding to them being filmed?

'Anyway, better back to the bar, otherwise, it will be my tiny ass on the firing line.'

'Which walls have eyes?'

'All the walls.' Joannie's laugh echoed down the hall as she went. Katherine stuffed the roses unceremoniously into her locker and headed back to the reception desk to finish her shift.

The Excelsior was one of Sam Sinoli's regular hangouts, he would meet his associates in the bar or restaurant, for private meetings he would rent a suit. When Sam noticed the new blonde-haired receptionist, he had quickly become obsessed with her. She couldn't ignore his charm offensive and Katherine found herself increasingly drawn to the enigmatic character. She was aware of his presence in a room without having to look to see if he was there. She could hear only his voice in a crowd of many and she could feel his gaze on her without turning around. Her inherent pragmatism tried to dampen the emotions that coursed through her when Sam was around. She sensed an undercurrent of some intangible menace, something unspoken about among the people that knew or were acquainted with him but pushed the thoughts to the back of her mind.

Despite his constant invitations Katherine quietly refused his advances but Sam didn't give up. Every time he saw the receptionist, he tried to erode her resolve and get her to date him. Katherine finally capitulated, she wanted the gifts to stop and quieten the rumours with the hotel staff so agreed to a date with Sam Sinoli if he promised to be discreet.

***

Irene Buckley finished the hem she was sewing and smiled to herself. Her daughter was still holed up in her bedroom doing her hair and make-up. She had paraded through the lounge for the last hour in various outfits, asking her parents about each one and the impression it might give on a first date. She knew her daughter was nervous and that could only mean one thing, she was head over heels in love with the man who was about to take her to the theatre.

Irene was equally excited about meeting the suitor, the build-up to this event had been going on for days. The house was filled with flowers and both Irene and her husband were intrigued with this mysterious benefactor. He was clearly a wealthy man.

Katherine finally emerged from her bedroom, paraded, and twirled for her parents once again. Irene peered over the top of her glasses and smiled.

'He will be here anytime. I'm not inviting him in, so don't ask. And don't be staring out of the windows either.' Katherine checked the street for her date.

'Why not? Are you ashamed of us?' Katherine's father chuckled.

'She is that. We don't have a fancy house and a fancy car and I'm sure he has both. Roses and orchids don't come cheap you know.'

'I am. Yes, I am. I know you dad. You'll be asking him all sorts of questions. He's not the type of person you give the Spanish Inquisition.'

'What type of person is he then?' Irene thought this was an odd statement. But she didn't get a reply. Her daughter and her husband were distracted by the sleek black Chrysler Imperial that pulled up to the kerb outside their home and she walked over to see for herself. The kids in the street rode up and circled the shiny motor on their bicycles. Expensive cars weren't a common sight in the backstreets of Brooklyn.

Her daughter's date was chatting with the kids as he eyed the house. Irene noticed her daughter's nervous excitement and she laughed when Katherine hurried to the door to intercept her date before she or her husband could get anywhere near the dark-haired handsome stranger. Her attempts were futile, Sam Sinoli briefly kissed her daughter and then turned a wide smile on her and her husband who were both standing in the doorway.

'Mr Buckley, Mrs Buckley. I'm very pleased to meet you.' He presented the large box of chocolates he was holding to Irene.

'Well thank you, Mr ...?'

'Sam, please.'

'Well, isn't that nice?' She used her smartest church voice and eyed her husband. He was considering the man who would be taking his daughter out with a father's wary eye. The two men shook hands and Sam invited them both to dinner the following week.

'The Four Seasons, or anywhere else you prefer.'

'Oh well, that would be fine, but please you must come to us for dinner first.' She diverted the invitation knowing she didn't have anything grand enough to wear at the Four Seasons Hotel.

'Yes, Irene makes a lovely roast chicken, and we would like to know about your business, Sam.' Irene saw her daughter's eyes widen and noted the hand that slipped under Sam's arm to pull him away.

'Looks like Katherine is eager to get to the theatre. Off you go now, otherwise, you'll be missing the start, and those kiddies might have the wheels off your car if it stays there too long.' She nodded in the direction of the growing crowd of kids around the car.

'Oh no, they're just minding it for me.' Sam put Katherine in the car and handed some dollar bills to the kids. Irene watched the car pull off and some of the older kids chased the Chrysler to the end of the street. He made a good first impression on Irene and her husband, but she had noticed an uncharacteristic reticence in her daughter. She put it down to nervous excitement and walked back into the house where a cloud of cheap perfume still hung in the air.

'Whatever business Sam's into, it must be a very successful one.' She shot a sideways glance at her husband, but he had already picked up the newspaper so didn't notice her slight frown.

'No doubt about that; God only knows how much that car cost.'

***

Several more dates followed. Sam took Katherine to the best restaurants, nightclubs and concerts. They were treated like VIP's, never waited in line, given the best tables and had constant attention in any place they visited. Katherine's wardrobe expanded, she acquired designer coats and haute couture dresses. Sam asked Katherine to quit her job at the hotel so he could see her more often. If his work got in the way of a date, he would send a messenger with a gift. He showered her with jewellery and expensive perfumes. She became a familiar face in some of the city's most exclusive boutiques. Katherine's parents were not left out of Sam's gift giving; he bequeathed Irene with pearls and silk scarfs, her husband received fine wines and whisky. The family passed along much of what they were gifted around the neighbourhood and their popularity increased. When Sam realized they were sharing their gifts he made a grandiose gesture by making a large donation to their church and the kiddies' club where Irene worked mornings. Katherine's brother was not left out, he acquired a new car at a discount price. He thought he'd got lucky at the sales lot with an apprentice salesman, but luck seemed to follow the family around.

The courting lasted several weeks and culminated with Sam asking Katherine's father for permission to marry his daughter. He was given wholehearted approval. The whole family were living a charmed life.

Chapter 23

The charm offensive continued well into the marriage. Katherine was revered by her new husband; she was enchanted by his devotion and affection. As soon as she got a driving license, he bought her a luxury car. Their house was full of expensive contemporary furniture and art. It took twelve months for cracks to show.

Sam was frustrated that his young and beautiful wife had not yet become pregnant, and he did what he only knew how. He threw money at the problem. The fertility treatment Sam paid for resulted in Katherine giving birth to twins a month short of their second wedding anniversary. Her husband was euphoric, and he doted on his children, a boy, and a girl. Katherine wanted her Irish heredity to be recognized and she suggested Gaelic names for the children. Sine and Sive. Sam agreed. Mixing his Italian heritage with Irish bloodlines had been a genius business strategy and he proudly showed off his first-born son with Irish ancestry. Sam affectionately nicknamed his son 'Sin Sin'; he thought it was hilarious, the wisecrack went over Katherine's head. An elaborate christening party was planned so Sam could show off his new heir to the Sinoli empire.

***

A few weeks after the christening, Katherine started to notice she no longer had her husband's full affection. He was working longer hours and divided his time between his children and his work. She became increasingly side-lined.

When he started staying out all night Katherine suspected him of infidelity. She tried to eavesdrop on his call, and it was during one of these covert spying missions she discovered that shortly before he met her, he had fathered a son with his cousin's wife. This exposed his obsession for her to get pregnant. She understood he was desperate for a legitimate son and heir, and she had been in the right place at the right time. He was looking for a wife but more importantly a mother for his children. It explained his tacit frustration when she failed to get pregnant in the months following their wedding.

Katherine tried to confide in a sister-in-law but instead provoked a warning that chilled her to the bone. She was told never to mention such things again by a clearly panicked kinswoman. Somehow word got back to Sam Sinoli that she had been gossiping and the argument that ensued closed the chapter on her enchanted marriage. She tried to blot out the ugly episode with alcohol. Her aching heart and growing uneasiness about her husband made her turn to the bottle frequently for comfort. Sam used the smell of liquor on her breath as an excuse to sleep in another bedroom. Katherine was convinced he was seeing his cousin's wife again and her snooping intensified. She not only discovered that he had several girlfriends she also learned the stark reality that her husband's business dealings were neither honourable nor legal.

When Katherine discussed the 'family businesses' with the other wives Sam suddenly bought a new house, a long way away from their respective families and friends. The isolation made her depressed and lonely.

It was only a few weeks after their move when Katherine found Harry in the house. Harry was one of her husband's most trusted employees; and it was not unusual for him to be in their home. Employees were always coming and going but this time his presence left Katherine terrified. She had left the house to go to the liquor store and realising she had forgotten her purse she had left the car running and dashed back to collect it. As she ran into the hall she bumped into Harry. He was hovering by the door that led down to a basement garage.

'Harry! For god's sake, you gave me a fright there; I didn't know there was anybody here!'

'Sorry ... er ...'

'God, what have you done?' Harry stood with his hands behind his back but there was a large fresh bloodstain on the front of his shirt.

'You've hurt yourself?' She reached out to examine his torso, but Harry stepped back, and his hands instinctively came up to halt her advance; he faltered but it was too late. She saw his hands and arms were also covered in thick wet blood. Katherine had to concentrate hard stop herself from gagging at the sight and smell.

'I ... I just came back to get my purse, I ... I ... didn't realise there was anyone home.' She backed away from him and her eyes moved to the garage door that was slightly ajar, her mind raced with the possibility of the horrors that lay in the garage. Harry noticed her gaze and his eyes widened with a warning. He shook his head slowly. In her panic to get away she knocked a large ceramic sculpture off the hall table. It shattered on the black and white tiles. She fled to her car and drove off as fast as she could.

That day was the first time she hit the hard liquor, she wanted to blot out what she'd seen, and the neat booze certainly did the trick. The incident was never mentioned either with her husband or Harry. The sculpture had been replaced with a large fern by the time she'd returned home. She did now, however, understand the little jokes and wisecracks that the men made about Harry. He oversaw their wholesale meat business, and she knew now that he was responsible for butchering more than just the cattle. Whenever she heard them talking about jobs for Harry she shuddered and pretended that she hadn't heard.

The Sinoli family Christmas was always an enormous affair and the one that followed the incident with Harry was traumatic for Katherine and marked the beginning of her spiral into a deep void. When it came time to carve the birds somebody suggested it was Harry's job. There were some covert smiles between the men, and Katherine scanned the women for any understanding of the hidden meaning. The other women were either oblivious or deliberately ignorant to the snickering between the men. When Harry took up the knife and began to carve, he looked up and caught Katherine's eyes. Cold empty eyes she thought. An evil smile played on one side of his mouth, and he seemed pleased that she was watching him. She shivered and refilled her glass.

Chapter 24

The summer of 1985 was a turbulent time for the mob families in New York. The FBI was slowly making inroads into disrupting the criminal cartels and raids were constant. One of Sam's cousins was arrested for the murder of a business rival, and it made the whole Sinoli clan nervous. Katherine overheard Sam discussing the arrest. He was hoping the kid wouldn't talk, he knew they would have big problems if anyone started talking. He was warning the whole crew.

Katherine suspected her husband was wanted by the FEDS and she knew that the familial bonds of silence were splintering and making everyone insecure, so it was no surprise to her when Sam installed a state of art security system throughout the house and grounds. Cameras and alarms were fitted to every window and door and the gardens were secured with an electric fence. The large iron gates at the bottom of the winding drive became manned twenty four-seven with armed security guards. If unwanted visitors managed to get through all that, metre high steel ramps could be deployed on the driveway. Sam acted like a schoolboy with new gadgets as he showed them off to Katherine and walked her through all the new security measures. His kids were his priority but as an ominous afterthought he told her the security measures could lock people inside the house as well as outside.

Katherine's drinking had become constant. It was the only way she could get through the day. She felt increasingly isolated in this Ivory tower. Sam was hardly ever home but when he was around, he tormented his wife about her drinking and her appearance. He accused her of neglecting their kids because she was always inebriated. He considered her to be a liability and decided to hire two full-time nannies that would rotate through day and evening shifts. It meant he could pretty much ignore her completely and she felt as though she was invisible. Her estrangement and bitterness grew.

Her doctor began prescribing her tranquillizers and she would disappear for days at a time into her bedroom. She only occasionally saw her husband in late-night visits to her bedroom. He wanted more legitimate sons. If she was sober, she could smell the other women on him. She tried to hang around his study to find out who his mistresses were. On one of her eavesdropping adventures, she heard her husband tell somebody, 'It's in the Cadillac, get rid of it.' The fog of inebriation clouded her judgment and she tiptoed directly to the basement to have a look for herself.

She found Little Jimmy, one of the Sinoli crew stuffed unceremoniously in the trunk of her husband's car. His wrists and ankles were tied with wire, and he had a bloodied bullet hole in his forehead. She had to race back to her bedroom, and she threw up until there was only bile left.

Somebody had seen her and told Sam. Later that night when he had come to her room it was not for sex, instead, he severely beat her for looking in the car. His blows held no rage, his punches were cold and controlled and he aimed for places he knew would cause the most damage and least evidence. She understood then that she was married to a cruel and sadistic man and the violence he bestowed on her that night told her it was not only his crew who bloodied their hands.

Sometime during that night, Katherine miscarried her third child. She had been drinking so much she had not even known she was pregnant.

Sam was beside himself with guilt and grief, he eased up on the bullying and for a while, she got more freedom to see her friends and family. On her mother's request Katherine took up some addiction counselling. She agreed mostly because it was an excuse to get out of the house, the regular appointments meant she could pretty much come and go as she pleased without any of Sam's crew questioning her activities.

It took some persuading, but by playing on Sam's guilt, she got him to agree to let the kids attend a nursery, she could sit and watch her children play without a nanny in tow. One of the other wives in the family sent her kids to the same place and one afternoon Katherine suggested they went for coffee. She knew enough to not speak directly about the family business to this woman but with cryptic questions she slowly and depressingly learnt that they all knew, they had always known - the wives, sisters, mothers - they all knew what their husbands and brothers did, and they all ignored it. They were too frightened to speak about it and by somehow not acknowledging the facts, it was all happening in someone else's life.

Chapter 25

Throughout 1986 the mob suffered, they were being squeezed from all sides and rival families were increasingly fighting for territories to replace the operations the FEDS were shutting down. Turf treaties between different families were violated or abandoned completely as the criminals competed for the most lucrative alternatives.

The FBI was winning the war on organised crime due to infiltrators in the ranks. All the major families seemed to be affected and it made for a febrile atmosphere. The families turned in on themselves and hits were prolific. Most of the major mob syndicates underwent a rationalization programme. They didn't retire people off with a gold watch, fat pension, and good luck card; Katherine suspected there were many more bodies in the boot throughout those months, but she didn't dare go and look.

The bloody carnage on the streets of New York started getting unwanted international press attention and the politicians threw more resources at the FBI to get organized crime under control. It made Sam even more irritable and brooding. Katherine was glad he wasn't around so much. Her free rein continued until she accidentally crashed her car into a neighbour's. The guy called the police. She was over the legal alcohol limit and Sam was livid that he had to put up with the cops in and out of his house all afternoon. His paranoia convinced him they were putting in bugging devices. He paid off the neighbour and the cops, but it was too late, they had already been all over his house. They had been in his office, and he was worried.

The incident was logged in the police computers before he'd had time to pay off the cops, which meant he also had to wrangle a deal with somebody in the justice department. Katherine avoided jail, but she would have to go into rehab. He agreed, he was more than happy to get rid of her for a while, she was starting to cost him valuable favours. Katherine spent four weeks in a residential rehabilitation centre and came out sober.

Sam was on a business trip when she was released and when she got news of his intended homecoming late one night, she stayed awake to give him the good news of her sobriety. It was two thirty in the morning when she finally heard his voice. As she pulled on a gown and dashed to the top of the stairs, she realized he was not alone, the house was in darkness but for one reception room. She could hear combined grunting and moaning. In bare feet, she crept down a few stairs and peered through the wrought iron balustrade. She could see her husband's discarded clothes on the floor, but she could not see who he was with. As she repositioned herself on the staircase, a woman came into her line of vision. She watched as her husband thrust himself into the nanny. The nanny's skirt was pulled up to her waist and Sam was holding her legs wide and high while he bent over her on the sofa. She watched for a few moments, then turned, and silently crept back to her bedroom. Katherine sat on the end of the bed until the shock subsided and turned into revulsion and loathing for her husband.

She pulled a bottle of gin from under the bed and cradled it. She desperately wanted to drink it and let the alcohol work its magic. This had happened before; she was sure of it. She felt an overwhelming sense of deja-vu but in her usual inebriated state, she was always confused about

143

what was reality or her nightmares. She tried to reason with herself that she was his wife and the mother of his children, these women would come and go. But it was the fact that her children slept in the rooms over their grunting sweating bodies that disturbed her. They were too young now to be aware of the debauchery and brutality that was their destiny in life, but their future held no promise of decency or goodness in this family. The realization spurred a decision. She had to get out and it wouldn't be easy. She replaced the unopened bottle back under the bed.

Chapter 26

A few weeks passed and Katherine kept up her routine. She would take bottles from the bar as usual, discard the liquid in her bathroom and secrete the empty bottles around the house. She took care to gargle with the liquid and splash it around her bed sheets and clothing. The bar was always stocked. She was unsure how much she was supposed to be consuming. The most difficult part for her was feigning inebriation, not to her husband; even when he was around, he paid scant attention to her, but she knew that she had to keep up the act around his employees, including the nannies.

She found it easy to keep track of her husband's activities, his schedules, the people that came and went for meetings. Most of his activities were nocturnal and she had to adjust her body clock to keep up with the endless late-night appointments in her husband's study.

On one occasion Sam found her loitering outside his study so she pretended to stumble and drop to the floor. He regarded her with disgust, stepped right over her and kept on walking. Another time she had been listening in on one of his calls, he became suspicious and sent someone around the house to check who else was on the line. Katherine was in one of the spare bedrooms. When she heard footsteps in the hall she lay on the floor and hoped they would think she had passed out. The bodyguard grunted and sucked his lips, he plucked the phone from her loose grip, replaced it in its cradle and left the room.

One afternoon when she went to collect her supplies, she noticed that the bar was devoid of its usual array of bottles and her mind went into overdrive. She was summoned to her husband's study and her legs trembled so fiercely that she could barely walk in unaided. It turned out the following day was a niece's birthday party and Sam wanted her sobered up and in attendance. The trepidation was replaced by relief; it would have been a gruelling mission trying to act inebriated for hours in front of the entire family.

The following morning, she was keen to get out of the house. She told Sam she wanted to help with the party preparations. He was in a good mood, he liked having the family all together, it made him feel more powerful. He scrutinized her carefully, calculating the degree of her sobriety and agreed she and the kids could go ahead early without him.

The party got underway, and more and more family members arrived, loaded high with presents and party food. Katherine was happy, her depression lifted, she was sober, and it felt like she was bathing in sunlight for the first time in months. She chased the kids from room to room on bikes and helped them up and down plastic slides. A few of the women had babies and while Katherine was taking her turn cuddling a new-born the mother came over to reclaim the baby.

'I'm so sorry, Katherine, I didn't mean to be insensitive, showing off our Mickey. I forgot about your baby.' Katherine was surprised. It was the first time anybody had mentioned her miscarriage directly. She realised they must all know and while she was coming to terms with this information the woman added, 'At least you have the twins.'

'It was really unfortunate losing the baby, but Sam and I are trying again now and I'm sure they will have another brother or sister real soon.'

'You're trying! Oh, Katherine, that's fantastic. I heard that the complications from last time meant it might not be possible, for anymore, oh that's great news ... I'll keep all my things crossed it happens soon, then little Mickey here will have another cousin to play with ...'

Katherine did not hear anymore, she was running the words over again in her head. The woman thought she was barren, from complications, who would say such things?

The rest of the afternoon went by with a blur for Katherine. She poured herself a couple of drinks, it would have looked suspicious if she had not. She wanted to get her sister-in-law alone, she wanted to quiz her about what the women were saying and learn what they knew.

The party seemed to go on for hours, endless rounds of party games and laughter, but Katherine did not feel like celebrating, she wandered in the garden professing the need to smoke. She ran her mind over and over her many hospital and doctor's appointments that had followed her miscarriage. She had been prodded and poked and tested on so many occasions she had lost count. Had they told her she could no longer bear children? She tried to remember; her constant tranquillized stupor that had followed her beating had blocked out all memories. She did know however that Sam had not returned to her room since the night of that beating. A chill spread through her body. She had suspected that it was down to his guilt and concern for her. Had he seen her medical records? Is that why she had been paraded before doctor after doctor? The only thing plain and clear to Katherine now was that a barren wife was not much use to a man who put dynasty and lineage above all else.

Chapter 27

It was a chilly autumn morning when they first contacted her. Katherine was on her way to see her hairdresser; it was a salon she had been using for many years because the owner was a friend from High School. She knew she was being tailed; it was not unusual. Most of the family were at some time or other; however, it had become constant and conspicuous. They had never approached her or made contact, so she tried to ignore them.

The night she discovered her husband with the nanny, she had toyed with the idea of the government's witness protection programme. One of Sam's crew had given evidence to the FBI and then disappeared. The family put a lot of resources into finding him and were enraged when the search proved futile. The FEDS had given him a new name, in a new place. It was unlikely they would ever get their hands on him.

The idea of getting herself and her kids away from Sam Sinoli was the only thing keeping Katherine sober. If she worked with the FBI to get her husband jailed the risks were high. If he got a whisper of her betrayal, she would certainly end up in the boot of the Cadillac. Even if she was successful and got the FEDS to relocate her and the kids, she feared for her parents, her brother, and his growing family.

She pulled her Chevrolet Camaro into a parking space in front of the small parade of shops. The car's tinted windows made it difficult for her to gauge the edge of the sidewalk, so she wound down both windows to get a better view of the curb; as she struggled to park the large vehicle, an agent stuck his head right through the open passenger window and offered her a card, it had a handwritten telephone number across the middle.

'Mrs. Sinoli I'm FBI agent Jim Cavell. I understand that you may be having some concerns about all the murders your husband has been committing.' Katherine felt the blood drain from her face. She glanced desperately up and down the sidewalk.

'Nobody's here, I checked.' The agent was in his late forties, his blonde hair already greying around the edges. 'Take the number Mrs. Sinoli. We know about the bodies in the boot and the abuse you get.' Katherine was mortified. If she was seen talking to this man she was done. How the hell did they know what went on in her home? The agent saw Katherine's eyes scanning the middle-distance, and her breathing had shortened, panic was setting in, so he kept it brief.

'We know you've got some trouble, Mrs Sinoli. We got people on our payroll.' He answered her questions. 'If you want out, we can help, just call the number. It can't be traced to us. It's a private number.' He turned and strode off as quickly as he'd appeared.

Katherine had not taken the card from him, even if she had wanted to, her hands were frozen, clasped around the steering wheel. He'd dropped it into the open window knowing full well she wouldn't leave it there, lying on the passenger seat. The overpowering urge for a slug of gin flooded her, so she stayed in the car for a few minutes to regain her control. It was hard, staying off the bottle, even harder since her relapse at the party. What she learned that day had knocked the confidence out of her and increased her anxiety.

She was on borrowed time, and she knew it. If Sam realised that she was not going to drink herself to death he might find he had to hurry things along a little. The courage that had germinated in rehab had all but disappeared.

Katherine fingered the paper with trembling hands. The agent told her they had somebody on the inside, she tried to think who that might be. Katherine got herself out of the car and fled to the nearest bar for the much-needed gin. It was her hairdresser that stopped her sinking into the abyss that day. From the large window of the salon Sandy had watched Katherine park the car, saw the agent have a brief conversation and then witnessed Katherine flee to the bar. She managed to shoehorn her terrified friend back to the salon where she silently got on with the hairstyling. Both women eyed each other through the mirror, wondering who would be the first to mention the incident. In the end, it was Sandy. She sent her gofer to the store for more cigarettes, there were no other customers in the salon.

'I know that guy. He's been here a few times. Always after you've been in.' Katherine's eyes expanded in astonishment.

'Wh ...?

'Asking loads of questions. How long have I known you? Why don't 'the others' come here for their hair-styling.' A knowing glance through the mirror communicated more than any words.

'I say nothing, only we go way back, to high school.' She smiled and rubbed Katherine's arm as if to reassure her.

'Somebody's talking to him ... somebody from ...' Katherine's voice trailed off to barely a whisper, '... from the family.' Katherine's eyes sought out her friend's.

'That's not good. Do you think Sam has any idea?'

'I don't know.'

'Well, I just hope they don't think it's you. Fellas like Jim out there making themselves a nuisance around you and somebody might get the wrong impression.'

The gofer returned, and the discussion ended. Katherine sat in silent contemplation and chained smoked while Sandy talked non-stop about almost anything and everything, which was usual. The subjects she covered were her kids, her parents, and the nuisance drug pushers at the end of the street whom she determined to be no older than sixteen.

Katherine felt shame, she knew that somewhere further up the line her husband was responsible for the powder those kids traded. She tried to look out through the salon windows, past the glossy photos of the women with flowing shiny locks advertising the newest shampoo and shine products. Each time her head was promptly tweaked back to face the mirror, she felt tainted by her husband's crimes. She was sheltered from the everyday consequence of their impact, but here in this neighbourhood, on these streets, there was no escaping their reality.

The conversation with Sandy was the first time she had talked to anybody about her deviant family and her husband's business. Now that it was out there, they had acknowledged and discussed it, she wondered what her friend really thought of her? Did she know that Katherine's kids would grow up to be murderers and thieves, no better than the pushers on the street corner that Sandy reviled? She wanted to talk more to Sandy but that would put her at risk, and that was unfair.

Katherine paid for her blow dry with the usual large wedge of notes that she never counted out. Sandy was a single mum and Katherine helped her the only way she could. She said she would be back the following week. Sandy followed her to the door and held her fur coat. While she put her arms in, she got close to her friend's ear and spoke softly so the gofer couldn't hear.

'What shall I tell the guy when he comes round later?' Katherine's eyes widened and she looked everywhere except at her friend. Words were impossible to formulate so she shook her head. The panic etched on Katherine's face told Sandy everything she needed to know.

'Okay. I'll give him that message. You take care of yourself, and I'll see ya next week.' It was raining and Katherine pulled her coat close around her body and ran to her car. She didn't turn around to see her friend waving goodbye, so she also didn't see the white blonde- haired agent walk by the window and barely miss a stride when her friend gave him a discreet nod through the rain-streaked glass. Katherine shredded the paper with the telephone number into a hundred pieces and let them flutter away in the wind as she drove off.

⊷•◄❮❯►•⊶

Chapter 28

The following week when Katherine returned to the salon she thought her friend welcomed her nervously and when she walked into the back room for her shampoo, she realized why. The gofer was nowhere to be seen and instead the blonde-haired agent sat in a bucket chair with a glossy magazine open on his lap and he greeted her as if it were nothing unusual for him to be sitting there.

Katherine had tried to flee from the salon, but Sandy stood in the doorway. Between the two of them, they managed to assure Katherine that she was safe, nobody had seen Jim come in or would see him leave.

It was the start of many such appointments; Jim Cavell would always be in the backroom of the salon and patiently try his best to convince Katherine he could help her get away from the mob if she helped the FBI and provided them with evidence of her husband's crimes. She wouldn't yield without guarantees that her parents, brother, and his family would be safe as well as her own kids. He tried to convince her that her wider family members would be safe, the mob didn't hit their own. Katherine knew better, she had seen Little Jimmy's crumpled body with her own eyes, and she knew how unhinged the Sinolis had become. In the last few months all mob rules had been abandoned. Katherine would only provide information of her husband's crimes if the FBI provided guarantees that they would all be put in the witness protection program.

Cavell took the proposition to his superiors and the suggestion that eight family members could be put into the WITSEC program made his boss baulk. It would be a massive cost for very little gain. The confessions of a drunk wife wouldn't stand up in court and the FBI knew that wives were not involved in the family 'business' dealings. Her information would be of limited use.

Jim was caught in the middle - he needed Katherine to talk, and he needed the government to make some guarantees, and he needed it fast. Katherine was spiralling into a hole again and it might not be long before his boss's sentiments became a certainty. The stalemate forced Jim to put his cards on the table at the next meeting with Katherine.

'I can't get any guarantees for your wider family, Katherine. The government doesn't think you have enough information about the businesses to warrant the massive cost of that. I might be able to sway them if you give me something I can start investigating, something that is indisputable in court.' He waited for some reaction to his words, but Katherine had retreated to somewhere distant. 'There is one thing that we could try. Sam spends most of his time in his car or his office, if we can get an ear in, a bug … then we can get the information ourselves.' There was still no reaction from Katherine, not even a question, and Jim wondered if she was listening to him. 'We can make it look like you just ran out on him, you, and the kids. This way you won't even have to give any evidence at all. We can get you far away, he will never find you, you'll all be safe, he'll never know who put the bug in.' Katherine leaned back in her chair and wiped her hands over her face as if clearing the past and bringing herself back to the present.

'Number one: You don't think he will put pressure on my parents and my brother to find me? Find his son? Do you really think that bastard will just let me walk away with his precious kids? It won't work; even if he's in jail, his brothers, the crew will do his bidding. Number 2: I can plant an 'ear' inside the Cadillac if it will get me the government guarantees but Mr Cavell, I have more than enough 'facts and incriminating evidence' to put Sam and all his cronies behind bars for a very long time.'

Katherine stood, lit a cigarette, and pulled on it several times before she started to pace the room. Jim waited; he could not read any emotion on her face. He watched as she put one foot in front of the other as if measuring out the floor tiles with each step and began reciting conversations, word by word, detail by detail, name by name.

She listed the dates and times of Sam's whereabouts when murders had occurred, or when people had gone missing. She listed as many of his employees that she knew about, and she detailed the timetable for routine drops and collections of his drug couriers. She told Jim about Harry's handy work and finding Little Jimmy in the boot.

Cavell remained seated in stunned silence. Katherine did not look up from her pacing, she was recalling the facts stored in her head like a child might relay the times tables for a teacher. She paused now and then to massage her temples or pinch the bridge of her nose as she recalled the memorised facts. Jim was afraid to interrupt her for fear of stalling the monologue.

When she paused to light a third cigarette, Jim put a hand up to pause her. He didn't know what to say. His mind was trying to process the implications this would have for the FBI. It was a goldmine, the names she had spoken had sent a shockwave through his veins. She could implicate a lot more people than just the Sinoli family and she had no idea even who half of these people were.

'Is this enough to get us all protection, Mr Cavell, my whole family?' It was a sincere question. Jim wanted to run back to his office and jump up and down on his boss's desk. 'Get me that bug or whatever it is. I don't want him to ever see the light of day. I want him away for the rest of his life, all of them!'

Every hair on Jim's body stood on end. He knew he had to get this stuff on tape as soon as practical. If the Sinolis got a whiff of what she was giving them, there was no doubt she was dead. With only one hour a week in the back room at the salon it could take weeks for him to get this evidence on tape and then corroborate it and pull them all in. He had stalled her monologue, how much more was there? His mind reeled as he tried to formulate a plan of action. He could also not risk corroborating any of the stuff she was talking about until the family were all safe. If the Sinolis' suspected a leak they would want to know where they were haemorrhaging and he might never get all the information. He would have to work fast, he also had to be discreet.

Katherine had revealed that some of the highest police officials in the State of New York, plus a senior official in the Justice Department were all collaborators with the Sinolis. It confirmed why they had evaded arrest and prosecution for so long. Katherine had also given him the name of someone on his team, someone in the heart of the FBI operational command. It was dynamite.

On his way back to the office he formulated a play of action. He needed to keep a small team on a need-to-know basis. He needed the guarantees for the witness program from his boss but made the decision to hold back some of what she had disclosed. She had named one FBI insider, and if there were one it was highly likely that there might be more.

As Katherine drove away from the salon that day, she for the first time in a long time did not feel the cold icy fingers of fear stroking her spine. A burden had been lifted from her; she knew what she was doing could get her killed but she also knew that would be her destiny anyway if she did nothing, so why keep all the horrors inside her head? Let Jim do what he could and let Sam rot in hell. She was already there.

Chapter 29

Jim got witness protection guarantees for the whole family. His boss agreed that the fewer agents involved with gathering the evidence the better. They would get it all on tape first, do some corroboration and verification and then extract the witnesses. Arrests and full investigations would come once the witness was out of the fire.

Jim assembled a small team of technicians from out of state and the storeroom above the salon was turned into a video and audio recording studio. Business in the salon went on as usual, except for the few extra customers that came in complete with bulging waistbands and electronic earpieces. Katherine showed up as usual every week for her appointment. Instead of getting her hair washed, a look-a-like agent would swap clothes with her and take the seat out front where Sandy would style and tend her hair. Katherine meanwhile would climb the narrow uncarpeted staircase where Jim and the technicians were waiting, ready to record her testimony.

After a couple of sessions, Jim told his boss that he needed more than the hour a week that the salon appointment would facilitate, he needed to get the stuff on tape a lot quicker. Katherine was struggling to stay sober. The terror of what she was doing was manifest in every utterance and he was worried her nerves would hold up for several weeks. It was nearer the truth that he was not sure his own nerves would hold up. If the information sat around on tape for a few weeks before they acted on it, it was a risk to everyone.

In addition, there were the technicians. FBI staff could be bought. Everybody had a price.

Various ideas were swapped including one to get her back in the rehab clinic for a week or two, but Katherine discounted that because she would be away from the children. She told them that her husband did not question or inquire about her regular appointments at the hospital and so Jim made a few phone calls, and the ensemble of technicians and equipment was moved between the salon and a suite of rooms masquerading as a gynaecology department on the eighth floor of the City Hospital.

Jim was astounded by Katherine's memory recall. Despite the slurred and sometimes quiet voice, the information flowed out of her without much leading or questioning. The less the agent coerced the better.

After the third week, whilst the technicians were checking the tapes and packing away their equipment, Jim showed Katherine the small listening device. He was getting enough evidence from Katherine, but it was damning, he needed to give her more protection. The microphone was no bigger than a large hat pin, its long needle was to be pushed into the underside of the passenger seat, only the small bauble microphone would protrude. Jim sensed some hesitation in Katherine's scrutiny of the device and asked her if she could go through with the operation.

'They sweep the house all the time for bugs, especially the phones, how do you know it won't be found?'

'It will be found if they sweep the car. If they can't find it, he will just stop using the car.' Jim saw the fear in Katherine's eyes.

'And he will have a very small pool of suspects, only a few of us have access to the car.'

'Katherine it's your call, I am not going to force you to do it.'

'Don't we have enough with the stuff that I'm giving you?' There was a tremor in Katherine's voice, she almost mumbled the words. Jim didn't want to tell her the other reason why he wanted an ear on her husband; it would worry her too much.

'We certainly do, but his voice ... his own words corroborating the stuff from you will be irrefutable in court. You see his lawyers will argue that the evidence we got from you was somehow coerced. They will trot out your medical reports and the rehab stuff and say we intimidated a vulnerable witness and that your testimony is unreliable ... because of your ... past addictions.' Katherine nodded. 'We don't want to give him an inch of wiggle room. If we corroborate one thing, just one little thing, it will make everything else you give more valuable.' Katherine's thin fingers took the box and put it in her purse. Jim jiggled a finger and held a hand to take back the box. He removed the pin and slid it delicately into the lining of her purse.

'Less evidence, should they go looking for some.'

She stood and made her way to the door.

'Jim. You have never asked me why I'm a walking journal of my husband's activities.' He walked over to her so that technicians were not in the middle of their conversation.

'You were planning to come to us, no?'

'No. I wanted out, but I was looking for a window, some slight window of opportunity when everyone would be out of the way ...'

'To kill him?' Jim was surprised. He looked directly into Katherine's eyes but did not see a killer.

160

'Maybe, but the priority was to get away, just me and the kids. He fathered a son with his cousin's wife.' Jim raised his eyebrows. 'It was before he met me. But I think they carried on. I thought if I could get proof and then tell his cousin ... well ... my biggest problem would be gone. But aside from that, my plan B, I figured by learning his routines, I could find a gap when I could just get the hell out of there. Time would be important, if I had hours, days, before he noticed I was missing I would have more success. A drunk wife is also an invisible wife, so spying on him wasn't too difficult. I also had a plan C. The information I had might be useful to his competitors, or the business partners he was screwing over.' Jim swallowed hard. She was playing a dangerous game. Sam Sinoli had no idea the biggest threat to his lifetime's work, his empire and his life was the enemy within. He considered Katherine's nocturnal enterprise meant she had more knowledge of Sam Sinoli's operations than even his closest hench men.

'You did the right thing talking to me, Katherine. You wouldn't have been able to live with that on your conscience and staying on the lam with two young kiddies would have been hard.'

'Just promise me one thing - if anything happens to me before I can get out, please just get my kids out, I don't want them raised in that life. Get them out and keep them safe and away from that evil family forever.' Jim studied Katherine's desperate, pleading eyes and made that promise.

Chapter 30

Katherine's hand shook as she raised the antique silver hairbrush and pulled it through her thick blonde curls. She didn't notice her reflection in the mirror; if she'd looked, she would have seen dull eyes and a washed-out complexion. A consequence of the tranquillizers that were a substitute for alcohol. She put down the hairbrush and reached into the drawer of her dressing table for the half empty bottle of gin that was hidden beneath Italian lace camisoles and silk stockings. Her shaking hands were too slow to catch the top as she unscrewed it, and she watched it clatter onto the glass-topped dressing table. After taking a large swig, she splashed some around her neck like perfume, then retrieved the bottle top and secreted the booze back beneath the lingerie before making her way downstairs.

At the top of the sweeping staircase, she took a moment to survey the house she would be leaving soon. The antiques, the artwork, the furniture, all chosen by her and shipped from all corners of the world. She hated them all. She smoothed down her Chanel mini-dress and descended. A few steps from the bottom she heard a car pull up outside, peering out to see, caused her to miss a step. She tried to grab the banister but tumbled down the last few stairs and lay in a dishevelled heap on the cold marble tiles. The front door opened, and the twins ran in, noisily, closely followed by Barney, their new Dalmatian puppy. They chased the excited animal around the hall and ignored their mother on the floor. Katherine was confused.

'I was on my way to pick them up from the nursery, why did you collect them?' She directed the words to the driver who had followed the children in and who now looked down at her with an accusing scowl.

'You're in no condition to be driving the kids today, or any other day for that matter. I'll be doing that from now on. You're not allowed to use the cars.' His voice was flat and his expression unsympathetic as he glared at Katherine. She clawed at the banister trying to pull herself up, she had twisted an ankle in the fall, and she struggled to stand.

'That's not your decision to make, Sam ...'

The driver curled his lip in disgust and grabbed her jaw. He held it in a tight grip while he threatened her.

'When I tell Sam you're too drunk to even stand up he'll agree. I'll tell him you are a danger to the kids. Don't fuck with me, he's already told me to keep a close eye on you, I can finish you anytime I want.' He hoisted her up the stairs two at a time and tossed her roughly onto her expansive bed, then growled at her to sleep it off, before slamming the bedroom door and locking it behind him.

Katherine's temples beat loudly. Her head was whirling, why had Sam delegated her welfare to this thug? Why had he been told to keep a close eye on her and what did finish her mean? She felt like a sacrificial lamb waiting for her husband to return home and make the final cut. Did they know she had been snitching to the FBI?

Katherine slid off the bed, her legs would not hold up she was shaking too much. She had a spare key in her jewellery box, she had considered locking Sam out of her bedroom on occasions but knew it would only anger him and elicit more beatings, so she had not used it. Even if she could escape her bedroom she would never get out of this fortress if her husband had ordered her confinement. She crawled on her hands and knees across the thick cream carpet to her closet and frantically started grabbing at the neatly arranged shoes. Jim's telephone number was hidden under the inner sole in a pair of stilettoes and she desperately tried to find the correct shoe. She was surrounded by shoes and had torn out the sole of almost everyone when her panic subsided enough for her to consider that if they suspected she was a rat then they would be monitoring her calls. Calling Jim would be an inevitable suicide. She called her mother.

'Mam? They won't let me out of the house,' she whispered into the phone. It was dangerous, but she had no option, her words were almost undecipherable as her voice trembled with terror.

'What, why, I don't understand?' Katherine heard the fear ripple through her mother's voice and regretted the burden she was now putting on her.

'I want you to call this number and give the guy a message. I need you to help me. Please mam, just do what I ask, pleeeease? Tell them I need an urgent appointment with the Doctor, stress that it is very, very, urgent, and I need the Doctor to make a home visit. Now.'

Irene Buckley tried to calm her daughter as she grabbed a magazine from the coffee table and scribbled down the number and her daughter's message. As she replaced the receiver, she considered waking her husband for support and accord, but the fear she'd heard in her daughter's voice spurred her urgency. She hurried into the kitchen, away from the din of the TV set, and picked up the phone on her kitchen wall.

***

The U.S. Marshal service had planned to extract Katherine Sinoli and her children when her husband was on a routine out of town trip, it would buy them time. The date had been set and was only two days away. She had been giving the FBI evidence of her husband's crimes for weeks and the carefully orchestrated meetings between the FBI and the wife of one of the most prolific crime bosses in New York City had come to an end. Arrangements were in place for the final de-briefing and the extraction. The U.S. Marshal's Service would be working closely with the FBI for the operation.

Katherine was supposed to bring her children with her to a routine hospital appointment. Only this time, they would not be returning home. Instead, they would be taken to a WITSEC holding facility where they would stay until the Sinolis' and their associates had all been rounded up and arrested. A final relocation, new identities, and new life were a few months away, but she was assured that she and her family would be safe. Jim Cavell had given her his word. Katherine had incriminated at least six members of the Sinoli mob family, plus some very senior officials in public office and law enforcement. With the evidence she had given the FBI they would all serve long sentences, but the prize for the FBI was Sam Sinoli. They knew with him out of the way the others would be easier to pick off one by one. The Sinoli family was responsible for countless murders, heists and racketeering throughout New York City and beyond, and until now they had been untouchable.

The hierarchy of the crime family was such that as orders were passed down, it was not uncommon for instructions to become distorted. On more than one occasion the wrong person got whacked. Nobody cared, they would just go right out and get the right guy and have a laugh at the error over dinner. The families of innocent victims would receive large brown paper bags stuffed full of used dollar bills. It didn't matter to the mob that children would be born bastards and wives would live the rest of their lives wondering how their husbands might have looked with the ravages of time.

The FBI was about to start rounding up the bosses at the top of the mob's hierarchy; if everything went smoothly it would be a major blow, not only to the Sinoli crime syndicate but it would have ramifications throughout the other crime families operating in New York and the entire justice department and political establishment. The handful of FBI agents in the know were frenzied with excitement, they could not have better evidence if they had infiltrated the mob themselves, and it was something they had tried many times. Jim Cavell had the head of one of the major families in his grasp. He had spent countless hours with the U.S. Marshals planning every detail of the extraction and subsequent round up of the Sinoli crime family.

Chapter 31

Jim Cavell practically skipped out of the office, he was looking forward to spending the afternoon with his wife and daughter. He had promised them a picnic, or now he was thinking maybe even the zoo. His wife's badgering about his excessive overtime made him feel guilty. The Sinoli case was about to go hot as the witnesses were pulled in and this meant his workload would be relentless, so he announced he was taking a rare afternoon off and headed out.

The Sinoli case was the biggest of his career. The FBI had been tracking the family for years, they were one of the most powerful mob families in New York State. They had successfully infiltrated the crime syndicate but only at the lower levels of the hierarchy. The information coming out was not much use; they really needed somebody in the upper echelons, somebody closer to the decision makers. When Cavell received a tipoff that Sam Sinoli's wife might be looking for a way out, he found out everything he could about her and put a tail on her. When he found the right time and place to make contact, he started grooming her to testify. The offer of a life of freedom from the mob's grip was a valuable bargaining chip, and she finally agreed to testify on tape. His colleagues in the FBI had initially discounted the woman as a drunk and doubted her worth, but she had turned out to be the best witness the FBI had netted in a decade.

Jim's phone started buzzing as he hung his jacket in the back of his car. He glanced at the screen but didn't recognise the number.

'Cavell.'

'Doctor Cavell?' A woman's voice addressed him, he didn't recognise it.

'This is Jim Cavell.'

'Hello, Doctor this is Irene Buckley, my daughter Katherine Sinoli asked me to call you.' Jim froze, the hair on his arms stood up.

'Yes?'

'She asked me to call you and said I should tell you … *She needs an urgent appointment with Doctor Cavell*. I must stress that it is very urgent. *She needs a home appointment because she is unable to leave the house.*' Katherine's mother delivered the message as if she was reading it. Jim replayed the words in his head.

'Doctor, I believe my daughter is in fear of her life, they have locked her in the house.' She whispered the last sentence, and he could hear distress percolate every word.

'Jesus Christ …' Jim cursed to himself. If Katherine wasn't already dead, her life was now in very grave danger. 'Mrs. Buckley, I can help Katherine, please relay the message to me again, exactly as she said it to you.' He sprinted across the car park and raced through the corridors back to his office while he held the phone to his ear. Katherine's mother repeated the brief conversation she'd had with her daughter. 'How long ago did she call you, Mrs Buckley?'

'Right before I called you.'

'Five minutes? ten?'

'Two at the most.'

'Where exactly is she?'

'She is in her bedroom; she is locked in the bedroom.'

'Was there anybody with her?'

'Erm I'm not sure, she was whispering, and she's very frightened.' Irene's voice almost broke as she spoke of her daughter's fear. Jim's mind ran through some scenarios of what could have happened for them to incarcerate Katherine in the house. If they knew she was a rat, they had very little time to get her out.

'Doctor, how much trouble is my daughter in?' Jim thought for a moment. He did not want to lie to the woman, but the truth might incapacitate her, and she needed to be strong to get herself and her family through the next few hours.

'Mrs. Buckley, your daughter is married to a very dangerous man. She, you all, are in a lot of danger. I need you to round up your family, pack one suitcase each of personal items and wait by the telephone. Do not go out. I will arrange for people to come and collect you and take you to a secure facility within the hour.'

'What's happening to Katherine?' The old woman's voice trembled.

'I will personally go and get her and the children, they will be safe. Do you understand what you need to do, Mrs Buckley?'

'Yes.'

'Stay by the phone, okay?' Jim hung up and slammed a clenched fist onto his desk. The violence brought questioning glances from the staff in the surrounding offices. Somebody dared to enquire if there was anything he needed, he didn't glance up to see who it was, his mind was too busy.

'I need the Marshal's SOG unit on the line, I've got an extraction to do.'

'Now?'

'Ten fucking minutes ago!' Jim glowered at the secretary standing in the doorway.

'Who?'

'To be advised.' Jim was mindful that the Sinoli family had long tentacles and until Katherine was under the protection of the U.S. Marshal service, he was not taking any chances with her security.

'On it.' The secretary retreated into the outer office and snapped instructions to several other administrators. The place burst with activity as people picked up phones and scurried in all directions.

***

The Deputy Director of the New York FBI office strode purposefully across the outer office, he started speaking before he was entirely through the doorway to Jim's office.

'What happened?'

Jim, aware of all the eyes and ears around closed the door and spoke to his boss with his back to the glass window.

'It's Katherine, I got an emergency message just now via her mother. She is at home, and they won't let her leave the house.'

'Do they know she's been talking?'

'I can't think of any other reason why they would lock her up. As far as we know Sam is upstate. She usually has more opportunity to come and go when he is away, not less.'

'Do we have real-time on his car mic?'

'No, it's going to tape, you said minimal bodies on this. It's only reviewed every eight hours.' Jim reminded his boss that the planned extraction was only a couple of days away and he had to work hard to stop his frustration exploding on the furniture again.

'If Sam Sinoli is upstate, we have an hour or two, yes?'

Jim shrugged in response and the director continued,

'I can't see him having one of his hoods deal with his own shit. Is there any way we can get her out of the house?'

'The only way I can see is we go in and get her and the kids out, the SOG might have some better ideas, but we need to get her out ASAP.'

'And the kids! Jeezus, Jim this is too risky, three bodies out of a probable fortress.'

'That's the deal, the information we have will be useless if we don't get the kids out as well, she will refuse to let us use it.'

'We won't even get into that avenue before they start shooting. Do they have a panic room?'

'They don't need one; like you said the house is practically a fortress. The entire avenue is covered by tight security. There are at least three mob houses in the vicinity, security arrangements include electric gates, ramps, cameras and armed guards in the grounds. Without an appointment, you don't get inside!'

The phone sprung to life and an assistant announced the arrival of the Special Operations Group of the U.S. Marshal Services. Jim's office wasn't big enough to hold everyone, but his assistant had already prepared an operations room and directed the agents to it.

***

Across the other side of the room, a young agent lingered at the water fountain and studied the scene. He glimpsed the strained and tense expressions on the men in the operations room before the blinds got pulled. The SOG team had been hastily convened and the department, was a hive of activity. Cavell's assistant was running around like a headless chicken,

171

and he noticed what appeared to be floor plans or architect drawings going in. Light from an overhead projector seeped out from the edge of the blinds, but from his vantage point, there was nothing he could glean. He suspected there was a witness grab going down and he knew some people who would pay a very handsome gratuity for his information.

The young agent refilled his water cup and let his gaze casually roam over the rest of the employees in the department. When he had determined the weakest link, he made his way casually over to the girl.

Chapter 32

Laurie Bannister was sweating and agitated, he paced the floor quietly behind his team of Marshals that now sat around the table in the special operations room at the FBI New York headquarters.

The deputy director had presided over the first, carefully drawn up plan for the extraction of Katherine Sinoli, her children and wider family members. This had been abandoned when he received the call from the FBI, and he had to hastily assemble the team to do an emergency extraction.

The various agents and Marshals were going through the minute detail of the house, the grounds, and the security they would have to navigate to get the witnesses to safety when Jim's assistant announced a sinister development. On news of Katherine's trouble, the FBI had increased resources and put an agent on intercepting in real-time the bug in Sam's car. The assembled men and woman seated around the oval table now heard that somebody had called Sam and warned him of an imminent operation. Sam Sinoli knew that there was an urgent joint FBI, U.S. Marshal operation going down. The informant did not know who was about to be brought in but suspected, because of the agents involved it was one of Sinoli's crew.

The news floored Jim and his boss. They were being careful, they knew they had compromised agents, but they had kept a very tight ship. The FBI director was both embarrassed and furious, Jim was too stunned to take it all in, the whole operation was turning into a disaster, the months of work, the potential arrest of numerous major crime figures - it was all about to come to nothing because they had a leaker in their department.

Sam yelled at his assistant to find the person responsible, they had their voice on tape, but that investigation would come later, right now they had to pivot to the changing circumstances and time was not on their side.

The SOG team appeared unperturbed by the dynamic situation, and the need to re-plan an operation from scratch. While Jim and Laurie were still reeling from the shock and trying to figure out the leak the Marshals had arranged for a new ops room and the team relocated two blocks south to the U.S. Marshal's office. With Sam Sinoli now alerted to an extraction of one of his own and on his way back to New York City the window of opportunity was closing on them fast.

The only silver lining was that Sam had not made any calls to his crew; the agents figured he was probably as unsure as they were about who they could trust.

***

As Laurie paced, he listened to the rasping voices of his Marshals checking their communication devices. Cavell's voice affirmed his earpiece was set and working. Laurie had tried to prevent Jim from going in, the Marshals' Special Operations Group were highly trained and highly specialized professionals, and an FBI agent was a spare part and would only be in their way. He was persuaded because the witness was volatile and mistrusting so he had agreed Cavell could go but ordered that he must stay in the van.

The whole extraction would last only a few carefully timed minutes. With no secure phone line into the house, any advance communication with the target was out of the question.

The FBI monitored the conversations in Sam Sinoli's car, while two Marshals sat in a private ambulance parked a couple of blocks from the private tree lined avenue that led to the Sinoli house and waited. Two additional Marshals sat alongside Jim in the back of the vehicle.

Katherine's mother nervously fingered the paper she was to read from when given the instruction. She was surrounded by Marshals that would be shortly escorting the Buckleys to a safe location as soon as Irene had completed the call to her daughter.

From the operation room, the commander gave the order to go and everybody in the room listened to a dial tone, several beeps as a number was keyed and then the ringing of the telephone in Sam Sinoli's house. A bored male voice answered, and Katherine's mother asked to speak with her daughter, her request was not acknowledged but they all listened as the line was transferred and Katherine's uneasy voice came on the line.

'Katherine, I have spoken with the Doctor, and he understands your urgent condition, he has sent an ambulance. When you see the ambulance coming down the drive you must get the children and meet him at the front door. Do you understand?' Irene Buckley read from the paper she held in trembling hands and glanced at the female Marshal sitting beside her.

''When? Here?' Katherine's voice was barely a whisper.

The agent sitting in front of Irene Buckley nodded and mouthed 'now'.

'Yes. Now.' The agent tapped the piece of paper as if to remind Irene of the dialogue. 'Our house number is the amount of time you have to start a distraction at the rear of the house.' Irene wanted to shout to her daughter to hurry, do it quickly, get the children, but the agent had given her strict instructions to say only what was on the paper or what she wrote down for her.

'I ... okay.' Katherine's voice was apprehensive.

The agent scribbled quickly for Irene, and she relayed the question.

'Yes or no?'

'Yes.'

The agent disconnected the line, and the Operation Commander told the ambulance to go. The clock was now ticking. The electricity would be cut to the entire area in three minutes and would be out for forty-five seconds. Once through the security gates the drive up to the front door would take an estimated ten seconds so that left the SOG team and Jim thirty-five seconds on arrival at the front door to get the three targets in the vehicle. The power outage would ensure the gates and security ramps were not activated. Under no circumstances could the team become trapped inside the property; a shootout was out of the question.

Katherine didn't have long to set a distraction for the staff and crew on the property and get the children by the rendezvous point. Laurie held his breath and prayed Katherine was sober enough to complete the instructions.

Irene Buckley, her husband, and two small suitcases were loaded into the large people carrier waiting outside their home. Their daughter in law and grandchild were being herded into a similar vehicle three blocks away. Irene's son was nowhere to be found. As a travelling sales rep, he was often out on the road and could be anywhere. The Marshals were not too worried, if they could not find him then the mob probably couldn't either. He would be picked up as soon as he contacted his office or returned home.

***

Katherine scrambled off her bed, unlocked her bedroom door and in stockinged feet ran across the hall to the nursery. Her daughter was in a playpen and Katherine moved through the room to locate her son. He was in an en-suite bathroom where the nanny knelt by a bathtub bathing him.

'Get Sin Sin in a towel. I have to go out.'

'You're not allowed to take the children out, Katherine; I've had orders from ...' The nanny was sneering at Katherine and for it, she received a hard smack across her face. Her head ricocheted sideways and crashed against the top of the ceramic basin. Stunned, she put a hand to her head to check for blood.

'You're a fucking drunk! Get out of here. When I tell Sam what you just did ...'

Katherine grabbed the woman by the throat.

'Listen to me you little whore, this is my son, my house and you do what I say. Do you think I don't know you drop your knickers for my husband and stuff white powder up your nose every opportunity that you get? If I tell my husband that you are putting his children at risk by leaving your crap all over their nursery, he won't fire you. He will kill you!' Katherine's anger was driven by raw panic. She hurried back out of the nursery remembering she needed to get the security guards away from the front of the house.

She found her cigarette lighter and raced to a rear staircase that led down to the kitchen. Sin Sin had started to cry when she'd hit the nanny and this, in turn, set off his twin sister. She wanted to run back and gather them to her, but she had to follow her instructions. They needed a distraction to get them all out. Her mother's house was number three, three minutes; she wondered how long she had left.

Katherine paused at the kitchen door. She could hear voices on the other side, the cook, and at least one other staff member, were in the kitchen. It would be impossible to start a fire in there, she opened the door to the basement garage and hurried down the concrete steps. She would need an accelerant if anyone was to notice the fire in such a short time span and so scanned the shelves for gasoline or a similar flammable liquid.

Her panic was making her hands tremble and she dropped as many items as she picked up. An invisible stopwatch was clicking loudly at her temples and Katherine reluctantly opened the trunk of a car parked in the vast garage to look for a gas can. She remembered the last time she had done this, and the ghastly memory brought bile to the back of her throat. Katherine bunched up some old dust sheets and poured gas from a spare canister all over the fabric. She threw her lighter onto the pile and used a shovel to push the burning mass under the rear of the car, she threw in the cannister and some bottles of paint and turpentine for good measure and retreated.

Back in the hall, she could hear her children howling, and on the landing, at the top of the stairs, the nanny was yelling at Rocco, one of her husband's crew, that Katherine was insane, and had attacked her. Things were not going well, she was nowhere near the front door, and neither were her kids, the most direct route would be past the nanny and Rocco but this was out of the question. Adrenalin and fear focused her mind. Standing by the door to the garage Katherine could smell the fire but it would take time to reach the upstairs landing. She pulled a nearby mirror off the wall and threw it violently onto the marble tiles to draw Rocco downstairs.

'See I told you, she has gone fucking crazy, get her back to that fucking loony bin.' The nanny screeched over the banister and Katherine waited another second or two until she heard footsteps running down the stairs and quickly ducked back up the rear staircase. In stockinged feet

Katherine had speed and stealth and dipped into the nursery to scoop up her daughter before the nanny, still standing on the landing holding her son in a towelling robe noticed Katherine behind her.

***

The ambulance pulled up to the security hut at the entrance to the private road leading to the Sinoli property. The array of multi-agency operatives in the control room listened. They were standing ready to intercept the call when the guard tried to dial through to the Sinoli house. However, the dim-witted guard failed to check with the residence and instead just opened the barrier and let them drive through. Laurie allowed a breath out. They did not have the luxury of contingency seconds, and this was a lucky break.

The guard at the Sinoli property wasn't so amenable, he halted the ambulance and retreated into the gatehouse to put a call up to the house. It was no coincidence his call repeatedly produced an engaged tone, on all the lines he tried. The Marshal driving the ambulance aware of the count down in his earpiece yelled for the guard to hurry up. In assumed alarm he yelled that they were called to see to Mrs Sinoli because she was suffering a miscarriage. The guard looked worried but not worried enough to open the gates without authority. The Marshal, hearing the seconds ticking away, asked the security guard if he wanted to be the one responsible for his boss's wife bleeding to death and losing a baby. He appeared to think this through and then pushed the button to open the gates, he told them to wait at the other side because he would come up with them. When the gates were wide enough for the vehicle to pass through the Marshal put his foot on the accelerator and sped up the long driveway.

The operations commander gave the instruction for the power grid to go down and declared forty-five seconds to all on the wire. Laurie had stopped his pacing and held a clenched fist to his pursed lips. The driver glanced in his rear-view mirror and broadcast that he hoped the security guard was not a fast runner.

As the ambulance approached the glass and wrought iron double doors of the sprawling mansion, the marshal in the passenger seat announced that the targets were not waiting as instructed. The ambulance stopped by the front door, and everyone could hear the argument inside. The marshal reported a yellow glow and thick smoke in the hall.

'What do we do? Smash and grab?' he asked the commander.

'Why don't you just try and ring the bell?' came a dry response that was followed by an enormous explosion. The glass in the doors blew out and the doors swung on their hinges. Grey smoke funnelled out.

'Nice welcome. I didn't know we were expecting pyro.' The driver had the luxury of humour, his job was on pause. The other Marshals and Jim did not hear the last part of his sentence they had all jumped out of the ambulance and entered the house. Their flashlights scanned the hall, the staircase and then when someone heard a low moan by the stairs, they rushed forward and picked up Katherine and a small child. The radio was busy with everyone giving a rundown of their situation. Someone declared that they had two targets on board. The driver announced that the security guard was indeed a fast runner and would be in firing distance imminently.

'Ten seconds to power up,' came the notice from the operations centre.

'Get me more time.' Jim was still in the house.

'No can do.'

'We're missing a kid.'

'Where the fuck are you, Cavell?'

'The second kid is not here, dammit.'

'Five seconds.'

'I've got to find the second kid.'

'Get out.' The exchange was interspaced with gunfire, the gate guard was getting closer, and the shots were becoming more accurate. Two Marshals yanked the protesting FBI agent into the back of the ambulance and dragged the doors shut as the driver floored the accelerator.

Chapter 33

Laurie Bannister started breathing again. The team were away from the house and heading south out of New York to the Fairton maximum-security compound in New Jersey. Katherine's parents, her sister-in-law and nephew were also on their way there in separate SUVs.

The operation had not gone exactly to plan; however, nobody had been injured and they had two out of three targets on board. As the ambulance had sped back down the driveway of the mansion at breakneck speed. Katherine realised that her son was not with them and let out a deep visceral scream, one that silenced any congratulatory proclamation the agents might have uttered. The two-and-a-half-hour road journey to Fairton was completed in silence but for the unremitting sobs of a mother in anguish. Jim tried in vain to soothe the woman. He promised to do everything possible to reunite her with her son as soon as they could, but even to him, this promise seemed futile. After what had just taken place any further attempts to get the boy out would be virtually impossible.

***

Katherine was kept sedated and under medical observation for several days at the witness protection unit. It would be the family's home until the paperwork could catch up with the operational activities.

Irene Buckley was grateful her daughter was mostly pacified; she was spared the family fallout that occurred in the days following their extraction. Katherine's brother was eventually located upstate New York and was picked up and brought to the compound several hours after the others. He was incensed that his sister had selfishly turned their lives upside down and he was refusing to enter the witness protection programme.

Jim tried to convince him that he would not be safe, the mob would find him and demand to know Katherine and her daughter's whereabouts. All the tactics Jim tried could not persuade the young man. It transpired that Katherine's brother was having an affair with a colleague and was now facing a decision whether to enter the programme and be with his pregnant wife and small son or forsake them to be with his girlfriend. Jim observed and refereed days of intense arguments between the family members. While it tore at Jim's soul, the Marshal assigned to be the family's liaison was indifferent to the unfolding drama, he told Jim that this was perfectly normal. The stresses on families put into a witness protection programme often tore them apart. The Marshal seemed apathetic to the misery that he attended every day.

Due to the high-profile nature of Katherine's testimonies, which would implicate senior members of the U.S. judiciary system and senior political figures, an unusual step was taken to ensure her total protection. The witness protection board had decided to move the witnesses overseas. Katherine's parents still held Irish passports, so the decision was made to move the family back to Ireland.

Despite the pleading from his parents, Katherine's brother decided against entering the witness programme. He would change his own name and move upstate to live with his girlfriend. With this news, his wife also refused to be relocated overseas away from her own parents and siblings. Katherine's parents made the heart-wrenching decision that Irene would go with Katherine and Sive, and her husband would stay in the United States of America to support his daughter in law, her unborn child, and his grandson.

***

The large plane waited expectantly at the end of the runway for its remaining three passengers, the engines whirred loudly in the humid Florida dusk. An internal flight on a chartered Cessna had brought the two women and child here and the next leg of their long journey was to be transatlantic. Mary, Katherine, and little Lucy stood clinging to each other on the tarmac, afraid.

Mary White had chosen her own new name and one for her granddaughter. She thought it better that Katherine keep her own name, her mental state was deteriorating, and she did not want to disorientate her daughter anymore.

Jim bounded down the steps of the light aircraft behind the women holding a cardboard file that contained the paperwork for their new life. Passports, medical records and birth certificates - all the documents for the life that they had never had but would have to pretend they had lived. He stopped in front of the two women and child and nodded silently in the direction of the waiting 747 across the runway. This was as far as he would be going, now they were on their own. Katherine pulled her daughter towards her and shivered despite the warm Florida breeze; she regarded the enormous plane and reluctantly started in the direction of the aluminium steps waiting for them. The fading evening light was pink with the promise of another hot sunny day tomorrow, one Mary knew they would not be witnessing. Eyes tortured with grief focused on the FBI agent they had come to know well.

'Where are we headed for Mr Cavell?'

'We've found you a beautiful little town on the Southwest coast of Ireland.' Mary tried but failed to keep the disappointment flash across her face. She understood the agent mistook it for fear of knowing anybody there.

'You don't have any relatives there; I checked that out myself, Mary.'

It didn't escape her that the agent was trying hard to keep his own emotions in check.

'There are some good people waiting for you. They'll look after you for a while in a convent, and then once things have quietened down over here, you'll get your own home.'

Quietened down, after the trial is over, she thought. Mary smiled at him a weary, but grateful smile that did not reach her eyes.

'You're sending us to a sleepy little place just like the one I spent half my life trying to get away from.' She glanced over her shoulder to see her daughter and granddaughter ascending the steps of the 747. She saw the flash of regret cross Jim's face. He was about to apologise, he had no idea. He'd assumed she would be content to return to a small town, where nobody would be likely to happen across them. Mary put a hand up to silence him.

'It'll be for the best. Ireland's the best place in the world to stay out of any one's way. A corner of the world where nobody ever goes to, only ever departs from. 'Tis a fine place to bring up the kiddie, I've got to thank you, Mr Cavell, you are gonna have my prayers for as long you're on this precious earth. You and your family. Take care now Mr Cavell, God bless ya.'

'Good Luck Mary.'

Mary's heart was already broken into tiny pieces and now it was about to be scattered across the globe. She put one foot in front of the other and concentrated hard to hold her emotions together and find the courage to turn the page on a new chapter of her life. For the rest of her days, she would live as Mary White and with only the memories of a husband, son and grandchildren in another place that she would never see again.

***

The three weary travellers finally arrived at The Sisters of Mercy Convent in Ireland after a long journey across the Atlantic. As their plane had circled the green rugged landscape over Ireland, Mary's stoic struggle with her emotions finally crumbled as she peered out of the window and remembered leaving this place with her husband many years earlier.

They had left as young newly-weds, hearts filled with excitement and ambitions for a family of their own. The future had held so much promise when they waved cheerfully to the small circle of family and friends that had gathered at the docks to see them off.

A small car delivered them to the convent, after what had seemed like many hours driving along winding green lanes and past too many farms to count. The nuns made a big fuss of the child; she appeared shy and quiet. The long journey, the disruption to her routine, and being parted from her twin brother had quietened the once rambunctious toddler. The separation would inevitably take its toll in the days and weeks ahead and the nuns tried their best to preoccupy the child and make her happy again.

Mary spent her days in quiet grief for the family that she had left behind, her sadness was compounded by her worry for Katherine, who never seemed to surface from the depression that hung over her. She would spend her time in the gardens of the convent alone or clinging to her small daughter, rocking her back and forwards until one or both fell asleep.

Their stay at the convent was supposed to have been brief. The U.S. Marshals had told them, that it was an interim stopover until their permanent accommodation was arranged. However, the weeks turned into months. Mary suspected it was because the trial in America was still in progress. The reality was that the nuns and the doctor were worried about Katherine's mental health and her addictions. They feared Mary would be unable to cope with the child and her daughter on her own.

The family spent a Christmas at the convent and then as spring came round, they were settled into their own cottage in the village of Anchora, about forty miles from the convent. The local priest agreed to take guardianship of the family and he was tasked with filing an annual update to the U.S. Marshal Service on the status and wellbeing of their protectorates.

Part 3

Chapter 34

She swirled the remnants of cold coffee around in her mug. Jim had spent all evening telling her about her family and the story of how she had come to live in Ireland. At first, it seemed like an account of someone else's life, a chronicle of somebody else's family, but as the evening wore on, she became more familiar with the characters and their congruence in her reality. For the most part, she just sat and listened to Jim, occasionally venturing a question, or pausing his dialogue to refill their mugs with hot coffee.

The man who had walked into her house earlier that day, and whom she had welcomed with suspicion and animosity had revealed a part of her history that she had wondered about since she had found her grandmother's letters. Never once had he referred to his files or sketched over details and she was grateful that he was candid with her, not only with the information but with his thoughts and feelings towards her mother and her grandmother.

'I wondered about the nuns; I was puzzled when I found some old photos of us all standing in a garden in the sunshine. I can't remember being there, but now you've told me about the convent it does seem familiar somehow. Or maybe it's just the photos. Do you want to see them?'

Lucy headed upstairs to get the photographs that she had found in the loft and with an afterthought she took her grandmother's letters downstairs as well. Sometime during the evening, the pair had moved into the sitting room and Jim now leant back into the sofa and studied the photographs Lucy handed him.

'You know I think we went back to visit the nuns a couple of times. I've got a vague memory. It might have been one Christmas. Probably to take some presents. I guess, it's the sort of thing my grandma would have done. I'm not sure when we stopped visiting, or why we stopped ...' Lucy's sentence faded away as she understood exactly why they had stopped going. 'I suppose when I got old enough to start remembering; because that would be a link to my past, wouldn't it?' Jim viewed her over the top of the photographs. Lucy tried to stem the rising anger that again threatened to overwhelm her, and she tossed the letters over to Jim unceremoniously. 'There. That was the mistake she made, keeping those, or even writing them in the first place.' Jim read each one in silence. She watched him intently, waiting for a flicker of guilt, a reaction of any kind. Some time passed before either of them spoke, and when Lucy got up to stand over the mantel and made a pretence of re-arranging the ornaments, she was fighting to keep back the tears.

'Why didn't she take us back to America after my mother died? She could have taken me back then, to my grandfather and cousins. We wouldn't have been in any danger, with that side of the family, surely? Even if my father had found us, it was my mother that gave evidence, not us.'

'That's a question I can't answer for you, Lucy. I suspect she probably struggled over the dilemma herself. It would have been a lot more upheaval for you, all over again. If you were my daughter, that would have been my biggest concern - with the turmoil you'd already had in your life, I would have tried to make things as normal as possible for you.'

'Not knowing my family is not normal! Seeing your mother slowly die a little bit every day is not normal!'

'There is also the impact it would have had on your grandfather to consider, Lucy. Imagine walking back into someone's life after several years without any contact. It could have been just as traumatic as leaving in the first place. You were still a young child. You had stability, routine, all your friends, and a chance to lead a good and honest life, away from all the corruption and murder. She saw your mother broken ...'

'I know she hated it here. I know now why she spent hours browsing glossy American fashion magazines whenever we went into Kearis. She loved watching American TV shows and she especially loved to hear my friend from Florida talk about America. Now I know she'd lived that life and gave it all up, for this!' She waved an arm across the room. 'This pokey, crumbling house in a dead-end backwater. All that time, she had known what it was really like to live in America, have a big family. I know she wanted to go back.' Lucy's tears were free flowing now and she sniffed and wiped them away.

'I don't think these letters were ever meant to be read by anybody, Lucy.' Jim's voice faltered. 'Sometimes folks write things down to ... as a way of helping themselves, a therapy if you like. I don't think she wanted to ... these are intensely private. Your grandmother was a strong and dignified woman. These pieces of paper reveal her feelings of guilt and torment for the decisions she made. I think that's why she didn't want you to see them, Lucy. If you hadn't found them, you would have never known her pain and sacrifice. She was proud of how you turned out and the opportunity you have for a great life.'

Lucy's body shook as the tears turned into violent sobs that shook her body. The pent-up emotion from all the revelations found a channel out. Jim took her slight body in his wide arms and held her until she stopped crying.

***

Jim left the cottage exhausted and with no doubts in his mind that Lucy would try to find and contact her family. The girl was like a jigsaw with one piece missing and her quest to be whole would drag her to every corner of the world to find that lost fragment of herself. He had purposely nurtured the web of intrigue and romance for her long-lost family. He had told her the truth as he remembered it but skirted around the facts of her father's ruthlessness and brutality. The facts that would make Lucy despise her father. It was a strategy, he had played the good cop, to gain her trust, her friendship, and in the days that followed all that would change. He knew that to stop her from seeking out her father and her twin brother he had to shatter the romantic illusions he had helped embroider today. He had built her up to tear her down, the bigger the fall the more impact it would have. He was going to have to use tactics that would deliver a heavy dose of horror to try and deter this young woman from being reunited with her family. It was not something he was looking forward to, the girl was still grieving, but he would do whatever was necessary. Twenty years ago, he had looked into her mother's eyes and made her that promise.

On the road back to his guest house Jim called the FBI headquarters and asked his colleagues to access the case archives and send him everything they had. It was a big favour, the historic material that Jim wanted was vast and in addition, it was being done off the record. As far as the FBI were concerned this was an old, closed case and Jim no longer worked for the government. They'd complained, the FBI was functioning under a tight budget, they didn't have the resources, staffing levels had been squeezed and it could take days to get him what he asked for. So, Jim passed it back to the Marshal Service. The support he needed could come out of their budget. Jim called Laurie Bannister and things started to move more quickly.

***

Steven Dolph wondered why he was sitting in a dingy basement gathering archive material, scanning, and sending it. Surely this was an administrator's task, but he kept the prevarication to himself. He had received a call from Seth, the old man laughed loudly after telling him where he was being assigned for several days.

Dawn was breaking; Dolph had worked around the clock in the dusty archives because Jim Cavell needed the material urgently. He was armed with the last batch for scanning before heading off to get some sleep when Seth swung by and told him to check his messages. Dolph choked on his own spittle when he heard Cavell's voice again; this time, he wanted Katherine Sinoli's video testimony.

'How the fuck am I gonna get that over to fucking Ireland by today?' A colleague walked by and made a joke about Dolph having a bad day. He was too tired to give a smart-ass reply. Video evidence was going to be a pain in the neck to get to Cavell. This stuff was old, it would be Betamax, it would have to be converted, that couldn't be done in one day.

Dolph called Cavell to ask if the court transcripts would be enough, it was the same thing anyway. In no uncertain terms, Jim told him to get him the video.

'If I wanted court papers, I would have asked for court papers. I need the video. I want to listen to her brittle voice, and I want to see the whites of her terror filled eyes. Do you understand? And I need it today!' He hung up without waiting for a reply.

Dolph called the technical specialists at the FBI. A bright young thing, clearly more on the ball than Dolph, noticed an entry in the records that said someone had requisitioned the evidence in the early nineties. A TV company by the looks of it.

'Huh, why are you telling me this?'

'Well, it means they would have been reviewed before they handed anything over so ...'

'So, what, why would they be requested by a TV company?' The lack of sleep had clearly slowed the Marshal's brain.

'They were making a documentary about the mob and wanted anything we could give 'em. Guess this case was one of the big ones, I remember the coverage on the news on this one, there's loads of books written about it. The file note says for research only not reproduction. But the point is, well, they would have been digitalized, the TV company would have paid to access the records and get them into the format they needed.'

'Falmer, you're a genius.' Dolph punched the air, all he had to do now was find out where the most recent copies were stored.

***

Jim drove into Kearis and found himself a print shop. He walked in and told the young man behind the counter to close the shop. He needed privacy for what he was about to do. The spotty teenager froze and eyed the telephone. Jim put 100 Euros on the counter and told him he would also need his expertise with the machines. He was a retired U.S. federal agent, not a print machine specialist. The boy stared at the white-haired, slightly overweight American and Jim waited and watched the boy's face while he decided if he was sitting

193

in front of threat or a fruitcake. Jim had no identification from the bureaux so said nothing and waited for the boy's inertia to expire. It took a while.

'Do you have an internet connection on that thing?' He pointed to the screen on the counter. The boy nodded silently, and Jim told him to key into a search engine, his name, and spelt it out slowly for the teenager. Several hits came back, the boy scanned down the page, Jim pointed to an article and told him to open it. It was a link to the University of Illinois website, and he knew it included a large photograph of himself.

'There you go; see that's me.' Jim mimicked the pose. 'Now read it.' He watched the boys' eyes scan the text and knew he was reading the short biography that revealed Cavell was a retired FBI agent and travelled the U.S. giving keynote speeches and training lectures for criminal justice students. His specialist topics included organized crime syndicates, FBI careers, negotiating techniques and so on. The young man in charge of the print shop kept moving his eyes from the screen to Jim's face and back again.

'We're cool?' Jim's patience was being tested to the limit. Wide eyes nodded back at him.

'Great, now let's get some printing done.'

Jim told the kid that there would be lots of photos and the nature of them would be gruesome, he should try not to look. As the glossy A4 photographs started to chug out from the machine one by one, the boy tried to avert his gaze. Several prints in and the boy had turned white.

'I told you not to look at this stuff.' Jim interjected and pushed the boy from his chair and took his place at the computer, 'Where we up to?' The boy gave Jim instructions to use the software from a distance over his shoulder.

Jim could have shown Lucy these sickening images on a computer screen, but he wanted to leave her with an enduring testament, something she couldn't just switch off with the click of a mouse. He wanted to leave the evidence of her father's handiwork in her hands, in her house, where the disgusting tangible proof could not be ignored.

Chapter 35

Frozen food parcels dropped to the floor with a thud. Lucy crouched in front of the freezer and pulled out various packets trying to find something suitable for lunch. She was expecting Jim anytime, and she felt guilty at the reception she had given the agent the previous day. Jim had spent the whole evening explaining how she had come to be in Ireland, in a witness protection programme and he had given her the much-needed insight into her mother's life with her father.

Lucy hardly slept, the information had played over and over in her mind. The new insights only provoked more questions, Jim Cavell had the answers she needed. She deeply regretted her initial hostility towards the American and today she was determined to make amends. She would show him some hospitality. He told her he would bring her some case files and trial paperwork and she was excited at the prospect of learning more about her family.

A loud rap on the front door interrupted her search in the freezer and she shoved everything back haphazardly in her eagerness to answer the door. The smile stretched across her face disappeared as she opened the door and discovered a courier in a shiny padded jacket standing there instead of Jim.

'Good-morning, I have a delivery for a Mr Jim Cavell.'

'Eh? Oh, right well, you better bring it in.' Lucy eyed the bulky cardboard box as she stepped aside to let the courier put the box in the hall. Large black letters across the box told Lucy it was a laptop, she held the door open for the deliveryman to leave but instead, he asked her where she would like it set up.

'Oh no it's okay, I can do that. Just leave it here. It's fine.'

'I have instructions to have it internet ready.'

'Oh no, we ... I don't have a connection here.'

'You will have in about half an hour.'

'That's not possible; it takes days, to order ...' Lucy stopped talking; realizing things would happen quickly if a government agency had requisitioned the service. 'I see, well ... I guess the dining table is the best place.' Lucy was impressed with the speed Jim worked.

'Are you FBI as well?' The courier was busy unpacking equipment and stopped what he was doing to look at her. She noticed he tried to hold back a snigger. Before resuming his unpacking without answering.

'Ah, guess not.' She left him to it and returned to her expedition in the freezer.

Jim arrived while the courier was still installing the laptop. Lucy overhead them discussing the equipment and then she saw cash changing hands. She wondered if she would get to keep the laptop. Her own was old and heavy compared to this sleek, new, and what appeared to be a very expensive looking model, then she remembered the eighty thousand euros in the bank. Being rich had slipped her mind with all the other chaos in her life.

'I've got some lunch out for later, but if you are hungry now, I could put in on the stove,' Jim nodded.

'I'm expecting another delivery soon.'

'Really! More equipment?'

'No. I asked for your mother's video evidence to be sent. The files are too large so they're setting up a portal for us, online, access should be dropping anytime.' She saw him scanning her face for a reaction. It was a bolt out of the blue and it knotted her stomach. She knew there was video evidence, but she had not expected she would get to see it. She tried to control her emotions.

'I see.' Lucy sat at the table and watched Jim tap away on the computer for a while. She could see he was having a digital conversation with someone and wondered who was at the other end of the dialogue.

'This is a good place for you to start.' He turned the laptop around to Lucy. His manner was colder today, business-like, but she shrugged it off. She hadn't exactly given him a welcoming reception the previous day. 'We can go through this stuff later.' He patted the pile of documents that were hot off the press from the copy shop. Lucy glanced over the screen, there were numerous image and document files, and she opened one and glanced at the typed words.

'Why are some words blacked out?'

'Redacted. They might be references to civilians without any criminal activities. Here, this is probably her doctor for example.' Jim pointed to a line about her mother's mental health. 'And if these people are still alive, we need to protect their identity. A lot of these records are requested by journalists and such.'

'Right.' Lucy started reading from the beginning. It was all there, much the same story that Jim had told her the previous day. Only this was the fine detail, pages and pages of details.

She found a report filed by Jim about his first meeting with her mother. It was just as he had described to her the previous day except in these notes, he had summarized that

Katherine was probably already addicted to prescription drugs as well as the booze. He wrote that her hands shook, and her concentration was erratic, varied between lucid and disconcerted. She was saddened that her mother had been in such a state at this point, even before the real drama of her life had unfolded. Her father's medical records were of no note although she read that he had been treated for Gonorrhoea in 1982.

Lucy opened file after file and read each one in silence. Only when she noticed the smell of the food burning in the oven, did she stop reading. Lucy found Jim sitting on her back doorstep and offered him the well-cooked food. They ate in silence until Jim pushed his clean plate away and looked at Lucy.

'It's a lot to take in, I know,' he said pitifully and Lucy offered him a feeble smile.

'I guess I'm lucky in one respect, there can't be many people around that have had their history documented in quite so much detail.'

'No. There aren't so many people in the world with such a notorious father!' That hurt Lucy and she ignored it.

'We've haven't gone through your father's criminal records yet.' He pointed to the cardboard document wallets he had brought with him. 'There's quite a lot as you can see.' Lucy was puzzled by Jim's tone. She cleared the plates away and said nothing. Jim rested against the counter while she washed the plates.

'Your father was incarcerated for sixteen years. He was extremely lucky he got off so lightly. If it wasn't for his lawyers, and the plea bargains, he would still be rotting in jail now.' His words ripped into her, he thought her father should still be there, in jail.

'I am fully aware; he did nasty things. People change; it was a long time ago.'

'Come and sit down, I want you to have a look at the nasty things your father did.'

'Why? Why are you doing this to me?'

'Because you have an idealistic assumption that this story is going to have a happy ever after ending. Because you are sentimentalizing about your long-lost father like he is fairy-tale hero. And because, Lucy, if you insist on going to find your father, I want to make damn sure you go into this with your eyes wide open. I'm going to make sure you know all the dirty little details about your nasty father.'

'Why? This isn't your job anymore, why do you care what happens to me?'

'I feel responsible. I failed your brother, he is stuck in that world of wickedness and I don't want to fail you. If you are still hell bent on finding your family, there is not much I can do to stop you. But I can, at least, tell you what the consequences will be.' Jim dragged a hand through his hair and sighed. When he spoke again there was no sign of his earlier frustration, and his tone has softened. 'If you find him, and you don't like what you find, there is no way back, no way out. They won't let you just walk away.'

Jim pulled one of the cardboard folders from the pile and extracted the contents. Glancing over the pages he threw the pile on the table, so they spilt out like a deck of cards. Jim pointed a stubby finger at one of them.

'In nineteen-seventy-nine, your father had these men murdered. They were two of his own crew, his hoods. Call them whatever you want. But they were on his payroll. He thought they had been conspiring with us, giving us evidence about some property deals going down in the Harbour area. The Sinolis' were extorting higher than market rent from some of the local businesses in the hope they would go bust and have to sell up.

The Sinolis' were contracted to collect the rent and received large commission payments for their time … you get it?'

'Yes, but what has this …?'

'We had one of our guys posing as a potential buyer of the units. We had the evidence of the dirty ops and your father thought we got our information from these boys. As far as he was concerned, they'd snitched and so he cut their tongues out. Look at the photos, Lucy. This is what your family did to their own!' Lucy had seen the photographs when Jim pulled them from the folder and one glance had turned her stomach. She didn't want to look again but her eyes were drawn to the gruesome scene.

The boys were about her age, they were tied in chairs and a large blood stain covered their shirts and had pooled into a puddle around the chair legs.

'These boys were innocent of the crime they were murdered for, but your father didn't bother to find out the truth.' Jim pointed to another photograph. 'This one … look at the pictures, Lucy. These two were a couple of innocent homosexual kids. They turned up at your father's hangout by mistake. They were lost and looking for a venue with a similar name but decided to stay for a quick drink anyway. The bartender was busy, a row started up and they were asked to leave by your father. When they refused, they were escorted to a back room and your father watched while they were raped and beaten. He eventually asked them to climb into their own body bags! It would save his crew the trouble of cleaning up the mess. The boys had no choice, they climbed in, and their murderers laughed before unloading a bullet into each one at close range. McKinsey ...' He pointed to one of the boys.

'... was still alive when the bags were found on the city tip.' Lucy felt as though all her hairs on her head were standing on end as she stared into the dead eyes of one corpse in a body bag. 'McKinsey lived for three more days in the hospital.' Lucy swallowed hard. 'Their crime, walking into the wrong bar and being a bit mouthy.'

'This one ...' Jim sat down now and hooked his feet up onto the table. He had slowed his words and appeared to be considering them carefully. 'Susan.' He pushed a photo across the table gently. 'She owned a deli in Greenwich. She was the girlfriend of a criminal your father did business with. Anyway, long story short, she was fed up with all the violence and murders, just like your mother, and she agreed to let us bug her store, a place where there were a lot of agreements made. The bug was found somehow, and this is what they did to Susan. That's her penance.' Lucy was afraid to look at the photograph, but a morbid curiosity drew her gaze. The woman had been stripped of her clothes and tied with barbed wire, it was unclear to Lucy what the cause of death had been, the plump woman's flesh was torn where the barbs had pierced her skin, white folds of flesh squashed through gaps in the wire and Lucy felt the humility the woman must have endured, being stripped and slowly tortured.

'I don't want to see anymore, you're sick!' She was becoming dizzy and could feel the bile rising in the back of her throat.

'These are your father's victims, Lucy, not mine.'

'Why didn't they just put a bullet in her and be done with it?'

'To serve as a warning, a murder like this would put off other informants or anyone thinking of helping the FBI.'

'So, the wire was a message then.'

'Exactly. For anyone else thinking of corroborating with us, like your mother.' Lucy winced at this. 'I'm not sure if they suspected your mother of helping us at this point, but she was already talking to us when Susan was tortured and murdered.'

Lucy felt Jim's gaze scrutinizing her face and she tried to hide the emotions threatening to overwhelm her. She felt shame, her father, a blood relative was responsible and capable of incomprehensible terror. She swallowed hard. There were still many more photographs in the pile, but she had seen enough, and she pushed them away. She watched him consider the pile and select just one more photograph.

'This is Sandy.' He didn't show her the picture but held it to his own eyes and inspected it again as if he was seeing it for the first time, a sadness shadowed his face. 'Your mother's friend. The hairdresser we talked about yesterday.' Lucy's eyes widened. 'We used her place for cover for your mom's recordings. After a few sessions we decided it was getting too risky for Sandy, so your mother would walk into the salon and then just keep walking. Right through the building and out of the back door to where one of our cars would be waiting. We had a look-a-like take her place in the chair and get a blow dry.' Jim passed the photograph to Lucy. 'She was your mom's best friend.' His voice held deep regret.

The photograph showed the woman sitting in a low-slung salon chair, her head was bent backwards over the wash basin and her throat was cut so deep she had almost been decapitated. Lucy ran to the bathroom to vomit. She wanted to cry but no tears came, she was numb. She wondered how many horrors Jim could have witnessed to make him so nonchalant to all those images. Had he seen each one of them first hand? Were those his bloody footsteps on the tiled floor of the hair salon? A gentle knock at the bathroom roused her from her angst.

'I'm leaving now, Lucy.' Jim's voice came from the other side of the bathroom door.

'Where are you going?' She was surprised he was leaving.

'I've set up your mother's video evidence on the computer for you, and I'm gonna leave you to watch it in your own time. Whenever you're ready. I know it's difficult, Lucy.' He cleared his throat. 'There are a lot of hours of recording. In the end, we could only use about an hour of the evidence at trial, but I've given you access to all of them.'

'Why?'

'Can we have a conversation face to face Lucy?' Lucy unfolded her limbs and softly pulled the door open.

'Why did we only use an hour at trial?' She nodded. 'At the pre-trial hearing, the defence lawyers claimed we had obtained the testimony under coercion. They used your mother's dependency on drugs and alcohol as a tool against us. The fact that it was your father that had driven her to that mental state didn't prick his attorney's conscience in the slightest. So, we used only the most … lucid statements in the hope the jury would reject the defence argument.'

'So, it was all for nothing, she went through all of it for nothing?'

'No not at all, it didn't go as well as we had hoped but your mother gave us a lot of information. We could corroborate a lot of stuff and the information she gave us on the hierarchy and workings of your father's businesses, gave us valuable intelligence. It meant we could round up a few more of the mobsters who in turn ratted to get their sentences shortened. We also weeded out all the crooked politicians and insiders working with the families. We would have never known about that if it weren't for Katherine's information. So, your mother's testimony was really valuable, Lucy. It was a turning point in our fight against organized crime in the 80's. At that time, things were starting to fall apart for the mobsters, but the stuff your mother gave us tipped the balance for us.' He crouched down to the bathroom floor where she was still sitting and took her hands. 'It wasn't for nothing.'

'Will you be coming back?' Jim handed her a card.

'Sure, that's my number, call me when you like, any questions. Day or night, okay kid.' She nodded and watched Jim walk away and down the stairs and she noticed for the first time that he had a slight limp.

***

As Jim pulled his rented car out of the small lane, he considered how like her father she was. Strong, self-controlled. He had expected a much worse reaction to those photographs. He'd hoped for horror, disgust, loathing, but whatever she had felt she had managed to control and keep from him. He considered her career choice might be a lot to do with the way she handled it. His ace had fallen short of the mark, and he was disappointed that he had underestimated her reaction.

He hardly noticed the beautiful scenery as he drove through twisting lanes back to his guest house, he had work to do. He needed her to stay away from her father, away from the mob. He considered the remaining tools in his arsenal. He would have to get Frankie to talk to the girl.

Ray 'Frankie' Franks had entered the witness programme eight months before Katherine Sinoli. He was the hood that told him Katherine was a possible weak link. He knew she was having trouble with her marriage; he knew she was getting a beating from time to time, and he knew she was looking for an exit route.

If Jim could get Frankie to talk to Lucy, give her first-hand experience of what it was like inside that family she might be more inclined to stay clear of them. Frankie had been a witness and contributor to the Sinoli brutality and he had also testified at the Sinoli trials. As a teenager he'd gotten involved with the mob, rising through the ranks, and only turning in on them when the killing spree in 1983 scared him witless. He was supposed to have been hit along with several others, but he wasn't where he should have been. That same day he turned up at the FBI office and never went back onto the streets. If Jim could get him over to Ireland to see Lucy and talk to her, it might help her see the reality of the family.

***

She watched the first few recordings from start to finish. The youthful face of her mother was alien to Lucy. Her mother wore expensive designer clothes, her hair and makeup were flawless and the manicured hands that lit up cigarettes one after the other were far from the chewed nails and yellowed fingers that she remembered. The woman she remembered was a sick and wasted figure; this woman on the screen was beautiful, intelligent and terrified.

Lucy was so focused on the images that she had to replay the recordings over and over so that the stories made sense. As she worked her way through the tapes her mother's appearance deteriorated. She felt anger welling up towards Jim and the FBI. They were forcing her into this, and she was literally wilting before her eyes. She could see why some of this evidence had been dismissed. Jim and occasionally others could be heard in the background assuring Katherine and expertly drawing more information from her with an easy camaraderie. As Lucy skimmed through the final hours of the recorded evidence, she noticed that her mother appeared exhausted and had to keep asking for breaks in the sessions. She was witnessing her mother's irreversible decline. She wanted to watch more but anger was pulsing through her veins. She was looking at a woman tortured with fear and guilt and being manipulated by government agents that would eventually rip her entire family into shreds.

Lucy vowed to herself that she would not be controlled or manipulated in the way her mother had been by these men. She would watch the remaining footage another day, now there was just one thing she had to do and that was to get to New York before they could stop her. Lucy was in no doubt that Jim would try any means possible to prevent her from finding her father. If he would come out of retirement and go to this length to try and persuade her from going to find them then there had to be a reason. Something had to be in it for them and she became even more determined that she would not be cowed into ignoring her past.

Chapter 36

He got the number from Seth; it had taken more time than he expected. Jim had been passed around several old colleagues who wanted to talk about old times, the good old days. When he eventually obtained the telephone number for Ray 'Frankie' Franks he keyed the number.

'Stevie Ward please.'

'Who's calling?' It was a soft female voice and Jim decided it must be a wife. He hesitated a moment too long and when the woman asked again, he could hear a trace of fear in her voice. He kicked himself. This family had been in the programme for over twenty years and still, after all this time, a slight pause from a mysterious caller could send shockwaves down their spines.

'Mrs. Ward, this is FBI agent Jim Cavell, there is no need to worry. I just would like to have a word with your husband please.' It was unusual for the FBI to call a witness, they mostly had one point of contact and that was only with their designated Marshal. But these were unusual circumstances. Jim reminded himself that 'Frankie' in his heyday had been a vicious killer himself and therefore put aside any compassion for the man and this unusual approach. Jim heard muttering in the background, and it was a short time before a man answered the telephone.

'Stevie here.' The man's voice rattled, and Jim could hear him pulling on a cigarette over the line.

'Stevie, this is Jim Cavell, I'm sorry to call at this hour but I need a favour.' Jim was fed up with the small talk he had endured to get here and cut to the chase. 'There's nothing for you folks to worry about, I got your contact details from Ed, your liaison.'

'What's the favour?'

'It's about the Sinoli case, I know it's twenty ...'

'Hang your horses, Cavell, there ain't no way I'm going back down that road again.' The man laughed into the phone, and it started him hacking and coughing.

'It's not what you're thinking, there is no involvement with the FBI or justice department. I don't want evidence, I just want you to talk to somebody.'

'Jim, me and my family, have been happy living a quiet life all this time. There is no way, I'm gonna risk it all, for any favour. Hell, we got grand kiddies now, yeah believe that, and I'm still alive to take 'em to the park at the weekend ... '

'You wanna turn down an all-expenses-paid trip to Ireland, Stevie? Your wife would love it here, beautiful scenery. When was the last time you treated her to a holiday, Stevie?'

'What's Ireland gotta do with anything?'

'It's the Sinoli kid, remember the daughter Katherine got away with? We put 'em in Ireland. Twenty years she's been in the programme and only just found out about all this shit! Can you believe that? Anyway, now she wants out. I'm having a hard time persuading her and I thought you might be able to help. I need someone telling her how it is, on the inside. The real deal, no holds barred. I need her to forget about any ideas she has in her head about wanting to find her pops. You with me?' The coughing had stopped and there was a heavy silence on the other end of the line.

***

Lucy didn't waste any time. She'd seen how her mother had been manipulated by the FBI and she wasn't going the same route. Having the internet at home had its uses. She'd found a flight and called the travel agent. Now she stood in the hall scribbling a note to Edith. She knew Jim would be back at some point today and she needed to buy herself as much time as possible. Her flight was not for another six hours, and she hoped by the time he knew she was gone it would be too late for him to do anything about it.

Creeping out of the house at dawn she gently pulled the front door closed and pushed the note through her neighbour's letterbox lowering the flap down gently, so it didn't wake the old woman. With only one suitcase and a ruck sack, she made her way swiftly down the hill to the bus stop.

Lucy was completely lost in her thoughts and did not see the small figure wrapped in a heavy coat until it was too late. She had no option but to try and bluff her way out of this encounter. She tried her most carefree happy tone as she greeted the woman.

'Edith, you're out and about early on this fine morning, how are you?' It sounded contrived and she knew it. She saw the look on her neighbour's face and knew she had drawn the suspicion that she had been trying to avoid.

'I got my cleaning job Thursdays and Mondays, nothing unusual about me being out this hour, and where you off to young lady? Looks like you're off on your holidays.' Edith's tone was warm, but she eyed the suitcase warily.

'I'm off into Kearis. I've got a meeting with the bank manager, funeral expenses, you know ...'

'Bank won't be open for hours yet.' The woman held her gaze steadfastly on the suitcase as if waiting for it to announce its own impending journey and Lucy's eyes fell upon it too.

'Oh this, yes, I've been clearing out some of grandma's things. I'm dropping them off at the charity shop while I'm in

210

Kearis. I've got a few odd jobs to get sorted this morning so I'm up and about early myself because my visitor will be back later ... and I don't want to miss him ...' Lucy's voice trailed off as she remembered the text of the note she had written and posted through Edith's front door.

'The American?' Edith's eyes narrowed as she gazed right into Lucy's.

'Yes, he's coming back later, could you explain if I'm a bit late?' She was babbling and appeared as nervous as she sounded. As she raised her gaze to Edith's she saw that the woman knew exactly who Jim was.

'You're in no danger, my dear. These men won't let anything happen to you.' Lucy was stunned; all her fibres wanted her to shout at the woman *Why didn't you tell me!* but she had to think on her feet.

'Edith, I'm going back to Cork for a few days, back to campus. I just want to be around my friends for a while ... all this ... it's a lot to take in ... I need a few days away from here. If he shows up later tell him he can find me in Cork, only I need a little space so please buy me some time, Edith? I would really appreciate it. Just to get my head together, you know. I left a note for you to say I was in Kearis today, I just don't want him around for a day or two. Please, Edith?'

'Aye, I can understand it must be difficult. Best you're with your friends for a few days that'll be nice. I'll avoid him as long as I can.'

'Okay thanks, Edith.' Lucy gave the small woman a bear hug and picked up the case and hurried away before the guilt in her eyes gave her away. She hated lying to the old woman but isn't that what they had all done to her, her entire life? She shrugged off the guilt.

Chapter 37

The light had been seeping around the sides of the window blind for over an hour and Lucy winced at the brightness as the passenger next to her now opened it wide on orders from the stewardess. Trepidation pulsed through her temples. They were coming into land and from her aisle seat she could only surreptitiously glance out of the cabin to get a view of her birthplace.

As the plane bumped into its descent position and the landing gear whirred from the undercarriage Lucy's nerves were matched with excitement. She stretched out cramped limbs as best she could in her economy class seat. There was a clamour of activity as people put away books and games and she observed other travellers and wondered where their journeys would take them. Was anyone else on a life-changing adventure or were they all heading home to happy families and familiar routines?

Her thoughts were interrupted as the plane touched down. The G-force pushed her weight into her seat, and she heard the mighty roar as the engines reversed. The other passengers appeared unperturbed by the lurching and whirring of the large aircraft, so she swallowed hard to try and relieve the popping in her ears and linked her fingers together to calm her jittery hands. The pilot announced their arrival and asked passengers to remain seated until the plane had come to a complete halt. A deluge of clicking around her indicated that nobody was taking the slightest bit of notice, but Lucy compliantly remained seated and fastened.

Eventually, the passengers were shepherded off the aircraft and Lucy followed the throng of grumpy and dishevelled people into the airport. She had imagined stepping out onto a concrete runway and smelling the New York air, in a symbolic homecoming ritual. She pictured her family collecting her, but the unglamorous reality was that she was alone in a strange city, and nobody knew she was here.

Lucy followed other passengers through the maze of arrival halls and joined a queue of bodies corralled by a maze of ribbons. As her turn at the immigration desk drew closer, she felt her hands grow clammy: ever since she had discovered her original identity, she had become nervous about all things official. She hoped that she'd had enough of a head start on Jim and he had not somehow managed to prevent her from entering the country. Paranoia stalked her and she imagined all the immigration officers' eyes were on her.

'What's the purpose of your trip today, mam?' The immigration officer took Lucy's passport.

'Erm ... I,' Lucy started sweating.

'Business, tourist ... why are you visiting The United States of America?' The officer was clearly disinterested in her reply.

'Oh, yes. I see. Ah, tourist!' Her accommodation details were checked and after what seemed an age of clicking on a keyboard, she was handed back her newly minted passport and waved forward - the passport she had fortuitously applied for only a few weeks earlier with the intention of spending the summer in Florida with Janey. She hurried swiftly out of the customs hall and allowed herself to breathe again.

Her dusty old suitcase was easy to spot on the baggage carousel; all the others were clean and modern. A few days earlier this case was in her loft and contained her grandmother's trinkets and belongings. In her haste to pack and get out of Ireland, Lucy had only given it a cursory wipe down. She found a taxi rank and gave the driver the hotel details. She had changed a substantial amount of euros for dollars while waiting for her flight and she examined the unfamiliar currency now and separated the bills she would need to pay her fare. Persuading the bank manager in Kearis to give her access to her grandma's account had been easier than she thought, but then he had assumed she wanted the money to pay for the funeral expenses. She smiled at her own cunning and sat back to enjoy the sights and sounds of the busy New York traffic.

Chapter 38

Edith heard the heavy knocking and cowered into her armchair unsure of what to do. The man knocked three times and each time it got louder and harder. Now she could hear him calling out for Lucy through the letterbox. She hoped the disturbance would not wake Jerry from his lunchtime nap. She had made a promise to Lucy, could she break that promise? On the other hand, she sensed that Lucy was up to something and if that something might put the girl in danger, she would never forgive herself. The American returned to his car but did not drive off. Edith picked up the telephone and called Father O'Reilly.

The priest listened silently as Edith relayed her story of finding Lucy rushing off at the crack of dawn with a suitcase and her tale about heading back to Cork. She told the priest how the American had been here for a couple of days, and he had been cooped up with Lucy in the cottage for most of the time. She couldn't be sure what was going on, but her bones were telling her something was amiss. She added that Lucy had extracted a promise from her to keep her secret quiet until the afternoon.

'What's to be made of it, Father? Shall I go and see the man outside?' Edith peered through her net curtains to make sure the car was still there.

'God help us Edith, I think she might have gone!' The priest was worried.

'Gone?'

'To America. Janey told me she was convinced Lucy had made up her mind to go. I called the FBI to try and stop her. She has a brother ... dear god. I never thought she would be so foolish, but she's a head-strong girl and she's determined to find her kin.'

'Brother! She has a brother, well I'll be ... I knew something was wrong. I've never seen her head off for the University with a suitcase, Father. She normally just has the rucksack, the girl might be headstrong but she's not a good fibber. She shouldn't be going to America on her own, what can we do?'

'That's not the half of it, Edith, God give me strength. Go and tell the man outside what you just told me, he might be able to stop her in time. I should have had a talk with Lucy myself so I should.'

**

Jim knew Lucy might try and make a dash to New York. He just had not considered it would be so soon. When the old neighbour had hobbled over to his car and told him that she'd seen Lucy leaving very early with a suitcase he had cursed loudly and sprung into action. His first call was to Martha; she accessed the flight passenger manifests of all New York-bound flights leaving from Ireland and relayed the details back to Jim. She also gave him the address and number of the booking agent where Lucy had reserved her ticket. Her accommodation details were not in the immigration system yet but by the time she was on the ground, they would know where she was headed. Jim asked for eyes on her at the airport just in case. Lucy had already outwitted him once and he needed the status quo levelled. He now headed to the vicarage; the old woman had given him directions on where to find the priest.

Chapter 39

Jim pulled into the gravel drive and by force of habit checked all the mirrors before jumping out. Lucy was in the air somewhere over the mid-Atlantic and he was confident things could be handled properly at that end, so he had just one final thing to do before he could join her in New York.

The priest took his time answering the door, and when it finally opened, Jim introduced himself and was shown into a lounge overstuffed with antique furniture. A fire burned fiercely in the hearth and the heat coming from it was in no way tempered when the elderly priest stood in front of it and scowled at Jim. Jim had never spoken with Father O'Reilly but knew from Lucy's conversations that the old man had played an important part in the girl's life. He knew it was he who had filed the annual reports and contacted his colleagues when the old woman died. He had offered his hand, but the priest had ignored it.

'You know what happened twenty years ago?' The priest spoke slowly but his accent was heavy, and Jim had to listen carefully.

'Yes sir, I was involved in the extraction of the family all that time ago. The last time I saw Lucy she was two years old.' A shadow darkened the agent's eyes.

'So, you're the one. Please, sit down.' The priest's hostility thawed slightly. 'Mary told me about you. She talked fondly of you; said you helped them much more than you needed to.'

'Well, I ...'

'She's gone, hasn't she? To America.' Father O'Reilly still had not taken his chair.

'I'm sorry; I didn't expect her to be so headstrong. I underestimated her.'

'You should have come to see me first. I could have told you that.'

'She's on a flight, yes, but we will be staying close, very, very close, she won't come to any harm, I've got the best agents in the field watching her every move.' Jim silently hoped his words were true. 'And I'm on an afternoon flight. I'll get to her before she finds them.'

'It should have never got this far.' The words were spat out with venom as though the priest had a bad taste in his mouth. 'All you have done is made the girl more determined, determined to prove us all wrong.' The priest faltered, he looked crushed, and Jim realised he loved the girl very much. 'She's not a stupid girl, it's just a strong draw, trying to find her family. Trying to find the twin brother she was ripped away from. But I could have made her see sense ... in time. Your meddling just pushed her into something too fast, too soon. What exactly did you feed her fertile mind with these last two days?'

'I misjudged the situation; I approached it completely wrong.' The agent's elbows were resting on his knees, and he wrung his hands over and over. He was too old for this game, he should have let someone else handle the situation, retirement had slowed his brain, the priest was right. 'I didn't know that you were so close to Lucy and her grandmother until yesterday. I would have come over sooner ... '

'Call yourself a detective.' The words sliced through Jim. ''Tis her family see, she is just as entitled as the next person to go and find them. If she is the woman, I think she is, she

218

will see them for what they are soon enough, Mr Cavell.' The priest covered his face and rubbed at his temples to ease the throbbing nerves. ''Tis the blood you see, stronger than any other tie, it is. You must know that from your own family.' The priest had been looking into the fire but turned his eyes to the agent. Jim didn't notice the scrutiny; he was a long way away. He was remembering the events from twenty years ago and the suffering and heartache from that time was reflected in his face now. The two men sat for a while in silence, when Jim eventually spoke his words came out in barely a whisper.

'I'm worried it will be too late then Father, she won't be able to walk away.'

'Oh, why not?'

'These mob families are ... tight, closed. It's how they stay invulnerable. Once they know who she is they will not let her out of their sights again. She will be a badge, a trophy for them. They will think they have gotten one back against the FBI and the government and most importantly of all, against me.'

'You? What is so important about you?' The priest was confused.

'They won't let her go again, even if she wants out.' Jim tried to make the priest understand what this would mean, and he thought he was getting close, but he needed to be more direct. The old priest needed to know what evil resided in that family. He should know what the Sinolis' were capable of and the retribution he had suffered at the hands of the Sinolis'.

'They'll threaten her, or if that doesn't work, they will involve her in something, implicate her in a crime so ... she will be stuck with the family, with no way out. They are evil and capable of the most heinous acts, Father. You mentioned my own family earlier. Well, the mob took them away from me. In revenge. In revenge for taking away his family, Sam Sinoli put a target on my own baby daughter. His daughter for mine, an eye for an eye, that's how they think. Sam Sinoli had my daughter murdered.' The priest gasped and clasped a fist to his mouth.

'Fourteen months old she was, slightly younger than Lucy ...' Tears started to roll silently down Jim's face. He felt the priest kneel before him and clasp his hands over his own. He was whispering prayers with melodic rhythm. Jim found the words comforting, and it was a while before his thoughts returned once again to the drawing room with its roaring fire.

The priest rose and for some time stared into the fire, his own eyes glassy from unshed tears.

'Any more souls suffer from this heinous chapter?'

'We had just the one daughter, my wife left me soon after.' Jim swallowed hard and could not bring his eyes to meet the priest's. 'She wanted no part in my life anymore. She hated me for what happened, resented my job, everything about me. I was a constant reminder of our daughter. She lives in Atlanta now, she married again, has a son and another daughter. I'm glad she found happiness.' Jim was comforted by having made known the burden he carried. He thanked the priest for his prayers and his compassion.

'She has no place in a family that would, that could do such a thing ... 'tis pure evil. Does Lucy know all this, Mr Cavell?'

'No. And she never should, it is not to be her albatross.' Jim's voice was quiet, his head hung low, and his eyes stared down at the carpet. The priest nodded and the silence stretched.

'How long do we have?'

'She is on her way to New York; they are a few hours behind us. But it could take her less than a day to find them, two or three days if we're lucky. The Sinolis' are not hard to find, but I'll do my best.' Jim stood up to leave.

'I know you will.' The priest thanked him, but his face was bereft of any hope. They walked to the door and Jim offered the priest his hand. The old priest clasped the agent to his body.

'Thank you, thank you so much, Mr Cavell, for taking care of Mary and Katherine and the little one all those years ago, the Lord blesses you and whatever happens now is the Lord's will.' The priest had been fingering a silver crucifix pendant throughout his prayers and he unclipped the chain now and put it into Jim's palm. Jim noticed the decades of wear and caressing had worn the most intricate details of the religious talisman. He understood this was a cherished possession.

'Let's just hope the Lord is on our side then.' The two men nodded and as Jim took leave his voice now masked the personal grief that was perpetually gnawing at his soul. 'I'll be in touch soon, Father.' Jim once again compartmentalised his personal anguish and covered it with a cloak of professional authority as he had done for more than twenty years.

Chapter 40

S he could barely contain her excitement as she took the steps two at a time into the hotel lobby. The travel agent in Kearis had given her a list of hotels and she opted for a modest three-star within walking distance of the major tourist attractions. She was booked in for six nights and had even purchased a return flight. She had no intention of being on that flight. She noted the check-in procedure carefully. Her passport was taken and the number keyed into a terminal. She nodded, thanked the receptionist, and headed for her room.

It was much better than she had anticipated for the budget, it had a great view and she stayed in the window long enough to be eyeballed by the skinny agent that had followed her from the airport and now sat in his car in the street below.

***

The wind whipped into the half-open car window and Steven Dolph zipped it up quickly and blew air into his fingertips to warm them. He had followed the girl into the baggage hall and despite having seen her at the graveyard several days earlier he double checked against the image on his phone and casually picked up her purposeful stride out to the taxi rank. While she stood in the queue, he waved his colleague over, and they slid their vehicle into the line of traffic behind the girl's ride.

The cab had offloaded its passenger at the Lamcy hotel, and it was here that Dolph and his partner sat. Their instructions were to shadow her until Cavell got there. The agents from the U.S. Marshal Service positioned their vehicle so they had a clear view of the front door. If the girl left the hotel, they would see her. The younger agent returned to the car with two large coffees and Dolph wrapped his hands around his cup to warm them.

'What's the story with this Sinoli family then?' The rookie agent offered the question to Dolph.

'Tsh.' Dolph blew air from his lips. 'Any self-respecting New York Marshal knows about the Sinoli family! Where you been livin'?' It was almost word for word what Seth had said to Dolph a few days earlier. Until his nocturnal spell in the archives, Dolph had been unaware of the significance of the Sinoli name in organised crime in the seventies and eighties.

'Well, they're mob, I know that, but what's with a retired FBI guy getting involved with this girl?'

'Jim Cavell brought the whole Sinoli house down. Pretty much single handed. He got a mole inside see, was workin' her for months. Divide and rule, the first major tactic of any war and Cavell worked this strategy; he turned the families in on themselves. Until then they had been untouchable. He managed to get enough intel to implicate the other five major crime families ... some judges, a Senator.' The younger agent whistled. 'Yeah, and the rumour is there were FBI agents on the payroll.'

'No shit. Yeah, I think I heard about that case! A big case that changed the way the fuckin' FBI is structured and everythin'.'

'Yeah, that'll be the one.' Dolph nodded.

'How do you know so much?'

'I was overseeing their fuckin' admin people at the FBI archives, getting them to dig out all the files so we could be in the loop because this thing has come live again. I had access to all the files, make sure they were pulling the right stuff together.'

'So, we're working with Cavell, Holy cow!' Dolph saw his colleague shift in his seat. His interest in the seemingly mundane tailing operation had suddenly been piqued. 'I thought they were finished, though, the Sinolis? I ain't hearin' anything about this mob family anymore.'

'Oh, they're still around, the old man got paroled. Had enough stashed away to pretty much pick up where he left off. So, their ops only really ever got stalled. Probably wrapped everything up in front businesses now, so it looks legit. Probably more Senators in their pockets, who knows. They don't go about gunning down their enemies in the streets anymore. They fine-tuned their murder tactics to more sophisticated MOs. Their dirty work doesn't make the headlines now.' The agent seemed deflated at this news. Dolph added, 'Doesn't mean it doesn't happen though.' The young agent turned his gaze to the hotel where the girl was holed up.

'So, what's her connection?'

'One of the got aways, but I'm sure we'll find out more when Cavell gets here.' Dolph smirked at his colleague's fervour. The truth was he was just as thrilled to be working for Cavell and was looking forward to meeting the legend face to face. As far as the rumours went the FBI had baited Jim Cavell with all kinds of perks and promotions to tempt him back to work. Positions that some agents worked their whole career for, but Cavell turned them down saying he had earned his early retirement. There were rumours abound too about how the Sinoli case had delivered some kind of bad luck for

Cavell and his wife left him because he was too devoted to the job. The agent had got promotion after promotion but never re-married; instead, he devoted his life and career to bringing down the mob and was now enjoying his retirement, somewhere in Wisconsin. What a coup, working with Cavell. Working this case would be worth a whole lot of bragging rights in the department.

Their instructions were clear; keep an eye on the target and do not let her make contact with any of the Sinolis. He was babysitting a kid from Ireland. How difficult could it be? He turned up the collar of his jacket; he would not take his eyes off the hotel doorway.

Chapter 41

Dolph was napping. It was his partner's turn to keep his eyes on the hotel foyer and the girl's first-floor hotel window. The light remained on. There was no sign of his quarry, and he was getting impatient. His stomach was growling, and he had hoped the girl would have ventured out for some sight-seeing or something by now; she had been holed up in her room for several hours.

'Wakey, wakey sleeping beauty.' Shifting his weight, he stretched. He had strolled the hotel corridors a couple of times, the girl's room was at the front, and he had checked the layout of the hotel and found the fire escape at the side of the building with alarm doors. The only other way out of the building was through the kitchen, so he was pretty sure if they stayed close to the lobby, they would see her leaving the hotel.

In his last stroll past her room, a couple of hours ago, he heard no television noise and assumed she was sleeping. Surely, she would be hungry by now? He checked if there had been any calls, in or out from the girl's room, room service, nothing. He needed to stretch his legs so got out of the car and strode as far down the sidewalk as he could while keeping the hotel entrance in his line of vision. On his third pass of the hotel lobby, he noticed that the desk clerk had changed. The evening crew must have handed over so he would risk another walk in and up to the girl's door.

He sauntered up the steps and into the lobby to ask the clerk if there were any messages for him, room 110. She shook her head and he thanked her and walked unchallenged to the stairwell, he jogged up the stairs, he needed the exercise after all the sitting around. As he approached the girl's room, he checked over his shoulder to ensure he was alone in the corridor. He pressed his ear to the door and waited. Still no sign of a TV, a shower, or even any snoring. There was something wrong, he could feel it.

He walked to the opposite end of the corridor away from the girl's room and called the hotel and asked to be connected to Lucy White, room 102 and then strode back to listen to the buzzing of the phone through the door. It went unanswered and the agent cursed. He knocked harshly on the door, several times and when there was no reply from within, he called his napping colleague and sprinted back down to the desk clerk, showed his identity, and asked for access to the girl's room.

***

Jim Cavell had unwittingly revealed the way to lose a tail when he had told Lucy about her mother's testimonies; her mother would walk in through the front door and then straight out the back door of the hair salon.

Lucy had done pretty much the same when she'd checked into her hotel. She found her room, hovered about the window until the agents in the street below had seen her then gave the room a lived-in look. She pulled back the bedspread and punched a few pillows, tossed one to the floor. She scattered some clothes and underwear around the room and left her toothbrush and comb by the sink. She splashed water about and screwed up the towels. She stripped down to her underwear then went back to the window, yawned, stretched and pulled the curtains. There was still daylight outside, but she switched on a few lamps, re-dressed, collected her lightened suitcase, and headed downstairs.

The kitchen wasn't difficult to find, and the staff had just pointed uncaringly when she asked for the back door. One or two of them had a question in their eyes but she ignored it and walked swiftly out and into the alley. She stayed in the narrow back streets until she was several blocks away from the agents and then strode out into the main street and hailed a taxi. She made the driver circle a few blocks before hopping out, she paid the driver, and walked across a small square. The trees and bushes eclipsed her view of the street and when she was sure she was out of sight from the taxi driver or anyone else that might have been following, she ducked into another hotel. The check-in procedure was the same as the last place. She had hoped a smaller place, off the main tourist drag might have overlooked the requirement for ID; but they hadn't. She would have to stay on the move. If she selected small hotels with manual checking in processes, she hoped it might buy her a couple of days.

This second room was basic, a single bed, a small dressing table, chair, and a wardrobe. She turned on the TV but didn't bother unpacking anything. She felt into the pocket of her coat to check that watch and her mother's wedding ring were still safe. She intended to show her father the jewellery; it would prove her provenance in case there was any doubt in his mind about her identity. Now that she had finally arrived in New York City, after practically running out on Jim, she would have to move quickly. She would need the internet, so her priority was a library or similar. She flipped through the assortment of tourist leaflets she'd grabbed from the first hotel, hoping to find a city map. Her eyes felt heavy, the lively passengers in the row behind her seat on the plane, had denied her any sleep so she let her body and mind float off, deciding forty winks would do her a world of good and shake off her jetlag.

***

Jim's phone started to ring as soon as he switched it on, and it was pressed against his ear for the entire journey from the airport to the Lamcy hotel on Manhattan Island. There was a problem, the agent had told him.

'Damn right there's a fucking problem! Find her.' He had hung up and immediately called Martha. Right now, he was on his way to the hotel; he had to see this with his own eyes. One entrance in and out of the hotel and the idiots had lost her! When Jim arrived at the hotel, he could hear an argument in the lobby while he was still outside paying the cab driver.

'This is too much disruption to my guests.' The hotel manager was backing an agent into a corner. 'You shudna put a criminal in my hotel. Who gave you permission to put a murderer in my hotel?'

'Sir, the girl is not a murderer … she …' The agent had his hands up but couldn't be heard over the manager's barrage.

'You shudna put a criminal in my hotel, if you knew she was bad news, why wasn't she arrested?'

'Sir, we were only minding her, she hasn't done nothing wrong … she's not dangerous.'

'My guests are complainin', they're checkin' out and my staff are not babysitters. They aren't responsible because she went out the kitchen, you understand?'

'Yes sir …'

'Who's gonna compensate me for this … I wanna speak with your boss. Who's in charge?'

Jim's pace quickened to swerve the ruckus and he hurried up to the first floor. Dolph was standing indignantly in the centre of the hotel room holding one of Lucy's t-shirts. He held it up as Jim strode into the room, as if the t-shirt was a shield, it was a pathetic attempt to hide his face. Jim tried to contain his fury, he wanted to floor the cowering agent but managed to control his temper. He snatched the t-shirt and threw it.

'I'm sorry sir, I didn't think she was a flight risk otherwise we could have had someone on the kitchen door.'

'You're paid to think, for Christ's sake! What's your name?' Jim checked the bathroom, opened the closet, and let his eyes scan over the already pulled drawers. There was not much sign of any luggage other than a few scattered items.

'Dolph sir, Steven Dolph.' He gulped. 'What should we do now? We can put someone on all the doors sir, we'll see her if she comes back.'

'What? For her fucking toothbrush?' Jim yelled and threw the offending item at the agent. Dolph squirmed under Jim's glare.

'You, Dolph, are going home. The rest of us are going to find the girl. I only want capable people on my team. You understand?' Jim turned to the other Marshal who had managed to get away from the ranting hotel manager and had joined them in the room.

'Let me talk to the kitchen staff.' Jim walked out.

They couldn't tell him much, she had asked for the rear door and left. That's it, yes, she had a suitcase. No, they didn't follow her out or notice the direction she took.

There was nothing Jim could do. Martha was checking all the hotels on Manhattan, but there was no guarantee she would have checked into any of them. Lucy could be anywhere. They were going to have to wait until she showed up and he knew exactly where that would be.

Chapter 42

The librarian pointed Lucy in the direction of a room adjacent to the main reading room in the New York Public Library. The Stephen A. Schwarzman Building of The New York Public Library was conveniently located at Fifth Avenue, only a few blocks from her hotel so she'd walked there. This building had been constructed at the turn of the last century and marble façade, with ornate detailing, and a pair of stone lions stood out amid the modern concrete and glass city scape.

Lucy gawped at the beauty of the place; the main reading room was lined with thousands of reference works on open shelves. She eyed the massive arched windows and grand chandeliers, and wished she had the time to wander and appreciate this iconic building but she was aware the clock was against her. This was the most obvious place for someone to hang out if they were researching their family history. Lucy scanned the other people at tables and browsing shelves, nobody was interested in her, so she pulled out her laptop and settled into a vacant docking station in the room with a sign that announced it as the Milstein Division of U.S. History, Local History and Genealogy.

Lucy spent several hours skimming through microfiche of New York newspaper titles from the early eighties. Much of what she found was just as Jim had told her. Her family were notorious and mixed up in every kind of organised crime that the city had suffered in the eighties. She had hoped Jim's evidence might have been biased, an edited and emphasized version for his own selfish ends and to make sure she would hate her family. All that she had found just corroborated Jim's versions of events, minus a few of the gory details that never made it into the public arena, probably for the sake of the victim's families she figured.

The articles she found had given her no clues to any addresses and even if they had she doubted they would still be relevant two decades on, so she switched back to the internet and focused on finding her brother.

It was much easier than she ever thought. She found a recent press article that mentioned the Sinoli name as a benefactor to a medical research facility and after a few hits in a search engine, a face, so like her own that she had gasped audibly, gazed out at her from the screen. There was no doubt this man was her brother. He had short black hair and more angular features, but the likeness had shocked Lucy. She sat for several minutes looking at the image before reading the associated text. She had wondered if she and her brother would look alike but she had not been prepared for this. She'd asked Jim for photos, information, but he gave her nothing; by design she thought, not because he didn't have anything.

The image that gazed from the screen was part of an article that led her to a scientific publication, it was allied with a university where her brother was studying. Several more clicks and she found him in another publication, Graduate & Postdoctoral Chemist Magazine. He was studying to be a chemist.

The first photograph had sent her reeling but as the shock wore off, she sat immobile and saddened. They had been ripped apart but chosen a similar career path in life and she wondered how else they might be alike. She had been denied a life with this person, her brother. She was flooded will all kinds of emotions she couldn't get a grip of, so decided to bookmark the page on her laptop and head out for some fresh air and a coffee. She had been here too long anyway.

Lucy spent some time wandering the streets, not only to stay on the move but she needed to digest all the facts she had found. Her father had been sentenced to sixteen years in jail but had been paroled after only eight. She didn't know if she was happy about that or disgusted. It was clear now that her mother was the one who had suffered the most out of this whole saga. Eight years and then her father was set free to pick up his life. Sine would have been ten years old when he got his father back and a stab of jealousy ripped through her.

Lucy made sure to double back or cut through a store now and then to avoid anybody following her, but her mind was numb, and she walked for a long time working through the flux of emotions. The weight of the laptop dragged into her shoulder and a groaning hunger directed her to a café. She chose one with an internet connection.

A few more clicks and Lucy found the name of the hospital where her brother was completing his post-graduate qualifications. He was a pharmacist at the Mount Messina Hospital, Newport, New York. Bingo. Lucy leant back and smiled to herself. She was jubilant. The waitress walked by and asked her if she needed a top up on her coffee.

'Do you do beer?'

'Sure do.'

'Then give me a beer, please.' She was going to celebrate and do some city sight-seeing for the rest of the afternoon and evening. She would go and find the hospital tomorrow. As Lucy turned her head away from the waitress, she caught the eye of a passer-by in the street who took a second longer glancing in the window than was normal. Lucy closed the laptop, laid out a few dollars on the table and on her way to the bathroom told the waitress the beer was for her friend who would be in shortly.

Chapter 43

Lucy eased herself out of the taxi and smoothed down her A-line cream linen shirt dress with matching tote bag. She eyed the hospital and was glad she'd spent a fortune in the high-end department store on her outfit. Her worn jeans and baggy sweater wouldn't have passed the twelve hundred dollars a night means test to get into this place. She had an appointment to visit the maternity department as a prospective client so needed the designer wardrobe to go with it.

The hospital website told her that the sixty-bed hospital had a reputation for outstanding patient care and innovative medical and surgical treatments. It boasted state of the art equipment and research facilities. It had specialist departments for Internal medicine, cardiovascular disease, orthopaedics, and maternal and child health. It was a long way from the hospitals she was used to working in and she knew she would not be able to just walk in and go wandering around the various departments looking for her brother.

She stood outside and gazed over the property, nervous excitement building, her brother was inside here somewhere. The hospital was a semi-circle of glass and chrome that curved around a central fountain outside the front of the building. Large silver letters across the top of the entrance glinted in the morning sun and announced that it was the Mount Messina Hospital. Lucy's heels clicked across the marble piazza, and she was too engrossed gazing at the property and architecture to notice the man quickly advance and present her with a small white card. She took the card with a smile and then shivered as she realized who this man was. How had they found her? How long had they been tailing her?

'Miss White, Jim Cavell asked me to give you this, please keep it close to hand.' Then he was gone. He'd departed as swiftly as he'd appeared. Lucy was too stunned to move for a moment. He hadn't tried to stop her entering the hospital. Her veins filled with adrenaline because she'd expected a fight. She thought the agent would have dragged her to a waiting van or similar. Hadn't Jim Cavell told her he would do anything in his power to prevent her meeting the family. But here she was, they had seen her, and they were going to let her walk right in. Lucy gathered her composure and hurried into the building and announced her arrival with the receptionist before they changed their mind.

***

Someone showed Lucy around. She was too unsettled about the episode outside to focus on the receptionist when she'd introduced the concierge. This nameless man walked ahead of her now, pointing to various departments and Lucy peered in through open doors, she was looking for more than just the patient experience.

Lucy had spent a lot of time in hospitals and clinics, but this was like nothing she had ever seen. Patient rooms were more akin to luxury hotel suites and waiting rooms were plush lounges with subtle lighting, contemporary art installations and fresh flowers. She was informed that every patient had a designated staff, they were rostered for twenty four-seven care and would always include at least two nurses on every shift. The various employees wearing pristine white, and lemon starched uniforms, nodded and smiled as she passed, unhurried and relaxed, a far cry from the harassed and exhausted colleagues she was used to working with. Lucy could understand the price tag.

Her concierge went on to point out the discreet CCTV cameras that watched every hall and every room. He told her that the hospital had its own permanent in-house security department, and this was a key selling point and why it was the place for many high profile VVIPs from all over the world. The Mount Messina Hospital put their client privacy, discretion and security at the top of their priorities. Mr Sinoli had been adamant that this was a fundamental principle underpinning the foundation. He turned and noticed Lucy's white face; she had stopped walking at the mention of her family name.

'Mr. Sinoli?'

'Mr. Sinoli.' The concierge nodded. 'He donated the building and set up the foundation which runs the hospital.' He said the sentence as if it were something she should have known. He opened the glossy folder she had in her hands and pointed to the inside back cover, which had details about the charitable foundation and the generous benefactor, Mr Sam Sinoli. Lucy was speechless. Her father had built this hospital and given it to a charity!

'Is everything okay, Ms White?'

'Erm, yes fine, I didn't see anything about this ... er benefactor on the website.' The concierge ignored her, indicating for Lucy to follow him again.

Lucy was floored this didn't fit the profile of an evil thug that she been conditioned to believe her father was. It did however explain why her brother was working here. She followed the concierge, now oblivious to his ramblings, she was thinking. She had planned to try and lose him and poke around the hospital to find her brother, but there was no way she would get away with it with CCTV covering every square inch of the property. If she suddenly announced her identity and requirement to find her long lost daddy and brother, it would look suspicious. This guy had more or less just told her that Mr Sam Sinoli was a multi-millionaire, she would be thrown out. They had arrived in the hospital maternity wing and Lucy asked if she could speak with the on-duty anaesthetist or pharmacist. The concierge seemed a bit perturbed but recovered his composure quickly.

'I'm not sure who we may have on duty and who is free, erm, may I ask what is concerning you?'

'I am unsure of what pain relief option I would like to use and how it will affect my labour and delivery.'

'I'm sure all that information will be discussed in detail once you are under the care of our medical team.' He was deflecting her request.

'Mr... erm, my friend recommended this hospital because your staff is approachable and accessible, shall I wait here?' She didn't wait for his reply and curtly walked to the last waiting area they had passed and sat down. The concierge frowned, then decided against any further argument and nodded once and walked away. She was glad she had bought new clothes; the diva routine would not have worked in jeans and hiking boots. She hoped that the next person to walk down the hall would be her brother. She couldn't contain her excitement.

***

The concierge returned but she didn't see him, she was fixated on the dark-haired young man following a few paces behind. She had been preparing for this meeting for days, yet it was still a jolt for her to see her own eyes looking back at her. Sine Sinoli offered his hand with a wide smile that she recognised. As the concierge introduced them she interrupted him.

'I'm actually called Sive. Sive Sinoli.' Nobody said anything. Her brother held her gaze, she could see him thinking. He was bewildered, his eyes roamed her face, her body, he let his hand drop away. The concierge had stepped a few feet away and was talking quietly into his phone. 'I'm your sister.'

'It's not possible.' Sine's face registered disbelief, and his head shook slightly from side to side. Lucy smiled at him, she liked his voice, she had wondered how he would sound. Remembering her own accent, she offered more information.

'I only just found out about you; I've been in witness protection in Ireland all this time.' He took a step back, his eyes widened with suspicion; he seemed to be getting his bearings back.

'Is this some kind of joke? Who sent you here? What do you want?' His voice seemed strained. Some security guards came running down the hall, the receptionist that Lucy had met earlier followed close behind.

'I just wanted to meet my brother ...' She argued with the guard who held her arm and started to pull her down the corridor. 'You know our mother was heartbroken she left you behind ...' She turned her head and saw a lost little boy standing in bewilderment. Lucy was at the end of a corridor being marched away by the two security personnel and had to shout to be heard. 'She never forgot about you Sine ...' Other staff and patients had emerged from rooms to see what the commotion was about and Sine, quick to quieten the unfolding PR spectacle indicated to the security guards to take her into a side room. He whispered for them to wait outside and then hissed at the receptionist, who was watching with hinged jaws to get back to her desk. She immediately left and Sine closed the door.

'Okay you've got my attention; now how much do you want to go away?' Sine ran a hand through his jet-black hair. Lucy laughed.

'This is not about money.' She pulled the watch and her mother's wedding ring from her purse. 'These were our mother's. Check it out with our father if you like.' Her brother took the jewellery and eyed the inscription she showed him.

'Where is she?' His eyes flashed with anger.

'She died, Sine. Years ago. 1988.' Lucy's voice was quiet. He never knew his mother. She understood the feeling, but she still had a chance to change her destiny, his loss was perpetual. He sat back into a leather sofa and fingered the watch and the ring. He swallowed hard and then pressed a button on his phone. A gravelly voice came on the line.

'Pops, did you give my mother a diamond and black stone watch once?' He watched Lucy while he spoke into the device.

'What? Who told you that?'

'Never mind about that, do you remember giving her a watch? Yes or no, pop? What did the inscription say?' Lucy was desperate to hear her father's voice. She moved closer to the phone but couldn't decipher the words clearly. Sine hung up; she could hear her father yelling when he disconnected the line.

'So, she died then?'

'I'm sorry, Sine.' It tugged at her heart seeing somebody grieving for someone they never had a chance to know.

'My name is Sin Sin, not Sine. Do you have any photos?'

'Sin Sin.' She tried the name. 'No, I don't. There … there were a couple; really old ones … that's all I have. We didn't have a camera back then and I … I only remember her a little bit.' Lucy kicked herself for being in too much of a rush to consider bringing the handful of photos she had of her mother.

'I don't remember her ... Pops wouldn't keep any pictures.' He seemed to be struggling and Lucy was unsure how to comfort him.

'She wasn't like us.' Lucy fingered her dark hair. 'She had blond hair, blue eyes. She was beautiful.' Lucy was remembering the couple of dog-eared pictures of her mother that she had treasured all her life. The ones that showed a smiling laughing woman, almost flirting with the camera or the man behind it. The ones that had been taken long before her life spiralled out of control. This was the woman she tried to remember as her mother, and the woman Lucy spoke of to her friends. The other memories were just for her, she kept them hidden and never talked about them. But now sitting in the same room as her brother, she divulged the unhappy reality that knotted her stomach every time she spoke about her mother.

'She was an alcoholic, she died from alcohol abuse. Towards the end of her life, she'd become so thin and fragile she fractured bones from just tripping up. She was a broken woman because she left you behind. She smoked and drank constantly. I remember a grey woman, a permanent grey pallor from the nicotine and alcohol. It's just fragmented memories. My ... our grandmother raised me.'

Sin Sin's phone started buzzing and it shook him from his thoughts, and he collected his self-control. He looked at the number.

'Come on, we have to go and see my pops.'

'Now?' She didn't feel ready; she would have preferred to spend more time with her brother. He didn't answer but walked out of the room, he expected her to follow.

Chapter 44

S in Sin steered the car erratically through the New York traffic to their father's apartment. Lucy didn't know the model, she was not familiar with sports cars, but the high-performance vehicle was clearly very expensive. Not something a medical undergraduate could afford, but now she knew Sin Sin was no ordinary medical student. They parked in an underground car park and Sin Sin walked ahead and pressed a code into an elevator. He had barely spoken the entire journey. Lucy didn't question the silence, she knew turning up in their lives would be a shock and she left him to his thoughts.

The lift had only one destination and when it bumped to its floor, the doors opened into a wide hallway. Mirror and chrome led the eye into a vast apartment, Lucy followed Sin Sin. The wall to ceiling windows offered a panoramic view of New York City and Lucy's eye was drawn to the view and did not notice the man sitting behind a desk until his voice interrupted her survey of the New York skyline.

'Why the fuck, don't you pick up my calls?' He didn't bother to greet his son and his tone showed his irritation.

'Good morning pops, I brought you a present.' Sin Sin flipped the watch on the desk and waved a hand at Lucy who had walked over to the vast window and who now turned to look at her father.

'What the? ...' Sam Sinoli had picked up the watch, but his gaze didn't leave Lucy's face. Sin Sin took a seat on a low sofa and put his feet on a glass table as if he was settling in to watch a favourite TV show. His father looked to him with a question and Sin Sin nodded to the watch.

'Where the hell did you get this?'

'She brought it.' Sin Sin leaned back with his hands interlocked behind his head and he looked at Lucy. 'Sive brought it home.' Sin Sin's voice dripped with sarcasm. Her father stood slowly and calmly walked over to his daughter, he walked around her as if inspecting a sculpture for fracture marks.

'Where is your mother?' He spat the words without trying to hide the venom in his voice. Lucy gulped.

'She died in 1988.' She felt intimidated but remained implacable under his scrutiny.

'How convenient. Or lucky, for her.' He sniggered. The man that circled her was much younger than she had imagined, he was fit and lithe. She had in her mind's eye a middle-aged man with a round waistline and thinning hair, a man who might embrace her and welcome her to his family. Her father looked younger than his years and his hair was still thick, his voice and face were filled with loathing and animosity. He clearly still hated the woman who had caused his incarceration and until now he had no idea was dead.

'She only just found out who she is!' Sin Sin raised his eyebrows and seemed to be enjoying the spectacle playing out before him.

'How is that even possible?' Sam's question was not directed at Lucy but at his son.

'We were sent to Ireland, we lived in Ireland, a place called Anchora. After my mother died my grandma raised me. I only found papers about my identity when she died, just two weeks ago.' The story made Sam Sinoli laugh. He released an exuberant guffaw and looked at his son as if they were sharing a joke. Sin Sin smiled but stayed silent. Lucy felt as if she wanted to run from the room. She held back tears. Sam wandered over to the window and looked at the vista for a long time before speaking.

'You like the view, huh? You like the view of New York, there is no better view than this.' He had his back to Lucy. She was unsure how to answer. He appeared to be ignoring the fact that his daughter had just walked into the room and was boasting about his apartment as if she were a business associate or employee. He showed no emotion towards her. She expected at least some questions or searching but there was nothing from him.

'It's the most amazing thing I've ever seen.' Her father turned now and looked at her, not with malice or suspicion but warmth.

'This view cost me millions of dollars. I worked my whole life for this view. Come, come, and look.' He waved at her to join him at the window. Lucy had the measure of the man, he needed to be flattered and valued material things. She took the cue.

'I can see you're very successful, you're lucky. If this were my apartment, I don't think I would ever leave.' Sam smiled at the view, nodded, and then turned and smiled at his daughter.

'New York is the best City in the world, hey? How long have you been here?'

'Two days.'

'Two days! You haven't seen anything yet. Where are you staying?' The conversation had started to flow, and Lucy relaxed a little.

'All over, I have kept on the move because the FBI is trying to stop me reaching you.' She saw her father's face darken suddenly.

'The FEDS!' He yelled it and the volume startled Lucy. 'You, you're the reason they're on my doorstep again twenty-four fucking seven. I shudda guessed.' He was angry again; the moment of geniality had passed. He walked back over to his desk and addressed his son, 'She brought the fucking FEDS sniffing around again.' He lowered his voice, and Lucy strained to hear the conversation. 'She might be working for them. You're gonna have to be her shadow.'

'No! No way. That's not going to happen.' Sin Sin didn't seem to mind if Lucy could hear him.

'She's a yokel, I don't want her roaming around the city using my name and getting herself picked up by the FEDS or the wrong crew. Put her in the Four Seasons and put Joey on her, I'm not a babysitter!' Lucy could hear her brother's protestation. She was a nuisance to them; it was not the homecoming she had expected.

'Okay, okay. I'll call Vera, she can stay with her in the burbs.' Sam Sinoli's deliberations were interrupted by the ping of arrivals in the hall and two of his associates entered the apartment.

'Joey, Mickey, come and meet my daughter!' The two men were surprised, since when did Sam Sinoli have a daughter? He took pleasure and pride showing off the new member of his family. Lucy felt like a prize bull at a cattle market.

There was a steady stream of visitors to the apartment, Lucy was introduced to various business associates. Her father recounted the story about how the FEDS had stolen her but now she was back with him. Not once did he ask her about her life or her upbringing.

When Sin Sin eventually got up to leave and told her to come with him, she was relieved to get away from the apartment. Her father was a show-off, and he was also a misogynist. Women had little involvement in any of the family's business affairs and to her it seemed old-fashioned. When she had told them that she was a doctor a couple of them had almost choked on the lunch they were shovelling into their faces. Her father sniggered and announced that the hospital would now have two Sinoli doctors. He professed to be proud and bragged that the family business had just doubled in a day.

For the most part, Sin Sin had stayed silent, but at this announcement he spoke up and told his father firmly no. It sobered the jovial mood of the men around the table and Lucy noticed that apart from Sam Sinoli everyone deferred to Sin Sin. Lucy decided she preferred his enigmatic personality over her father's big ego and brash nature, despite the fact he had just vetoed any opportunity for her to work at the hospital.

Chapter 45

Lucy woke sometime in the early hours; her body clock was still catching up with the time zone and the emotional roller coaster of the last three days meant she passed out as soon as Sin Sin had shown her a bedroom in his own apartment. Now she pulled on a borrowed t-shirt and took a seat in the window to watch the enchanting city nightscape. The blaze of yellow twinkling lights stretched into infinity, broken only occasionally by the black ribbons of the waters circling the city. She watched the vehicles moving about in the streets far below and wondered what everyone was doing at this hour. The view was spectacular, but it would have been even better from her father's apartment with his one-hundred-and-eighty-degree vista. She felt a stab of regret that she might not get a chance to see it again because she was being packed off to the suburbs in a few hours.

As she sat hunched in the window watching the night-time scene, she heard murmuring voices and strained to hear more. The voices were coming from within the apartment, and somebody wasn't happy. She opened her bedroom door and could hear the ruckus more clearly. It was coming from a room on the other side of the apartment. There was a crack of light coming from under the door and she could make out Sin Sin's and a female voice.

Her brother had not divulged any information about a girlfriend, and she did not want to pry so she hadn't asked. Muffled noises told her the two people were having sex and she was about to return to her room when the woman

247

howled, more anguished and muffled screams followed. A series of bangs and thumps sent Lucy's apprehension coursing through her mind, and she hovered in the lounge unsure of what to do. The woman was arguing and crying. Lucy tiptoed closer to the closed door.

'It's not enough, Sin Sin; I can't work with bruises and swelling. No wonder the others don't wanna know you, Sin Sin. I need more money.' The woman's voice had a heavy accent, and Lucy had trouble making out the words.

'We agreed what we agreed. You know the score Sal, take the fucking money and get out.' Her brother sounded bored and uninterested in the woman's demand. Sin Sin muffled something else. She couldn't hear the words, but the tone was menacing, and the bedroom door was flung wide open and bright light illuminated the lounge. Lucy ducked as far into the shadows as she could. A woman launched from the room and stumbled; a bright red stiletto followed her. She bent to pick it up and Lucy could see a leather mini skirt and torn tights. The woman hurried to the door and fled. Lucy stayed in the shadows trying to figure out what the feelings permeating her thoughts were. She was shocked. Her brother had battered and bruised a prostitute. Aversion and unease washed over her, and she crept back to her room.

***

She wanted to get out of her brother's apartment as soon as possible; she would collect her things from the last hotel and check into one close by. She didn't want to be in anyone's home, least of all an aunt in the suburbs, whom she had never met. But she wasn't ready to leave New York either.

The shock of her brother's nocturnal depravity made her want to put some distance between them. Her plans were halted by a call from her father. He initially spoke with Sin Sin but her brother passed the phone to Lucy. He was the charming gentleman she had seen flashes of the previous day and he told her she would be helping him with some business. Lucy was delighted; she was told in no uncertain terms the previous day that women didn't get involved in the family business; now he was asking her to help him. Ultimately, she would be working under Sin Sin at the hospital, but he had a few things he needed her to take care of first. A car would be sent. Lucy was enthused. When she finished the call and asked her brother about the new arrangements, he just looked at her in silence for a long time and with an expression that Lucy could not decipher.

'My father thinks I'm like him. He wants me to be the same, I'm not. I'm nothing like him and he has spent countless hours and efforts trying to mould me into his mini-me. He will try and do the same to you now.' A spark of hope flickered in Lucy. Was her brother opening up and talking about the family's past crimes? 'The medical profession gave me a different perspective on ... things, I prefer to work with my brain and not my hands. I think you might be the same?' His eyes narrowed as he scrutinized her reaction. She nodded dumbly, remembering his handiwork in the early hours. She was also unsure how much she should profess to know about the family's previous business enterprises, mentioning the FBI and their influence operation on her had only enraged them and increased their suspicions the previous afternoon.

'I would love to come and work with you at the hospital. Healing and helping people is what I've spent years working towards, it's my passion.'

'Come along later, anytime, I'll show you around. The staff tour this time ... not the client tour.' They both laughed and Lucy pushed the episode in the night to the back of her mind. She would try and rationalize it later, she suspected, against all the odds he was shunning the family business and wanted her to be a part of his world.

***

A car waited in the street and Lucy hovered on the sidewalk until the blacked-out window lowered and her father's smiling face protruded from within. She hopped in and the leather seats and walnut trims told her that this was a very expensive car. He greeted her like she was a treasured possession; it was how she imagined her first meeting with him might have gone. She was already aware of how quickly his mood could change and was wary of not gushing back at him. The words her brother had spoken at breakfast also swam in her head like a warning. They were going to see an elderly relative in a nursing home on Long Island. Enjoy the ride her father told her, take in the scenery. In the front of the car alongside the driver was Vince, one of her father's employees she had met yesterday. He had sat across from Lucy during lunch, and she disliked him a lot. His eyes were constantly on her, and he never smiled when any of the others cracked a joke, she wished he wasn't here.

The journey passed quickly because her father asked her about her life. She hoped that he was genuinely interested but she quickly realised he was just passing the time. When the car finally pulled up outside the nursing home his tone changed. The sign declared they were at the Medhaven Nursing and Rehabilitation Centre. As Lucy started to get out of the car her father pulled her back. He spoke carefully like he might address a child. The man she was going to see was an old friend, he was in his seventies and recovering from a heart operation. But he was being sedated too much and held against his will. She was to go and check on his condition. Lucy nodded. It seemed like a reasonable request. She would check his vitals and his med sheet and then tell her father if she agreed with him. Her father pulled out her passport and handed it to her. You need ID to visit patients. Lucy frowned; they had been to her hotel.

'Who the hell has been rummaging through my stuff? How did you get this?' Her father patted her knee. Vince grinned. It was the first time she had seen any expression on his face.

'Hush now, hush. I did you a favour; I know you didn't have time to collect your things. That place is a flea pit, no daughter of mine stays in a flea pit from now on you hear me?' Lucy was furious and her mind raced. She suddenly hated Vince with a passion she didn't know she had. His hands had been all over her personal property. Her anger was distracted when her father pulled out a syringe in a case and held it out for her.

'We want you to bring him round, then we can walk him out of here.'

'What!'

'This will reverse the meds they are giving him.' He tried to put it in Lucy's hands.

'What's in that?' Suspicion set off alarm bells at full volume in her brain.

'It's an injection, you do know how to give an injection don't you?' He baited her and tried to shift her curiosity.

'What is in the syringe?' Lucy took the case and popped it open; she examined the vial for information.

'I don't know what's in it; the doc gave it to me. He knows his stuff, I trust him.' He brushed off his daughter's questioning. Lucy looked at her father directly, she didn't believe him.

'Who wants him sleeping?'

'One of our competitors, they think the longer he is out of action the longer they have to run his business into the ground. We're just looking out for family, that's what we do,

Sine.' Her father was becoming impatient. His genial tone was wearing thin. 'What's the problem?'

'I don't know what's in the syringe!' Nothing added up for Lucy about this story.

'Jeezus fucking Christ, I told you I don't know either, we trust the doc. I ask him for something he gives it to me. This could be your job one day; you look after the whole fucking family … try startin' now!' he yelled in her face. She wasn't sure what would happen if she refused. She went to take the case, just to decompress the atmosphere and give her some space to think. He shook his head.

'Just the syringe, put it in your pocket.' The car door opened, and Vince stood over her like a tower and his gaze implored her to get out. She eased herself out of the car and started walking towards the hospital. She had to concentrate to put one foot in front of the other. Autopilot took her to the hospital entrance. Vince was close behind her, barring her way if she should turn and run.

'Get the fuck away from me.' Her hands pushed hard into his gut, but he didn't shift.

'You can't carry the old man out by yourself can you!?' He took her elbow and careered her into the building.

'Where are they going?' She noticed her father's car pulling away.

'They can't park out front; I expect they will find a space in the lot.'

Lucy mutely handed over her passport and signed the guestbook. She watched as her escort made an illegible scribble in the registration book before he took their passports back and hooked a hand under her elbow and pulled her towards the private room where the old man was sedated and hooked up to a machine. Lucy picked up his notes but had them snatched out of her hands.

'Give him the injection, we don't have time for all that.'

'What! If you think I'm giving him an injection you're sadly wrong, it's not goin ...' The syringe was taken from her and plunged into the skinny white arm of the elderly man. Lucy stood immobilized with shock for several seconds.

'What the fuck?' The heart monitor flat lined. She jumped towards the elderly man and started to resuscitate him but was dragged off. She hit the emergency call alarm and was thrown across the room. She tried to stand but her legs failed her, and she collapsed again. Two nurses ran into the room and started to attend to the body lying on the bed. Lucy was grabbed and carried out of the hospital.

The car sped along roads she would never remember travelling. She threw up in the footwell of the car and Vince cursed and curled his lip. Her father's car had long gone, and she had been thrown into another car that was parked close to a back door of the hospital. It was all planned carefully. She eyed the hands on the steering wheel beside her, he had worn the brown leather driving gloves the entire time they were in the hospital, she was the only one that would have prints on the syringe. Her father had been careful to touch only the case.

She leant back in the car, her t-shirt was soaked through with sweat, and she shivered. Vince threw her combat jacket at her. The panic attack had left her immobile and unable to speak for a long time but as her mind started to function, she knew only one thing and that was she had to get away from this car, she had no idea where she was being driven. She had to get away fast. She tried flexing her leg muscles to make sure they wouldn't let her down again and when the car paused at the next stop sign, she opened the door and ran as fast as she could. Vince could only yell after her, the cars behind started blasting their horns inpatient for him to pull off.

Chapter 46

The receptionist who a couple of days earlier had almost had her thrown out by security now offered her a wide smile and greeted her warmly.

'Good morning, Ms Sinoli, it's nice to see you back again so soon.'

'Thanks, I'm looking for my brother.' The receptionist nodded and smiled again; the bright red lips seemed to split her face in two. Matching red nail varnish tapped at a keyboard and she called Sin Sin's office.

Lucy wasn't sure coming back to find her brother was the right thing to do. If he was complicit in her father's trap, she would be walking right into another dangerous situation. She had seen a glimpse of his violence, but she had questions, and he was the only one who could answer them. She hoped that her brother, her twin, her own flesh and blood would have the instinct to protect his own. She needed a safe place to gather her thoughts, without her passport she couldn't just head to an airport and keep running.

There was no reply from Sin Sin's office and the receptionist asked Lucy to take a seat while she would try and locate her brother.

'Oh, I can go and wait for him there, what floor is it on?'

'Ah no ... erm so sorry, Ms Sinoli, but he might be some time and we are not allowed to let people go unescorted to restricted areas.'

'My father's on his way to meet us both here.'

'Oh, okay … I guess it will be okay.' The woman reconsidered.

'Thanks.' Lucy made to leave and walked toward the elevator.

'But if he is not in his office he might be in the lab.' The receptionist looked uncomfortable.

'Which is where?'

'In the basement.' The receptionist pursed her lips as if in thought, her eyes slightly widened as if she had committed a faux pas and could not undo it.

'Basement? Okay well, I'll find him. Thanks.'

Lucy took the elevator to the basement. The doors opened onto a utilitarian corridor; it was a stark contrast to the upper floors of the building. Dim strip lighting and shabby paintwork told her that only staff used this part of the property. Rubber track marks on the painted concrete floor and walls indicated countless trollies had been wheeled back and forth. She tried a few corridors but found only stores and equipment. She was about to return to the reception and check again with the girl where the lab was located when she noticed a door slightly ajar at the end of one corridor, light shone out from inside. As she neared, she noticed the labels on the boxes stacked high in the corridor, ammonium hydroxide. She pushed the door open.

He had his back to her, but she recognised the jet-black hair so like her own. She cast her eyes around the room. It wasn't the typical lab she was expecting, the array of shelves over the workbench that her brother was bent over held more boxes similar to the ones stacked in the corridor, more very large quantities of the same ingredients. There were some large stainless-steel drums, more typical of an industrial kitchen, not a chemist's lab. Blue hazmat suits hung from some crude hooks on the wall, and she noticed breathing

255

hoods and goggles. Lucy realized what Sin Sin was cooking up down here in the basement and gasped.

Her intake of breath alerted her brother to her presence in the room and before she knew it, he had paced the room and yanked at her neck, she could neither breathe nor talk. He had moved swiftly, his grip relaxed a little when he spoke, but he didn't let go.

'What the fuck are you doing creeping up on me like that?'

'You told me to come and see you at the hospital, Sin Sin.' Her voice was barely audible. Lucy was frightened by her brother's violence and by what she had seen in this lab. 'I needed to come and see you, something terrible happened.' Her voice pleaded and he released his grip but stayed close. Too close, he was still in her personal space, and it made her edgy.

'How did it feel?'

'What?' She felt the dread well up in her. 'Do you know what they did?' Lucy's eyes widened. Her brother smiled but said nothing. Her instincts were right. She had walked back into the lion's den. Her brain bypassed any rational thinking and the impulse to run, and she rounded on him, with the pent-up fury from the day's events.

'You're no fucking different, are you! This … I know what this is.' She jabbed a finger at the equipment and boxes.

'Like what you see?' Her swelling rage did not daunt her brother, he was not even slightly intimidated and seemed to savour the confrontation. He stepped forward until his face was inches from hers and his voice held a menacing undertone. 'So, you want to join the family business, eh? Let me acquaint you with the largest crystal meth factory in North America.' He was proud.

'Are you out of your mind? You could blow the whole fucking city up with what you have down here!'

'Clever, little sister.' A howl of laughter broke from his throat. 'I know what I'm doing. Pop made sure I studied with the best. It made sense to cut out the middlemen, the Mexicans were getting greedy and were asking for too much margin. Pops saw a gap in the supply chain and sent me off to study chemistry. The hospital is a cover. Here we are hidden in plain sight, right in the heart of the city. Now you're here we can really bump up production.' He laughed. She now understood the malevolent smile that had graced her father's face when he announced she could join her brother and go and work at the hospital.

'I'm not going to help you, Sin Sin, I'm not staying here. I'm going back to Ireland. This is ...' He yanked at her arm and pulled her close, so his breath hit her face.

'You really are so fucking stupid. Do you think you have a choice?' His fingers bit into the tops of her arms and Lucy winced at the pain.

'Please let go ... you're hurting me.' She had said the wrong thing, there was no distance between them, they were the same height and Lucy felt the stirring from his groin. She was embarrassed, almost ashamed of his sexual arousal, he refused to put any space between them. Instead, his grip tightened. She remembered the words of the prostitute and the scene she had witnessed in his apartment and recognised his desire to inflict pain. She tried to mask her fear and the burning sensation of his fingers tightening their grip on her arms. It would only drive his arousal. He looked at her mouth and bent his head to get his face into her neck where he inhaled her perfume deeply. This wasn't normal, this was her brother! Fear and disgust surged through her, and she pushed with all her strength at his body.

'What the fuck do you think you're playing at, Sin Sin?' She hadn't shouted but had ground out the words through a clenched jaw. The push succeeded in putting some distance between them, but his hands now had a firm grip around her waist. His eyes were locked on hers and she could see a hunger and lust that terrified her. The sadist was stoked, and his mouth closed over hers hard. She turned her head away and he released one hand from her waist to pull her head back. It gave her room to pull out of his grip and she stumbled several steps backwards. Her panic increased his lust and Lucy cried out with terror as he pushed his groin into her once again. She was choking on tears and screaming when his mouth covered hers effectively silencing her. She slammed a kick into his lower leg, and he stepped back.

'You bitch!' He spat the words and she realised all she had succeeded in was unleashing his anger. Panic took hold, she had to get out of his grasp and out of this room. There was no reasoning with the black eyes that flashed with fury. From some hidden depth Lucy found an anger she had never known before and with a deep guttural howl she had wrenched her wrists free and smashed the heel of her hand into his face. She heard and felt the snap of his nose. He fell back against a workbench and Lucy grabbed a stainless-steel trolley and ran at him. She kept hurting him, she smashed the trolley over and over until he was a crumpled unmoving heap on the floor. She stepped back and observed the still figure. She felt no emotion but could hear her own breath coming in short sharp gasps. He groaned and raised a hand to his face; she couldn't see his expression. His face was covered in blood. She turned and ran for her life.

She sprinted down several corridors blindly until she found a lift and once the doors had shut, she began to gasp for breath and the sobs started as the fear and anguish found a vent.

Lucy feared the receptionist might prove loyal to her brother so didn't head for the front door, she knew CCTV covered every corridor of the hospital, she was trapped and terrified. She pressed the button for a lower ground car park and leant against the wall of the elevator. Her legs refused to hold her up and she slid down and sat in a bloody heap. Her brother's blood covered her clothes and her hands.

The lift bumped to a stop, and she held her breath while the doors opened and then closed again. There was only one way out of this mess, she pulled off one of her boots and picked at the insole for the small white card with a telephone number handwritten across the middle.

She tried the number but the steel box she was sitting in prevented a connection, so she reached up to open the doors and crawled out. She was in an underground carpark, and she inched away from the lift and tucked herself between the lift shaft and a parked car. She hoped the cameras didn't have sight of her. She heard footsteps, she knew Sin Sin would have alerted security and she pressed her phone into her leg so the glow from the screen would not be noticed. When the guard was far enough away not to hear, she dialled the number. It connected immediately and hearing the voice overwhelmed her.

'Jim Cavell.'

'It's … Lucy.' Her voice was a shaky whisper. 'Please help me.'

'Where are you, Lucy?' She knew he had been expecting this call. She understood in that moment he had known the outcome of her quest to find her family.

'I'm in the basement carpark of the Mount Messina Hospital.' She kept her voice low.

'Are you hurt? Can you move? Can you see daylight, Lucy, and get into the street?'

'I'm hiding, there are guards everywhere, and they are looking for me.' Lucy tried to keep the sobs from breaking into her speech. 'I'm by the lift.'

'Okay, stay right there. I'm on my way.'

***

For the second time in his life, he dialled the U.S. Marshal SOG unit and requested an extraction for this girl. The van mobilised in minutes, he had already put them on notice, and they were expecting this call. It approached the hospital and didn't stop for the security barrier of the underground parking lot. It screeched to a stop in front of the lift shaft.

'Where is she?' One Marshal hissed and desperately looked around. Their entrance had attracted attention and Jim pointed at a security guard running towards them from an upper level. Jim opened the window and yelled her name; she appeared in his wing mirror.

'Back-up, six o'clock.' The black SUV roared into reverse as shots ricocheted off the steel crash barriers that separated the parking floors. The side of the SUV slid open, and two Marshals grabbed the girl and pulled her into the vehicle. Gunshots hit the back of the SUV as it screeched back up the ramp to where a galvanised steel shutter was unrolling. It proved to be no match for the heavily armoured SUV, the vehicle blew the shutter off on impact and for a few seconds bits of the frame travelled into the street with the vehicle.

'She's hit, she's hit.'

'We need a hospital pronto.' Jim swivelled round in a panic to see the agents examining Lucy in the back of the vehicle, she was covered in blood, crying and her words were difficult to decipher, she was trying to pull off her t-shirt, the agents were checking for bullet wounds.

'It's not mine.' She howled the words; she had pulled the garment off and threw it, her face contorted with revulsion and loathing. 'It's not mine.' This time, the words were barely audible, and she leant back into the cushioned seat exhausted.

'Scratch that, we're back on for Fairton.' Lucy didn't know it, but she was about to experience her second stay at the witness protection custody unit in Fairton, New Jersey. The agents relaxed into the journey.

⟶⟨◆⟩⟵

Chapter 47

Jim found Lucy sitting in the yard. She was huddled in a chair with her chin resting on her knees and she was deep in her thoughts, she didn't notice his arrival for several seconds. His heart broke for this young girl as he observed her from the lounge. He cleared his throat to catch her attention. She flashed a sad smile when she turned to see him and uncurled her legs to come inside.

It was the second time she had been in this apartment, but of course, she didn't remember the first. The witness secure unit was a place where countless new identities had been conjured and where witnesses were processed and prepared for their new lives. The large open plan lounge, separated from a kitchenette by a counter had played host to many distressed families over the decades. Two bedrooms opened off the main room and a small yard with a twelve-foot-high concrete wall afforded a view of a small patch of blue sky. Bland and functional furniture gave the facility the appearance of a budget hotel.

'I slept a whole day and night! No pills, just ... exhaustion I guess.' She had changed. The intonation was missing from her speech. They all did. All the witnesses he had seen come and go over the years. Being incarcerated in here waiting for their lives to start again was purgatory. While people waited to find out who they would become their psyche and personality was somehow set in a holding pattern.

'The paperwork is going to be easy, Lucy, but we need you to choose a name. Are there any you like?' She was silent, he thought she hadn't heard him. 'I have also been looking into Dubai for you, it's a mixing pot of cultures and nationalities. I think you would like it there. We could get your qualifications sorted and you could continue your medical studies.'

'Just like that, just like nothing ever happened?'

'It will never be like nothing ever happened. Your life is starting over. You can't go back to Ireland and pick up where you left off. It's the first place they will come looking for you.'

'I know that.'

'You can't risk putting your fam … friends at any risk. You must leave everything behind, there's no going back. Not for anything.'

'I know how it fucking goes!' Jim inwardly flinched, he deserved that, but he was relieved she was showing some normal emotion.

'Give me a name, Lucy, so we can get started on some paperwork for you. Another few days in here will send you stir crazy.'

'I don't care about a name, you pick one. You choose the location too, isn't that what YOU do. You tear up my family and send them off into far-flung corners of the world. You killed my mother. How does that sit on your conscience? You tore her family apart and caused her slow suicide, what if I might do the same, does that not prick your conscience?' Jim took a deep breath but said nothing. She would never know what this case had done to his conscience or his life. The evil her father had bestowed on others was not her burden to carry.

'You're not like your mother, Lucy.'

'Meaning she was weak?'

'They, he, spent months, years wearing her down. Making her dependent, that makes anyone weak.'

'I am like them, aren't I?' Jim was at a loss; he couldn't answer this honestly and be kind to her at the same time. He had seen her singular actions in Ireland. She had easily walked away from her friends, the priest. She had shown little emotion for her father's victims and more recently he had learnt of the rage and violence that she was capable of. He had worked with enough criminals over the years to pick out traits and behaviours of a psychopath. 'Is there evil inside me? I have the same blood, was I born bad?' She had read his thoughts. Jim crossed the room and pulled a chair up directly across from Lucy.

'I don't subscribe to that school of thought. I believe you are what your environment and your parents mould you into.' It wasn't exactly a lie. He had produced a paper which he'd presented at criminology lectures which offered some evidence that genetics play a part in behaviour. Some scientists theorize that criminality can be predicted in individuals with high levels of rage and violence from birth. But he had used it to open discussion on the theory, among his students, not as validated facts.

'That's what she was afraid of, isn't it? My ma thought I might be like them?'

'Lucy, your grandmother gave you a decent and loving upbringing. You were raised close to the church, and you know the difference between right and wrong. Everyone has a choice on which path to take. You made that choice. You are not them; you are not capable of doing what they can do.' He wasn't convinced of his own words. She had put her brother in ICU, it was touch and go if he would make it. This wasn't something he wanted to share with Lucy. She hadn't asked, so she may never know whether her brother lived or died.

'It runs deep though, doesn't it? I am capable of ...'

'You are still grieving, and on top of that, you had a terrible shock. What you had to deal with would throw anyone off kilter.'

'But I have a twin brother, how can we be so different? He told me we were the same, he told me that.' Jim could feel the angst in her words.

'Your grandmother did a great job of keeping you on the right path. Nobody is ever born evil, Lucy. Your grandmother and Father O'Reilly influenced you, but your brother grew up in a cold, unloving, mercenary environment, it's not surprising he's less empathetic, and more inclined to violence and crime. You are different. Your mother knew that growing up with violence and murderers would have moulded you. Getting her children out of that situation was the single biggest driver for her. She put her own safety at risk for you. Failing to save her son devastated her.'

'That's why she didn't tell me. My ma, I mean. She was still petrified, after all these years, that they might get to me, wasn't she? I understand why she didn't touch the money, the jewellery, and why she tried to get rid of those letters ... she didn't want me touched by their evil.'

Chapter 48

Jim walked down the corridor. He was looking for a familiar face, but she found his first.

'Jim Cavell! Honey, we miss you.' A middle-aged, round woman hurried over to him, her short arms didn't reach around his girth as she gave him a hug. Jim laughed loudly; he was genuinely pleased to see Martha. 'I'm glad you came by to see us! I heard you were rushing off back to that godforsaken cabin without even a hello.' She was chastising him with mock horror and Jim realised how much he missed his friends. They stood and chatted for a while about her husband and their two boys. As she was introducing Jim to some of the new faces in the department an office door opened, and Laurie Bannister appeared, he stood with his arms folded across his chest observing the scene with a warm grin from ear to ear. When Jim noticed him both men broke into a familiar chuckling and bear hugged one another fondly.

'I knew you'd be back, couldn't keep your nosey ass out of here for two minutes huh?' Laurie gestured for Jim to enter his office.

'Just following orders, I was told to get my backside down here pronto or you wouldn't release my expenses. Nothing changes I see.'

'Yeah? That what they told ya? Well good for them, worked a treat. Was thinking that you might jog off there to that backwater without seeing how we're managing without you.'

'Looks like you're managing just fine without me.'

'This one was a tough cookie, eh?'

'Yes, she was, I underestimated her from the start. Or maybe I'm just too rusty for this game now, Laurie.'

'Maybe, but nobody can come close to your persuasive skills, Jim.'

'What did you say to her to make her leave them?' Laurie's eyes bore into Jim's, his face posing an invitation. Jim's eyes cast around the room as he tried to ignore the sick feeling rising in his throat; he let his eyes settle into the middle distance out of the window, a trick that he had learnt years ago, it prevented anyone being able to read them.

'Wasn't my doing. She got her fingers burnt. She made up her own mind; we were just there in time to facilitate.'

'Hmm, well whatever it was, it worked. And you busted America's largest narco factory, without even trying! The FEDS are all over that hospital like flies, and the story is all over the press. You have pissed off those Sinolis all over again.' He laughed but Jim didn't sense any humour. 'You just watch your ass out there, you hear me? Anything you need you call me, okay?'

'You can count on that, Laurie. But there isn't anything they can do to me that matters.'

'You headin' home today?'

'Yeah, a couple of people to look in on and then I'll be headin' back.'

'Okay, well next time I want some bourbon time, you hear me?'

'Yeah, I hear you, give my love to Simone, and don't forget to sign off my expenses.' Jim kissed Martha and headed off towards the lift.

267

'Expenses, what expenses? Martha, you know about any expenses?'

'Be in your account next week Jim.' She winked at Jim, and he strode off. He missed these people, but he needed to get back to his cabin. He couldn't breathe in the city. The last couple of weeks had worn him down. He no longer had what it takes. This was a younger man's game. His eyes were off the ball. He had made elementary mistakes and when you were playing with people's lives, you couldn't afford to make any mistakes. He was going back home to the lakes and his modest but comfortable cabin, and his dog.

***

Jim put the small posey of mixed pink flowers into the heavy earthenware pot and looked around the grave. It was well tended, and he wondered who took such good care of all these lonely plots. Whose deft fingers plucked the weeds and cut the grass around the headstones. He wished he could thank them. The sun was low in the sky and the graveyard stretched for miles into the distant, headstones that marked the final resting place of countless bodies, sparkled white in the weak afternoon sunlight. He sat for a while in silence, Jim had never been one for words and departed souls did not need to hear, they could read your heart. As he gathered his jacket up and stood to leave, he cast his eyes once more over the chiselled words adorning the marble.

Emily Cavell

Our Little Angel

Sleep in Heavenly Peace

10 April 1982 - 13 October 1983

Jim walked with his head bent, back to his car; he was lost in his memories and didn't notice the two men watching from a sleek black sports car parked in the cemetery. He had been engrossed in his thoughts earlier too as one of them had slunk out from the vehicle and casually walked up to Jim's car, inserting a small parcel under the wheel arch by the driver's side before he continued up the road for a fair distance, only to double back through the trees and once again take his seat in the black car and wait.

Jim unlocked the doors and threw his heavy frame into his seat and inserted the keys in the ignition. In his wing mirror he caught the outline of two heads peering intently at him from a car some distance away and as he recognised one of the shadowy figures his heart jumped out of his chest and adrenaline sliced through his body. Once again, Jim had taken his eye off the ball, he had forgotten to check his car, he had forgotten to eyeball the cemetery and check his surroundings before walking back. His hand instinctively went to the door to flee from the vehicle, but it was too late, the explosion froze the terror on Jim's face. The blast sent pieces of the vehicle high into the air, a golden fireball followed, and then thick black smoke curled upwards. The black car pulled out slowly and the dark-haired passenger smiled as the black smoke filled the view in his mirror.

***

Seven thousand miles away a young woman offered her passport for immigration clearance at Dubai International airport. She was apprehensive until the young Arab woman had finished with her deliberations and computer checks and handed the shiny new passport back with a thin smile. Emily Black took the document and kept her gaze ahead, ignoring the many duty-free shops. Her shoes clicked a brisk tempo on the shiny modern concourse until she emerged from the cool air-conditioned terminal building into the muggy heat of dawn in Dubai. Emily put on sunglasses and ignored the cloying humidity that picked at her clothes.

She pushed her hands deep into the pockets of her jacket and felt the cold hard metal of the jewellery that had compelled this journey. She pulled the items out and formed a tight fist around them. Jim's words echoed in her mind. *'You must leave everything behind, there's no going back,'* he'd said. This jewellery held a key to her past, a past that had now been wiped away. Keeping these and the letters had been her grandmother's mistake. She spotted a garbage bin and without breaking her stride she tossed the items into the canister. Her load was immediately lightened, and she felt a small smile tug at the corners of her face as she strode off into another new life.